Spoonfuls From Heaven

A COLLECTION OF *Short Stories*

DanScribe Publishing

Spoonfuls From Heaven

A Collection of Short Stories

ISBN: 13:9781500289348

www.danneyclark.com / www.danscribepublishing.com

The persons and events portrayed in this work of fiction
are the creations of the author, and any resemblance
to persons living or dead is purely coincidental.

Cover design:
Larry A. Patrick

Photo credit:
Shutterstock.com

Printed in the United States of America

DEDICATION

Dedicated to all who follow Jesus even when it is difficult and those who work tirelessly to achieve and advance God's kingdom here on earth.

ACKNOWLEDGEMENTS

My sincere thanks always go to God our Creator and provider, to my wife and family, close friends, and those who continue to read and buy my work. Special thanks to my cover designer and friend, Larry Patrick for his technical skills and moral support.

A Grandfather's Love

What a wonderful day, what shall we do?
Said the lovely little girl, just turning two.
What's so great about it? barked the old graying man,
limping along, a cane in his hand.

Oh, the sky is so blue, and the sun is so warm,
Said the sweet little child, as she clung to his arm.
It'll be a hot one alright, not a cloud in the sky,
He responded to her, raising his gnarled old hand, to shade his good eye.

Could we walk by the brook, or wade in its stream?
Came her reply, as though in a dream.
No, you'll not see me a gittin' all wet, but under a tree by the water I'll sit.

For my joy now lives not in doing a deed,
But in watching you grow and live life at full speed.
He questioned himself, but scarce could recall,
Was he also once young, lively and tall?

How quickly time passed, like a loud clap of thunder,
Like lightening it's here, and then it is gone, makes a man wonder,

Why we cling to the past, and things we can't change,
And long for tomorrow, which is oft full of sorrow.

While wasting today, the time we can live,
And saving the love, we've been given to give.
He took her small hand, with spring in his step,
His energy renewed, although he'd not slept.

He scooped her up, not saying a word,
Onto his shoulders as light as a bird.
He stopped at the shop, with one twinkling eye,
It's ice cream we're needin' while feigning a sigh.

A grandfather's love, which cannot be learned,
oft' given away, is always returned.

A House on a Hill

Just after the turn of the 19th century, a young man named Thomas Light immigrated to America from his native England. The son of well-to-do parents who owned and operated woolen mills, he arrived with a desire to succeed, and the God given gifts to make it happen. He was only nineteen, but had grown up in his father's mills, learning their operation from the ground up.

America had recently achieved its independence, but was still suffering from the ravages of a bitter war. Arriving on its shores with a dream, a small amount of investment capital, and the ambition to survive, Tom bought a parcel of land. It was on a hill facing toward the North Atlantic Ocean and overlooking the Connecticut River. Several hundred feet above the wind driven surf below, it received nature's fury in nearly every season and was thought to be unbuildable as a home site. Only miles away, in New London, he acquired a warehouse near the dockyard and began fitting it with the looms and machinery necessary to make the fabric his new homeland so badly needed.

Although cotton acquired from the southern states using slave labor would eventually come to provide fibers to his looms, sheep's wool was now his main source of raw materials. The rocky soils of Maine and New Hampshire much resembled Ireland and Scotland and seemed a natural home for sheep. Heavy woolen fabric also seemed well suited to the harsh winter climates and the fishing fleets whose homes were nearby.

At the first year's end, his land remained barren and Thomas was living in the back of his mill while waiting for it to become operational. His funding had run short before he could get it off the ground.

A knock on the door brought with it a potential chance for the fulfillment of his dreams.

"Mr. Light?" said the man, "I have business to discuss if the time is right."

Of course the time was right, God's timing always is. Thomas was offered a contract to weave 1000 woolen blankets for the newly formed United States military. A sizable deposit accompanied the order, which allowed him to complete the remaining details to make his factory operational. A ship should arrive in the harbor in a few days with the necessary bales of raw wool intending to become blankets. With it came the promise of future orders if the first was satisfactory.

~ ~

Ships of commerce arrived daily, bringing and sending goods and supplies. The Atlantic coast states were interdependent, with the ocean providing fast and economical means to transport both goods and raw materials to and from states farther inland. Light Mills, now a prosperous and growing fixture in Connecticut, opened a second mill in Virginia to accommodate the south's new cotton industry.

Thomas himself, now approaching thirty, was a wealthy single young businessman of considerable vision. Developing Christian roots in England while growing up, he brought those values with him to his new homeland. As his good fortune continued, so also his desire to remain faithful to God manifested itself tangibly in the small community.

"God," he prayed, "show me Your will, that I can honor You by my service."

Almost immediately scripture came to mind that magnified God's desire that His children care for their less fortunate brethren. A need was obvious in the community, particularly for the widows and orphans of those lost to the sea and of the casualties of revolutionary war.

Thomas rented, and then later purchased, the warehouse beside his mill. In the beginning it was just enclosed space where the homeless could get in out of the winter's chill. Then a kitchen was added where meals were served, and finally accommodation made for sleeping. This required of him an ongoing personal commitment because the need was also an ongoing one. He learned right away that a one time financial consideration was not enough. He often hired from their own ranks, the indigent and homeless, to work in the mill and also at the shelter. The dignity they found often became more valuable to them than the charity he provided.

Among them was a young woman who, soon after her marriage, was widowed when her husband became one of the first casualties of war. He had noted that her blue eyes had regained a sparkle, replacing the look of hopelessness they had when she roamed the streets in search of food and shelter. Anna, Anna Pincheon, was her name.

She was put in charge of the kitchen, of ordering the necessary food supplies, of keeping order in the shelter, and of organizing dependable volunteers to serve and clean. Dan Bernard, a giant of a man who had lost a leg to a musket ball, was her 'enforcer', helping her keep order and police their motley crew of guests. As their numbers grew, so too the number of arguments, fights, thefts, and inhumane acts they attempted to perpetrate upon each other, the stronger preying upon the weaker.

Thomas required, as a condition of his charity, that all who accepted food and shelter also attend the Sunday morning church service provided there for them. He himself often joined them for both the meal and the worship. It was there that the seeds were planted by God which blossomed later into love between him and Anna.

~ ~

Five years after the land had been first purchased upon his arrival in America, the house was completed. Until that time, Thomas had continued to live in quarters at the mill and Anna at the shelter. Some months after meeting, however, a type of courtship had began. Thomas invited Anna to dinner, then to the theatre, a picnic, a carriage ride, and of course to church with him. He was pleased to find her a delightful companion who shared his passion for Jesus.

Two years after their first meeting, Tom asked Anna to marry him, and she accepted, but remained working at the shelter. Finally, as the new home neared completion, they set a date and made arrangements at their church. Anna, besides being widowed at a young age, had no living relatives. Both her mother and father had hopefully passed on to a better life.

After their marriage, life changed considerably for the young couple in many ways, but not their passion for Jesus and each other. Their home sat on ten acres of wooded land, tucked back into the native trees, but with a breathtaking view of the ocean. One of the first in the area with indoor plumbing, it was designed to endure the ravages of the coastal climate.

The mill continued to prosper and grow as they expanded to a third location in Pennsylvania. Cotton, linen, and wool were woven in abundance and shipped throughout the states and the world. Tom and Anna were married just over a year when their first child was born, a son. Two years later, twin girls joined them, bringing the family to five.

June 2, 1998, two hundred years after Thomas Light first arrived in the United States, ten generations of Lights had lived in the old mansion on the hill. The current matriarch, Phyllis Light, aged 93, still occupied the home, living alone but with two service people. Her family was scattered worldwide and numbered in the hundreds. Her own two children, both retired, lived in Charleston, their three children and their progeny were grown and had children of their own.

While all three of the mills had been torn down and replaced with other structures and businesses, the house had endured. The "Light House" as it had been called for generations, was owned and maintained by a trust which was perpetually funded. Although it had been rebuilt, remodeled, expanded, and modernized no less than thirty times over the years, it was never occupied by any other than a member of the Light family.

Thousands had been affected by the vision of a single man, hundreds had directly benefited from his love of the Lord and His generous nature, and the world was indeed a better place because of the light on a hill that could not be hidden.

Abide In The Light

It is not only that which resides in the darkness, but also that which we perceive in our minds to live there, that causes mankind to fear it. The light of day reveals what the darkness of night conceals.

~ ~

His footsteps echoed in the deserted alleyway as if magnified in some way by the surrounding darkness of night. Their hollow sound held emptiness, almost loneliness. He could have easily been the last living human on earth if one were judging by the surroundings. The walls of the buildings on either side rose like the walls of a canyon, vertical cliffs, almost seeming to touch, where they were met the by the dark cloudy sky above.

Lights, if there were any, were not visible to him. However, a luminescent quality at the end of the seemingly never ending tunnel in which he walked, spoke of illumination from some distant source. Street lights possibly, he thought to himself, where the alley merged with a narrow street somewhere ahead.

For a moment, the sound of his footfalls was over-shadowed by the mournful cry of some stray cat in heat. It was the sound of an animal in need, but alone like him in the darkness. A kind of other-worldly pleading for release from its torment, like the tortured souls of men suffering in Hell.

A scurrying, not a sound exactly, but the movement that should have produced one, alerted him to the presence of rats seeking sustenance among the garbage that lined the corridor. Dirty, he thought, possibly riddled with disease, their beady eyes fixed upon him without fear. He hastened his foot steps.

For a moment, like the arrival of a lightening bolt, his domain was flooded with light, then pitched into total darkness before red taillights signaled the passing of a large vehicle on the cross street ahead. He was almost encouraged by the thought that another, like him, existed. He moved freely onward while the darkened structures stared vacantly at him.

He seemed to have been walking forever, he felt no fatigue and although his destination seemed no closer, he knew he'd eventually break free of his confinement. He tried to recall how he'd gotten there, what events had preceded this journey, he could not. He questioned, looking for answers to questions not yet asked. He touched his clothing, finding comfort in their familiarity, and at the presence of his arms and legs underneath. Yet, even as he tried, he could not picture himself in his entirety. No features filled in the blanks as his mind sought to remember his face.

Once again, the now familiar sound of the cat echoed down the canyon toward him. He looked upward, nearly losing his balance as he did. He was rewarded only with the grayness of the sky that replaced the blackness of the walls of his prison. Somewhere ahead the sound of a falling garbage container assailed his senses as a cat or dog overturned it in its search for food. In the recess of a darkened doorway the body of a man lay motionless as he passed. He did not stop or slow his pace. He had no thought of mercy.

~ ~

Like mold or mildew, the darkness shrunk back from the light as the dawning sun announced itself to the world before then appearing in person to take away the chill of the night. The shadows seemed to cower and hide before they disappeared and daylight took their place. One by one the street lights winked out as their sensors also embraced the sunshine.

Even as the young priest awakened from his slumber and opened his eyes, and the last vestiges of sleep retreated from memory, a faint recollection of his dream remained. He asked himself, "Where does the darkness go when it is replaced by light?"

The question was immediately answered. "Into the hearts of men."

Angel Kisses

On that button of a nose, placed with tender care, were four or maybe five little brown specks on her otherwise nearly white baby soft skin. She was nearly four when she began to understand what Daddy meant when he teased her about her 'angel kisses'. With a tickle and a wink he'd have her laughing and squirming with glee.

Like all children, her blue eyes seemed far too large for her face. Sometimes, when in a serious mood, she'd appear almost "all knowing" with those large eyes, as if she could see something far away and distant, which no one else could. It was seldom that the twinkle left and gave this perspective, for she was far too full of the joy of life to remain sober for long.

At first, the pigtails stood almost straight out, but as her hair grew and her first two front teeth were traded to the tooth fairy, they could be braided and decorated, giving her a special persona. Life seemed so simple then, no thought for the future. Each day was full of itself and that was enough.

Waking with the aroma of bacon cooking in her upturned nose, the sound of water running in the bathroom next door, life was filled with wonder and joy. As Daddy laid down the razor and washed the remnants of soap off his smooth chin, she'd run to him and hug his leg. He'd scoop her up, lay a kiss on the waiting nose and they'd be off to breakfast.

Holding hands, heads bowed, they'd begin each day the same way, gathered around the table in the kitchen. If there was a world beyond these walls it mattered not, for everything they needed was here in this room.

Then, suddenly, like a well rehearsed play, Daddy would swallow his last gulp of coffee, jump to his feet and grab his wife like he had never met her before, lifting her off her feet, swinging her around like a new bride. With a soft kiss he'd sit her down, grab his hat, and head for the door as if to leave.

With a squeal, pony tails bobbing as she ran behind him, she'd pursue him and catch him at just the last minute as he grasped the door knob. Turning with a smile, he'd sweep her into his arms and plant a soft kiss just where the angels had left theirs, on that little upturned nose.

She awakened with a start, as she always did when rudely jerked from her favorite place of comfort back to reality. It must have been the slamming of the front door first, then the yelling and screaming which brought her back. The man who took Daddy's place after he had died had never been a father, just a man who had at first comforted her mother in her grief and paid the bills. As time had gone on, he had become increasingly more distant, angry, and had sought alcohol as the remedy to the demons that had followed him home from Viet Nam.

From her room she could hear them arguing and the sound of furniture being thrown and broken. Now 15, she knew the routine and had endured it silently for 10 years, each time swearing it would be the last. She wept as she knelt at her bedside, her hands shaking as she pressed them together in prayer. Yet this prayer was different, not for her salvation from this hell, but for forgiveness and salvation from eternal Hell.

She waited, it seemed for hours, until the house quieted and she heard her mother walking softly to their bedroom. She heard the door close and knew he would be passed out again on the couch. Quietly she reached into the closet and withdrew two bags which she had previously packed, then tip toeing down the hallway, she roused her mother. Holding her finger to her lips for quiet, she wrapped a thin coat around her mother and made her way out the front door to the waiting car.

She started the car and left it running as she reentered the house, making her way quietly to the kitchen. She blew out the pilot light and turned the knob to on and left with a tear running down her cheek and onto her 'angel kissed' nose.

Angels Among Us

He sat down at the table alone. A few others were already eating and talking noisily across the tables to one another. The small diner catered to the locals and an occasional tourist who had missed a turn off the freeway and were looking for directions. Having no reason to change, it looked no doubt much the same for the last 40 years, with faces replacing one another as each generation came and went.

A small country diner, it smelled of cooking oil, whatever soup of the day lingered in the air, and brewed coffee. Although sanitary, it looked far from clean. Its worn appearance belied the efforts which went into the constant cleaning necessary to keep it so.

Without asking, a plump, young blonde waitress sat a cup of steaming coffee in front of him. He nodded acceptance and gratitude without saying a word as she returned to the counter, clearing away dirty dishes and filling empty cups, with practiced efficiency. Over the din he heard a shout from the kitchen in the back that something was "up", making her turn to accept it into her waiting hands.

Re-entering the seating area with three platters heaped with their steaming contents, she began sitting them down in front of the eager teens seated at a table on his right. Something was said and laughter rocked from the table. She turned away smiling and gently cuffed one of the boys across the top of the head as she did, causing yet another round of laughter. Private joke, no harm - no foul he guessed.

Very much aware of his financial situation, he looked first at the right hand side of the menu, making mental calculation as he went. Subtracting the cost of the coffee, which was nearly gone already, he chose the half order biscuits and gravy, which left him just over a quarter for a tip. It would have to do, at least until he could find a few hours of work. Careful to not attract attention, he took two packets of jelly and two of sugar and put them into his shirt pocket. Hardly a meal, but energy food none the less, if nothing else came along. Surprising how little one needed to survive if they were careful.

He had just returned to his coffee when she reappeared with a friendly smile, "what can I get ya?" she asked.

"Not too hungry," was his reply, "just the half order of biscuits and gravy will do fine." Most of the coffee hitting his empty cup, she was off to turn in the order to the kitchen without another word.

Drinking his water down and holding the glass in both hands, as though warming them, he allowed his gaze to circle the room. It was a comfortable and friendly atmosphere with patrons talking from table to table. There seemed to be no age barrier, as often is the case in the big cities, for the seniors joked and visited with the kids as though they were peers. The teens showed proper respect but joked right back about this and that.

As she set the platter down in front of him, something akin to panic grabbed him and for the first time he looked up into her blue eyes.

"I... I only asked for the half, and not the eggs and juice."

"Oh, my mistake," she offered. "Sorry, just eat what you can, I'll just charge you for what you asked." She turned away, refilling cups along her way to the counter.

Head spinning, he dove right in, marveling at his good fortune.

Four homemade biscuits, three eggs, and rich creamy gravy bursting with fresh sausage pushing it's way into his mouth. Feels like a Thanksgiving dinner, he thought to himself.

After several bites and a big swallow of juice, he finally raised his eyes to look around, connecting immediately with her soft blue eyes across the room. She immediately looked away and returned to some task at hand, obviously embarrassed at being caught staring at him.

Finally, finishing the last bite, he leaned back with a contented sigh dropping his napkin into the empty plate. Then, in looking around, he saw no sign of the young waitress, who had evidently been replaced by an aging woman with red hair and freckles.

Again, the panic gripped him. What if she'd forgotten to change the bill before going off shift? How would he ever explain the mistake? Slowly getting up, leaving the promised quarter on the table, he made his way to the cash register. The woman looked up as he offered, "half biscuits and gravy and coffee" and motioned to his vacant table.

"Yeah, got it right here", she said with a puzzled look, "but it's already been taken care of, paid in full."

"Who? How?" he questioned. However, she had already turned and was serving pie to a young couple sitting at the counter. As he left, he forced himself to swallow the lump in his throat and walked slowly toward the freeway on ramp.

As evening fell, he found a small dry creek bed with an oversized metal culvert running under the road. There, he took out his meager belongings and settled in for the night, glad to be warm, dry, and well fed. Before sleep enshrouded him, she once more came to mind. He resolved to return in the morning for a proper thank you and a more generous tip.

Working the cramps out of his aging muscles, he arose at daylight, folding up his kit and packing it away. His eyes searched the empty diner for his patron friend but saw no one, then hearing a noise from the back, let out a tentative "hello."

A rotund man in white apron stuck out his head and replied, "have a seat, be with ya in a minute." He sat at the counter while the cook finished what he had been doing and returned.

"Coffee?" he asked.

"Yes, thank you." With a practiced grace, the large man filled the cup without spilling a drop, smiled and asked, "breakfast?"

"No thanks, just coffee."

"Oh, does that young waitress who was here yesterday work today?" he asked.

The cook frowned, "young? You mean Alene, the red head? She's old as you, comes in at 9:00."

"No, I mean the younger one, the blonde," the traveler replied.

"No one like that here," offered the cook, "just me and Alene."

"But, but, she served me breakfast. Biscuits and gravy, just yesterday"said the man. "Juice too."

"Can't help you there friend," answered the cook, "no one like that has worked here since Cathy and she's been gone near two years now. She was killed in a car wreck."

The Bitter Cup

It was winter, 1918, a particularly savage and cold winter when Sarah Kate Jackson made her first appearance into the world. Like most of the rest of her life, its beginning was also hard and laborious, almost 15 hours. Her mother died later that day from complications of childbirth, in the old farmhouse, with her husband and neighbors by her side.

It would be the first and last child of the unlikely union and though healthy, strong, and eager to get at life, she never was able to fill the broken heart of her father. He died several years later, some said of grief, most thought of consumption. Consumption was the term of the times when Mother Nature took one early who had trouble breathing.

So it began, on a low note, and followed by others. Sarah Kate was sent off to live with her maiden aunt in the community of Houston, Texas. While she was cared for, the hands which held and provided for her needs were never to have been called loving. Aunt Mildred, Millie to some locals, but never to Sarah Kate, did not possess the capacity, it seemed, for love.

Possibly the years alone, the obvious scorn of her peers, or the lack of suitors early on, produced the environment for a solitary existence. It any event, Mildred, never having the opportunity to marry, wisely chose to remain single. With age and a sense of resolution also came bitterness and loneliness. Rather than finding solace in the child, it was just one more reminder to her of her own barrenness, and another cause for her self pity.

Sarah Kate, as she was always called, never Sarah or Kate alone, began her schooling nearly two inches taller than the biggest boy in the class of 12. With her size and unlikely family, she also became the subject of the children's taunting and ridicule. Like her Aunt Mildred, she bore the cross quietly and turned inward and spent much time alone. Her world existed in her mind and in her books.

To her joy, her home was filled with thousands of books which she was encouraged to read by her aunt. If she ever wished things were different or more conventional, one would never have known, for she did not complain. Intelligent, quiet, and purposeful, she learned easily and retained the knowledge for some still unknown purpose. Aunt Mildred, a shopkeeper and dress maker, was as frugal as were the times and even during the 'great depression' they fared well and were able to endure and even prosper where others failed.

Twice, while in high school, she was asked out by young men, both times it ended in unhappy memories. Though always tall for a woman of the day, five foot seven, she grew into herself nicely and was not unpleasing in appearance or build. Her fine red hair was her joy and she took hours brushing and finishing it, just so. Her eyes a dark blue and her features clear, she could have been called pretty if there were someone special to notice. There was not.

Sarah Kate was of course expected to learn the household chores and performed them easily and naturally, and then was schooled in the fine art of millinery to which she was less fitted. She worked alongside of her aunt and did an adequate job under the expert eye and tutelage of the master, but never acquired a fondness for the job.

On her eighteenth birthday it seemed that the possibility of normalcy was on the horizon. Aunt Mildred had made arrangements for her to be educated further in a nearby woman's college. In that day, women of fine breeding, or those who sought to be known as those of fine breeding and aristocracy, always were sent away to school. Sara Kate fortunately saw this as a chance to learn and grow in knowledge, setting her apart from her peers who only attended out of duty and had interest only in young men and mischief.

While she studied quietly with her books, others in her dormitory would sneak out and find their male counterparts in unlikely places. She pretended never to listen to the hushed tales which they told, as they returned breathless from trips afield. Sojourns often included stories of fallen tresses and eager hands fondling proffered fruit. If she longed for such encounters, no one would have known, for her lips spoke not a word.

The school shut down completely during the Christmas season. In the first year she went home to see Aunt Mildred. She was not warmly greeted and seemed to slip right back into the mold which she had just left, and little was said about her progress at school. When school began again she was more than eager to return to her independent life style. Interestingly, though she never tried to develop friendships among her peers, she did acquire many friends. Many of the young women looked to her for advice and knew well their secrets were safe with her.

Tea was all the rage and women of breeding were always taught the art of entertaining and how to host a proper tea party. Sarah Kate, always the rebel, had no taste for tea and would join the workers after hours enjoying the hot thick brew of the south called chicory. She would laugh and visit and fit in well with the blue collar laborers who made sure the dormitory was properly cared for.

Her first kiss was from a young man whose job was to help care for the grounds, and who joined the group in the evenings after work. Quite unexpectedly, as they walked across the grass toward the dormitory, he leaned down and brushed her lips with his, then apologized and turned away.

Her heart beat wildly that night, and her head swam until early morning with thoughts and desires long repressed. She planned how to duplicate the encounter and played over in her mind how far she might let him go when it did. The recounted stories of the other young women gave her a taste for the passion she had never known, but longed to feel. But, it was not to be, the summer came and went and with it, his job. She never saw him again.

Sarah Kate graduated third in her class, with honors, but without the presence of family or friends attending the ceremony. Her aunt, now gravely ill at home, sent word of her condition and urged Sarah Kate to come home to care for the business. Within a few days of her arrival, she attended to the details and burial of her sole remaining relative, grieving the loss in her own way.

Her education and proclivity for hard work, applied to the small sew shop, soon bore fruit. As WWII began, she hired many wives whose husbands were sent overseas and soon the shop became a plant, landing its first military contract. She was able to pay her workers each Friday in cash, and began a tradition of enjoying Fridays with her staff in her home over coffee.

Many lonely young women and mothers with small children enjoyed the comfort of her too large home and the wisdom and company of their employer. Her home became a social gathering place for the entire small community, and its library God's gift to children eager to learn and read. She purchased a large commercial coffee pot of elegant design and quality, nickel plated, and holding more than fifty cups. It was always full, brewing surprisingly good coffee, and became the focal point of the large sitting area where she entertained both guests and strangers passing by.

As time passed and the war ended, husbands and lovers returned home and began to join their families at her home. Many a man, embarrassed to ask, found a wad of bills in their coat pocket on their way home after sharing their family's situation in the post-war economy. And so it went, year after year, with old friends being buried and new ones taking their places at the table over steaming mugs.

That brings us to the present, 91 years since she moved into the large house with her aunt Mildred, and the final day of her earthly life. As always, the door stands open, the aroma of brewed coffee fills the house, but today hundreds of guests, young and old came and went. Some, sitting quietly in small groups, visited and talked in hushed tones, others tended to the serving and brewing of the steaming black liquid.

Today, however, something was different. To the rich dark grounds three drops of vinegar were added before the brew was started . . . creating a bitter cup which echoed the pain in the hearts of all present.

City of Refuge

She felt older than her thirteen years, the weight of them seeming to crush the youth and vigor from her. She had little recollection of a carefree childhood, if there had ever been one... only the weight of responsibility meant for adults. Pet owners refer to the sire and dam of the litter, not to their mother and father, and yet most animals had more affection for their offspring than her parents had for her. Upon few occasions had they ever indicated a connection with their children at all, except to vent anger and rage. Karen was the oldest of the six spawned by lust, living in squalor in the old farmhouse down the rutted lane, far from the state highway.

Had their home bordered the coastal highway, possibly someone may have taken notice of the nearly naked urchins with haunted looks in their eyes in the grass-less front yard. Photographs of Holocaust victims mirrored the hopeless expressions in their drawn faces and lifeless eyes. Little Timothy was the youngest, nearly two, but barely able to walk, and unable to speak. He weighed less than the fat tomcat that had the run of the house. As she reminisced, Karen thought that the conditions seemed to be getting worse. Less food, no attempt at cleanliness, worn out clothes seldom replaced, and medical care now a rarity.

For the first several years she and the older ones had gone to school where the system had made accommodation and furnished a minimum of their needs. She had been able to secret away extra food to share with the younger ones. Kind hearted teachers and aids had slipped extra clothes and shoes into their lockers, but things were different now that they no longer attended school, much different.

She knew little of economics but had knowledge that those on the outside worked for those things they needed or wanted. She had seen examples in the form of the other children's parents and even her teachers. She felt guilty that she was unable to work, wanting somehow to better the lives of her brothers and sisters.

It's a wonder how the system became so corrupt that it perpetuated the very conditions that it was created to correct. But such is man, inherently evil it says in the Bible somewhere. Whatever a godly man can invent for good, an evil one can use for his own profit. The system, once in place, seemed to be on autopilot without oversight, checks or balances.

When they had first moved to Oregon, he had worked within eyesight of the Pacific ocean, albeit only occasionally and between short stays in the county jail. His drunkenness and foul mouth had invited fights and those fights had been the source of his police record. She, on the other hand, quickly learned to play the part of the hapless wife and was easily counseled by others like herself how best to work the liberal system.

To those with Christian hearts, she was a martyr, and she played the part well. She couldn't divorce because of her Christian convictions, and couldn't work because of the needs of the children. Having only four children then, but with their income well under the poverty level, the welfare system sprang into action. Social workers even took time to help her understand it well enough to abuse it. They got food stamps, welfare checks, access to pantries and food banks, and aid from churches and charities of all sorts. He never worked again after getting out of jail.

They met strangers in the Walmart parking lot and sold food stamps to them at a discount, pillaged food banks, then traded food for alcohol, and filed for federal programs which refunded money they had never paid as tax credits. The federal system furnished breakfast to the children and often lunch as well, making it unnecessary to feed them as much at home. The children learned to exist on one or two meals a day. Then came the twins, more welcome dependents, but an unwelcome burden to their mother.

They opened another avenue of income, WIC. They hoarded cases of formula and baby food, selling the surplus to others with babies, who had little interest in where it came from. Timothy rounded out the half dozen. He was born sickly and undernourished with a malady called failure to thrive. Had the doctors, or anyone, taken time to look at the other children, it would have been obvious that they all failed to thrive. Father was pushing three hundred pounds, his wife two-thirty, with the total combined weight of the six children less than one-fifty.

God's first blessing came when mother developed a cyst on her ovary, forcing surgery that included a complete hysterectomy. The baby factory shut down, she did learn however about the benefits of free, or rather tax-payer subsidized, healthcare and drugs. The upside was a new profit stream, selling prescription drugs which had been meant for the children. The downside, that the system kept records on the children by name for each visit. When alerted by a visit from HEW concerning the frequency of illness, they stopped going altogether before a case could be made for child abuse.

They had moved shortly thereafter and rented a post office box. That is when the children stopped attending school. They simply dropped out of sight, the landlord included the utilities in the rent, leaving no record of where they lived. But, while the checks kept coming, the food for the children did not. It seemed their parents were unaware that the children needed fed, having assumed they'd gotten by previously while going to school.

Karen and the older children were delegated to help carry in the food from the car after their parents' visits to town, most of which they'd never see. It was not unusual that a box of this or can of that might fall from the bags and slide under the porch before the food was relayed to the kitchen counter. There was such a surplus that those went unnoticed.

Karen had dreamed of running away, but knew she could not. She couldn't leave the little ones behind without anyone to love and care for them. Despair dispels hope, wrapping itself around you like a cocoon, making you unable to think or function. They did not have a phone, leaving her no way to call for help, no way to attract attention to their plight. Karen had only one ally in the world, her sixth grade teacher, Mrs. Rice.

Karen knew that Mrs. Rice suspected things were not right but lacked the evidence to do anything about it. Even Karen, fearful of retaliation, had lied to dispel Mrs. Rice's suspicions. Then they had moved and quit going to school. Still, Karen had her phone number memorized for the day when she might need to call.

It was the fifth grade she thought, when the Gideons had came to class and passed out the little red New Testament Bibles. She had hidden hers after they had found and taken away Jake's. Jake was a fourth grader, or was when they had quit school. Karen was an intelligent child and had done well in school, unlike some of her siblings who seemed to have learning disabilities.

God had given her an understanding of things well above what her schooling and intellect provided. He had allowed her to understand His Word, to interpret passages which were unclear to many others. When the children gathered around her in a small circle she read the gospels to them. She had a unique way of explaining to them what she was reading. It seemed that each, no matter what their age, was able to take comfort from the encounters.

Sometimes, it seemed it would go on forever, the marginal life that they shared. She was too young to see a tomorrow where she was an adult, where the children would be grown and escape their torment. Once, when a stranger had come to the house lost and asking for directions, Karen had considered slipping him a note, but was fearful that she'd not be taken seriously and their parents would be alerted. When their teacher had asked where they lived when one of the children had a broken arm, he had told her. Of course the official story had been that he had fallen from a swing and the child fearfully confirmed the story.

It was sometime during the night that Karen had been awakened by her younger sister. The baby was crying and convulsing on the floor. It was obvious that he had a high fever but beyond that Karen had no idea of what might be wrong. She tried to cool him with a damp cloth before mustering her courage to wake their parents. Nothing she could do worked and he seemed to be getting worse.

When mother finally lumbered into the room, flipped on the light, and checked the boy, she screamed at Karen, "you should have woke me earlier", then hit her across the face. The smaller children were crying and the older ones cowered as the household came to life. It was nearly an hour before they were loaded into the old Dodge Caravan heading toward Newport Beach and another before they pulled into the emergency room entrance.

Timothy was taken right in with his parents following, the other children were told to stay in the waiting room. An hour passed, then another. The small children had curled up in the chairs and gone back to sleep, Karen and Jake remained awake. When a nurse had caught Jake taking and eating sugar packets from the coffee bar, she offered him a banana from her own lunch bag. He hesitated, looking to Karen for affirmation before taking it, and wolfing it down.

Karen asked her, "is Timothy going to be alright?" The nurse smiled and answered, "let me go have a look and see how he is doing." She left, then upon returning, wasn't smiling. She knew she must not scare the children.

"They are giving Timothy food and water through his veins to help him with dehydration", she said, hoping Karen would understand the terms. "Has he been sick long? Has he been throwing up?"

Karen thought, "no, not lately", she answered truthfully.

"Has he had a good appetite, does he drink a lot of water and juice?"

Karen was beginning to see where the conversation was going and was trying to find a way out. "You'll have to ask mother", she said finally.

The nurse looked at her oddly, then asked, "how old is Timothy?"

"He just turned two", came Karen's answer, "last month."

The nurse was holding the admission form, reading it carefully. "I need your help," she finally said. "Your mother and father are busy with the doctors and forgot to give your address and phone number."

"We don't have a phone," Karen said, "we use a post office box in Lincoln City."

"Oh," came the nurse's reply, "I'll make a note, no phone. Do you know the box number?" Karen told her. "And we need a street address in the event we have to dispatch an ambulance" the nurse lied. Karen gave her the address without hesitation. "Thank you," the nurse said, "are you hungry?"

Karen hesitated, but the nurse continued. "We have extra fruit and cookies in the break room that we'll probably have to throw out," she said.

"Are you sure it's okay?" Karen asked.

"I'm sure," said the nurse, "do you want to wake the others?"

It was like the Christmas they had never had, cookies, oranges, apples, bananas, and all the small cartons of milk they wanted. The five of them ate like wolves as soon as the nurse left the room. When she peeked through the window, they were filling their pockets also.

When she reentered the break room there was no sign of anything edible anywhere. She smiled and said to Karen, "is there someone we can call in an emergency who you trust, since you don't have a home phone?" It seemed natural to her to give Mrs. Rice's name and number, so she did.

"Thank you. Now I need all of your names and ages," she said as if it were a game. One by one they gave the required information without hesitation, as she wrote them down on a paper. "Okay, now back to the waiting room and thanks for helping me get rid of the extra food, but let's keep our visit here private, just between us," she said.

The children had no problem keeping it private, knowing they'd get a beating if they were found out, but didn't say so. They had gone back to sleep in the waiting room when the parents finally joined them. The morning was just breaking as they got into the car, leaving the baby behind in intensive care. No one spoke until they arrived at the house when Jake asked, "is Timothy alright?"

"No, he's not alright," they answered harshly. "If he was alright he'd be coming home with us, now go to your room!" The mother and father lumbered to their bedroom and returned to bed, leaving the children alone.

Karen waited to hear snoring before she spoke. "We need to hide the food carefully, if they see it they'll know where we got it and we'll get beat sure." Each child took out the food they had brought and handed it to her reluctantly. Karen put it all in a shoe box, then onto the shelf in the closet under a tattered blanket. "We'll share it tonight after they go to sleep," she promised.

"Mrs. Rice?" was the question on the line when she picked up the phone. "This is Nurse Linda Baker at Newport General Hospital, do you know Karen Brown?"

"Who?" Rice replied,

"Karen Brown, age thirteen, says you are her teacher."

"Was," Mrs. Rice corrected. "She's no longer in school here, is she alright?"

"Yes, thankfully she is," Nurse Baker said, "but she listed you as an emergency number since she has no phone."

Mrs. Rice was confused, "emergency number? Is there an emergency?"

"No ma'am," Nurse Baker replied, "but I have reason to suspect she may be in trouble."

Mrs. Rice was interested now, recalling the frail little sixth grader who had looked so thin and so hopeless. "What do you mean trouble? the teacher asked. "I can't imagine her getting into trouble, she's such a dear child."

"Mrs. Rice, may I be candid with you and ask you to keep our conversation confidential?" the nurse asked.

"Yes, certainly," Mrs.Rice answered. "What is this all about?

"I have reason to suspect she and her siblings may be victims of child neglect," the nurse said, "but in these matters, if we move too fast, the evidence disappears and the children suffer reprisals." She told of little Timothy who had come in near death, dehydrated, under nourished and half the weight of a child his age. Of how all the kids seemed hungry and fearful but unwilling to ask for help.

"We all tried to help them," Mrs. Rice volunteered. "We could see they lacked food and clothing but had no substantial proof of neglect to take to child protective services, then they just disappeared. We thought they moved out of state or something."

"Will you visit with the other children's teachers and get a feel for their support, should we need it?" the nurse asked. "I am going to push the doctor to turn his findings over to the state for investigation and they may want to get your statements and observations.

"I cannot promise except for myself," Mrs. Rice said, "but I will ask around quietly and see if they are able to support our suspicions."

"Thank you," Nurse Baker said, "thank you so very much." When she hung up, she paged Doctor Danes, the head of pediatric medicine.

The house was quiet except for the snoring and heavy breathing from their parent's bedroom. The children had all slept and were now awake and hungry when Karen carefully took down the shoe box from the closet. Four dirty little faces looked up at her hopefully as she shared the hospital's generosity equally among them.

She herself took a large red apple for her part, savoring each juicy bite, chewing it slowly, enjoying its texture and sweetness in her mouth. Great care was taken that no hint might be left behind for later discovery. Orange and banana peels went into a plastic bag, wrappers joined them, before being hidden under other family garbage. When the feast was finished they enjoyed sly smiles together knowing they had endured another day.

Dr. Danes took the call, listening intently, then promising to discuss the case with the ER and attending, then get back with her. Dr. Danes was a good man, he had been a good choice to replace Doctor Walker when he had retired, she thought. He was one of those who had chosen medicine for the right reason.

Linda was also one who had chosen the medical field to serve others, but didn't see herself as extraordinary in any way, just committed. She and Daniel had married young with high hopes of a big family, a farm with lots of animals, and plenty of love to go around. Nearing forty now, they had two of the three, but no children of their own. That is the reason she had gravitated to pediatrics in an attempt to fill the hole in her heart.

Dan was a 'custom farmer', meaning he had the equipment and know-how to plant, till, and harvest the crops of others for a fee. Small acreages no longer turned a profit if they purchased and maintained all the equipment it took to raise crops. They themselves only owned forty acres, hardly enough to make a living by the time you fed your own livestock and yourselves. Linda provided for the extras, which always seemed to come around, from her nursing job.

It was a little after 3:00 p.m. when the heavy footsteps indicated their parents were awake. The toilet flushed, the refrigerator door opened and closed, and the television went on, beginning the cycle that defined their lives. Karen was feeling a little daring after pulling off their unscheduled meal without detection. She slipped from the ten by ten room that they shared and walked up to mother.

"Mother," she said innocently, "may I get some milk for the children?" She wisely stood a safe distance away as she asked. Her mother turned, her voice laden with venom. "Certainly not! We just have enough for your father and I for our breakfast cereal. You children always waste or spill it anyway. Have some crackers if you are really hungry."

"Thank you, mother," she said sweetly, "and cheese too?"

The obese woman would have beat her had she felt the energy to get up from the lounger, instead she sighed a heavy sigh and said "cut a small one, and don't waste it or your father will have it out with you."

Thank you, mother," Karen said politely once again, making sure her tone didn't bring retaliation.

In the kitchen she was light-hearted, knowing that mother had no idea of what was in the kitchen. She took an entire brick of cheese, four tubes of saltines, then cut the end off a tube of lunch meat. She had never felt so daring before or willing to risk getting caught. She slipped the food into an empty grocery bag, then returned and cut some more baloney and sliced cheese and placed it on a paper plate with crackers.

Then she cautiously reentered the living room where her parents were watching the 'smack down' on WWF. She placed the food between them. then exited before they could comment.

She had used the ploy before. By giving them the same food she stole for the children it made it hard for them to question what had happened to it. Inside their room, the children had their second meal of the day, eating and grinning as they did.

Doctor Danes went over Timothy's chart carefully before examining the boy himself. It read: age 25 months, 22 inches long, 12 pounds 9 ounces. Surely, he thought, the numbers must be wrong, until he uncovered the decimated child. He seemed long and angular, underdeveloped, more like an old man than a child. It was evident that the child was under nourished and had been for some time.

Nurse Baker had been right to question the child's safety. The ER and attending concurred, saying that the child had taken nearly two pints of liquid before his kidneys had begun to function. His temperature down, the child slept fitfully, a monitor recording an irregular heartbeat.

The four gathered in the break room to discuss Timothy and the other children. The attending was ambivalent and seemed afraid to make waves, the ER sided with the nurse, having seen first hand the condition of the child before being stabilized. Dr. Danes seemed indecisive, knowing that such charges were serious and sometimes separated families forever.

Nurse Baker pulled a disc from her pocket that she had gotten previously from security and slid it into the DVD player. It showed the family entering together, the mother carrying the baby, the five children following behind. It showed the children alone in the waiting room and the parents in ER with the doctor, finally it showed the children acting like locusts, attacking the food in the break room. They looked like they had escaped from concentration camp, their clothes in shreds. Dr. Danes made the call.

Before their shift ended, Brenda Nelson arrived from child protective services with forms to fill out, questions to answer, and pictures to take of little Timothy. She interviewed them first together and then privately. When it was Linda's turn, she made mention of her conversation with her teacher Mrs. Rice. Nelson's eyebrows lifted before she smiled and said, "nice work, need a job?"

Linda smiled, then said, "No. I have a husband, a farm, and a full time job here, barely time to get to church on Sunday.

"No children?" Brenda asked, "you're just a part-timer." They laughed together as they continued to go over the forms.

"P.O. Box, huh?" Brenda said. "It figures, they don't want us visiting them." Then she saw the note Linda had made with the physical location. "How'd you get that?" she asked.

"From Karen, the oldest daughter. I told her we needed an address in case we needed to dispatch an ambulance or something."

Brenda smiled and made some notes. "Good idea, I'm going to lobby to make that mandatory on all HEW forms where the family is receiving any kind of subsidy or aid. I'll speak to the hospital admin as well and suggest they add that line to their forms if they expect any kind of state or federal reimbursement."

"When do you expect the baby will be well enough to be released?" Brenda asked.

The nurse started to answer and then said, "you should ask the attending, he'd have a better idea. The family didn't even ask when they left and haven't called or returned yet."

Brenda smiled again, "I'm going to make sure that we arrive at the home unannounced, just as he goes home, they won't be expecting us and won't have time to prepare. Meanwhile I'll give Mrs. Rice a call and arrange a visit with her." They exchanged hugs.

It was 10:00 a.m. three days later that mother and father finally realized that Timothy was still at the hospital. This time, however, they left the children at home in Karen's care, with instructions to straighten up the kitchen. The kitchen was always a mess with half-eaten food and dirty dishes filling every available space, and certainly not because the children left their food and dishes lying around.

Karen loved it the few times they were left behind and had the run of the house. They always ate well and were able to hoard food for later if they were clever about it, especially canned goods and non-perishables.

Linda was not on duty when they arrived , but the staff had written instruction to call Brenda Nelson day or night before discharging the child. Timothy looked to the staff like a child's inflatable toy that had been re-inflated. As his body had been hydrated and given nutrition he had blossomed and thrived, finally being able to stand in his crib after four days. Nurses affectionately called him "Timmy Toy," because of his size and sweet disposition. He had gained over three pounds in four days, nearly 25% of his body weight, indicating the near-death condition he had been in.

The attending and Doctor Danes met with the parents in a carefully scripted conversation, asking innocent sounding but vital questions. Questions such as what brand of formula do you buy, how many ounces of liquid does he drink at a sitting, who is his pediatrician, has he had the full series of shots?

They, of course, made most if it up, having no real knowledge of what or how he got by day to day. They should have asked Karen or the older children if they expected answers. Doctor Danes excused himself to take a call that turned out to be Brenda Nelson, then returned to the conference.

When Timothy was brought to them, mother made a show of picking him up and awkwardly juggling him up and down. One might have wondered how a woman could have delivered six children and gained no sign of motherly instinct. The staff rushed to find a car seat for them, unwilling and unable to release a child if their car was not equipped with one. The couple, with their son, left but stopped by the market for beer and snack foods, leaving him in the car seat in the vehicle before heading home.

Karen and the older children had finished eating, cleaning, and destroying the evidence of their meal in the burn barrel well before the aged Caravan came down the dusty lane. They would have loved to have bathed, but were allowed the privilege only once a week and then only with permission. It would have been too obvious to hide had they dared. When mother and father entered the house they surveyed the kitchen but made no comment before handing the baby to Karen and scattering the opened snack bags across the counter. The children were overjoyed to see their brother and made no argument when told to "go to your room and take him with you." Mother and father settled in their chairs in front of the television and popped a beer each to wash down the pork rinds they had with them.

Karen had spied the case of infant formula that the hospital had given them and filled several bottles right away for later use, before hiding the rest in the closet. She was fearful it would be sold or thrown away if she didn't protect it. Originally, there had been a bunk bed and one other which they had all shared. As the bed frames fell into disrepair, the mattresses had been pulled onto the floor. Karen and Jake had arranged them side by side and against one wall giving them room to exist in the small bedroom.

The bed frames still lay out in the back yard where father had thrown them. The only furniture in the room was an old wooden rocking chair which they shared when they took turns with Timothy. Their meager assortment of hand-me-downs were in the single closet, some hung on nails, others on the floor, all well used and dirty.

Karen took the chair, settling in with Timothy and a full bottle, as the younger ones formed a semi-circle around her on the floor, content to touch or interact with their brother. Timothy was not oblivious to the attention, smiling at his siblings and making happy noises in his throat. The single window let light and a faint breeze into the room through its dirty cracked pane.

The sound of vehicles disturbed their reunion but was not loud enough to hear in the living room over the television. The first vehicle was some sort of large van, much taller and longer than their Caravan, the second identified itself as a county sheriff vehicle by the lightbar on top and markings on the outside. Karen watched as several got out of the van, recognizing only one, Mrs. Rice. Two deputies exited their cruiser.

The knock was heavy and loud but wasn't answered the first time. It was not until the second which was louder and accompanied by a man's voice that father answered the front door. Karen and the children strained to hear what was being said through the wall but could only hear when the conversation became heated. They heard father and mother curse and yell a couple of times and then the responding sound of a man's voice filled with determination and authority answer them. They supposed that one of the two deputies was speaking.

When the bedroom door finally opened, both the children and the intruders were taken aback by what they saw. After what seemed a long pause, a woman stepped into the room alone, knelt and said, "I'm Brenda Nelson, we are here to help you." Behind her in the doorway, Karen could see Mrs. Rice standing quietly with tears running down her cheeks. Karen, with Timothy still in her arms ran to her. "I prayed every night, I knew you'd come," she said to her teacher as they both burst into tears.

Outside the house, mother and father were being led, handcuffed, to the patrol car and helped into the rear seat. The man who had driven the van and the other officer were busily taking hundreds of pictures of the house, its contents, the children, the yard and even inside the cupboards and closets. The children were each given a chocolate bar, a toy, and a loving hug by Brenda. There were tears in her eyes also when Jake asked her, "what will happen to us now?"

She thought before answering, watching as the younger children turned to hear her, "just good things, only the good things that God has promised for you."

At first it was hard for the children. As bad as they hated their lives, the fear of the unknown was somehow worse. The fear of separation was paramount because all they had ever had was each other. Brenda fought hard to be honest with herself and the children, knowing that they could not bear deceit or more pain. She knew the chances of finding a single home for six children was nearly impossible and that any foster home was only a temporary stop. Once in foster care, she knew they'd just have time to settle before being uprooted again and most probably separated.

They were taken back to the hospital where doctors and nurses carefully assessed their medical condition. They were allowed to bathe, then received new clothes, before eating dinner in the cafeteria. Nurse Nelson came on duty and made a special point of joining them for something to eat. They gained a feeling of celebrity status as their prayers just seemed to continue to be answered.

Brenda was working feverishly behind the scenes to find accommodation for them among the few fosters in the small communities up and down the coast nearby. She had all but given up when Doctor Danes approached her. "How are you doing in your search for housing for the children?" he asked.

She shook her head, "not good, I am afraid. Either they have the heart and not the room or the room and not the heart. All of our fosters are committed, but their level of commitment often wanes when we are talking six from ages infant to teen.

"I may be of some help," the doctor said. We have a beach house which we rent out in the season that lies vacant most of the year. My wife and I could volunteer its use until something better comes along.

It is large, clean, and well furnished. I cannot, however, provide for their care and supervision. Brenda felt like the very hand of God had lifted her up when she answered, "may God bless you. It is a good start, now I'll pray for a willing heart to provide for their care."

It was Friday evening, Brenda knew it was unlikely that she could expect to recruit help from her fosters on such short notice, coming into the weekend. She got the keys and directions to the doctor's house, his personal contact information, and called her husband.

"Bill," she began as she had done many times over her years of service, "I need a favor."

"He sighed, "okay Bren, what do you need?"

"First," she said, "I need you to give me your weekend, then I need your help."

He nearly laughed, how many times had he called off a fishing trip, or left the bowling alley early to lend a hand? "Yes!" That is all he said, waiting for her to respond. He had learned some time ago to just say yes, if you waited to think about it a dozen excuses came to mind right away.

"I need you to grab the kids, their sleeping bags, change of clothes and meet me on the beach." She waited but then continued, "I have a beach house for the weekend and we're having a little get away.

"Yeah, right," Bill finally said, "what's the catch?"

"No catch," she said demurely, "I've invited some friends to join us for the weekend, the kids will love them."

"How many?" he asked, seeing through her ploy.

"Six, just six and they are very well behaved," she entreated him.

"Six? You gotta be kidding," he answered, "this better be some beach house to fit ten of us."

"I'll meet you there at 7:00," she answered, giving him the address.

"I gotta stop and get them a few things and order a few pizzas.

The whole gang loaded back into the van this time before Brenda took the wheel. She dropped her partner off at the office where he had parked his car, then headed to town. They hit the new Walmart at 5:45 where she struggled to remember names and associate them with faces. Tooth brushes, tooth paste, shampoo, and soap; then off to the children's wear where they chose pajamas, under-clothes, t-shirts or tops and casual jeans. There would be time later to buy real shoes so they each grabbed a pair of flip-flops and slippers. She included paper plates, napkins, and cups, then topped off the shopping cart in the junk food aisle before checking out, using her official credit card. The children were quiet, subdued, riding in back together. She supposed they were overwhelmed with it all, as she was.

Her last stop was to order four large pizzas to be delivered to the doctor's residence on the beach. The children had been no help ordering having never eaten pizza, except at school. She ordered two pepperoni and two meat combos and left at 6:45 for the rendezvous. When they pulled up, Bill and their two were waiting for them as the sun began to extinguish itself in the ocean's horizon.

The ten went inside together, walking from room to room, looking but not touching the finely matched furnishings. Brenda and Bill were impressed, she could only wonder how the children who had slept in squalor on the floor must have felt. Their two were boys, 10 and 12, and were no strangers to having guests over for the night who needed a place to stay. But this was over the top for them as well, a mansion on the beach and six children, wow. Brenda stayed inside with the baby and the two younger ones, while the older ones helped Bill and her sons unload the cars. In fifteen minutes, the living room was piled high with clothing and packages.

The two cases of soft drinks went into the refrigerator with the baby formula and those perishables that they had just brought with them. The kids were just starting to get familiar with each other when the doorbell announced their dinner had arrived. The ten sat, Timothy using his car seat in the chair, around the massive table where they blessed the food before Bill began filling plates and Brenda paper cups.

It felt like the TV show the 'Waltons' from the '70s only in nicer digs. Brenda cautioned the children to eat as much as they wanted but to remember they could have more later if they were hungry. She was fearful they'd over eat and make themselves sick.

Brenda asked Karen and the two younger children to help her clear the table while Bill began scoping out the bedroom arrangements with Jake, his brother and his two sons. By 8:00 they had settled in and become comfortable around each other. Bill put the Chronicles of Narnia DVD of "The Lion, The Witch and The Wardrobe" in the player and all sat back to watch the big screen.

Of course the Nelson family had seen it several times but the other children had only seen occasional glimpses of whatever their parents were watching. It must have seemed that they had been transported to a different world where they are valued and loved.

The younger ones nodded off half way through the movie, while the older ones fought to stay awake, not wanting to miss any part of it. The pizza kept disappearing as the night wore on. By a quarter of eleven all ten of them headed to bed, exhausted but happy.

Bill and Brenda awoke at 7:00 to the sound of "Sponge Bob Square Pants" on the television and the giggling of several of the younger children. Her sons were taking joy in 'parenting' the younger girls and watching their antics as "Spongie" did his thing. Bill made a run to the store while Brenda put on the coffee. When he returned he had a six pound bag of pancake mix, five pounds of bacon, two gallons of OJ, butter, syrup, condiments, dogs and buns, and various kinds of lunch meats and bread.

Dr. Dane's gas BBQ had a reversible grill plate that welcomed two pounds of bacon, then converted to a flat top on which to cook the pancakes. The bacon had hardly begun to sizzle before the aroma filled the air and children were coming out of the woodwork.

Brenda could tell that Bill was enjoying himself, looking much like Santa Claus at Christmas, with the expectant children surrounding him on the deck. Timothy had slept through the night but gave a lusty cry, indicating he needed food and attention. Brenda joined Karen who had already risen to provide for her sibling as she always had. She felt sad knowing much of her childhood had already been stolen from her, vowing to do all she could to make what was left as happy as possible. She also knew that she and Bill were not the long term answer to the children's needs.

Half of the bacon didn't make it to the table, being 'sampled' before it got there by the wolfish crew outside. Brenda guarded the remainder inside while Bill started filling paper plates with pancakes, two at a time. They all waited anxiously until everyone had theirs, the food was blessed, and juice poured, before diving in. It took longer to cook them than it did to eat them. In the end, nearly half of the 200 cake bag of mix had been exhausted. Looking around the dining room at the beaming faces, Brenda wished they could just quit her jobs and do this full time.

After clean-up, they all walked down to the beach where the tide was at low ebb, giving everyone a chance to find treasures in the sand. Bill and Brenda held Timothy's hands, forcing him to walk between them until he became exhausted, then took turns carrying him as he slept.

It was good to see Karen laughing and playing with the other children, while trusting her brother to their care. Eventually they returned to the house where the three younger ones watched the last half of Narnia, which they had missed. They all cried when the lion died and cheered when he came back to life.

Sometime later when they woke from naps and joined the older children, Bill fired up the grill again and began roasting hotdogs. Karen, his two sons, and Jake got cushy jobs as assistants, which gave them rights as tasters, bun grillers, and masters of ketchup and mustard application. Brenda and the younger kids handled the drinks and chips. Once again the Lord was thanked for their bounty and everything edible on the table disappeared. Brenda took mind of the plagues in the book of Exodus where the locusts came and destroyed nearly everything in Egypt.

A second job, he said, waiting for her reaction. Brenda looked at Bill puzzled.

"I better get a second job," he repeated. "We are eating close to $50 per meal."

She laughed. "It'll settle down when they finally get the wrinkles out of their little stomachs."

"Yeah, right," he answered cynically, "like a St Bernard only eats while it's growing. I've heard those stories too."

That is one of those things she loved about Bill, he seldom took himself too seriously and would do anything for anyone in need. She had little doubt that if it came to it, he'd get that second job before letting the kids go back to relive their nightmare existence.

"Have you got any ideas?" he asked. "I mean, for next week and the weeks after that. Do you have any possibilities?"

She shook her head then added, "God will provide." She was sure of it, He always did, but had no clue how.

The older children were playing outside together and the younger ones, including Timmy, were asleep in front of the TV.

Both Brenda and Bill were Christians, from Christian homes, who tried their best to live it to their boys. Brenda's father was a Baptist preacher from Roseberg and Bill's family attended as part of his flock. They had met first in AWANA, then became close as they moved into youth group together. They were juniors in high school when he first told her he loved her, and seniors when he gave her a promise ring.

They fought frustration and separation as they attended different colleges, but remained faithful to both God and each other. "Equally yoked", was the way it was described in the Bible, two bound together pulling in the same direction toward the common goal. They had always been equally yoked.

The children only had the single change of clothes that they had been given at the hospital and with all the activity of the past day, were becoming 'human'. Not that they would have noticed it themselves, having worn rags days at a time without laundry or baths. But Brenda and Bill had plans to attend their church in the morning and wanted everyone to feel clean and comfortable. So, off they went to 'Wally World' again to find some economical clothes for the six children.

They were especially proud of the way their own sons jumped in like siblings, with offers of help and suggestions for the other children. The 'company' credit card took another sizable hit in spite of Brenda's thrifty nature. This time new shoes, underwear, and socks were included with the new outerwear. They finished out the day with a movie rental and several 'bags of burgers' from the drive-in of the same name.

As Sunday morning came, they finished off the remaining bacon and pancakes before taking turns in the various bathrooms of the spacious home. Bill said it was like his time in the military, getting ready for deployment, as they readied the family for church service. Indeed it was a campaign to simply feed, dress, load, and unload the family at church. Of course, like everything else they had done together, it was all new to the children. They had been so sheltered, so restricted from real life that they had little concept of the nature of church.

Only Karen and Jake knew of, but not about church, the others did not. This was not the first time Brenda and Bill had arrived with 'extended family' but was the first time it filled an entire pew. Brenda kept Timothy and the two younger children with them while the other four followed her sons to Sunday school class. Bill walked with them, explaining to the teacher that they initially needed to stay together, rather than go to separate classes by age groups.

As usual God, through the pastor, furnished an appropriate sermon topic regarding Jesus' instruction concerning His love for children. Brenda kept waiting for instruction, for a sign, as to God's will for the children, but none came. She secretly hoped that Bill might offer to extend the care of the children beyond the weekend, but when he did not, part of her was also relieved. She saw them as a 'joyful burden' but a burden never the less.

Karen and Jake were all smiles as they rejoined them after Sunday school, hands full of colored Biblical figures and short stories. Each had been given a children's Bible with larger print and many colored pictures of Bible characters. In addition, they were worded age appropriately, allowing the young to get an easier feel for their message.

The dread of the end of the magical weekend hung over Brenda like a looming black cloud, she knowing it was maybe the only single shining spot in the children's lives to date. The thought of putting them into the system, separating them, and relying upon even loving strangers for their futures filled her with fear. She prayed, heard no answer and prayed some more. Still God seemed silent, unhearing, uninvolved.

"Pietsba" was the first word that Timothy had ever said, except possibly to Karen. He smiled as they returned to the beach house with pizza for lunch, eager to put his tiny teeth to work. The family laughed, repeating him over and over as they asked for yet another slice. The children took turns holding his hand as he walked short distances between pieces of furniture. It seemed that he had taken on the mantle of his new surroundings and was blossoming all at once. His once hopeless little life now had hope.

Bill gathered the family together in the living room after eating and took out his well-worn Bible. Several of the children took out their new ones as well. They he restarted the Narnia movie, stopping it often to explain the context where it paralleled the Bible. Over the next few hours the family came to appreciate C. S. Lewis' biblically realistic fantasy and gained a new appreciation of the movie.

This time the younger girls did not cry when the lion was killed, knowing he would live again, this time everyone knew who he really represented and why he had died. Brenda was amazed that no one interrupted, none dozed off, everyone including herself and her boys sat enwrapped in the tale.

Nap time found them all ready for a rest. While she lay beside Bill, eyes closed, she tried to imagine how the little strays were feeling. If they were wondering if this were somehow just a dream from which they would soon awaken, finding themselves back in the old farm house. "Bill, she said softly, are you asleep?"

"I was," he said, sporting a grin and opening one eye.

"You were not," she countered, "what were you thinking about?

"Oh, not much," he said. "About the impossibility of life, about the future, the past, and what to feed the horde for dinner."

She threw her arms around him and hugged him. "You are such a pussycat," she said, "all big and strong but really a cream puff on the inside." He kissed her without answering.

In the county jail, both mother and father had been booked on charges of child neglect and endangerment. In addition they were pursuing charges of fraud, willful misrepresentation, and whatever charges stemmed from the children dropping out of school. They'd spend some time, no doubt, back on the public dole being fed and cared for in some secure state institution.

"Clam chowder," Bill said aloud.

"What?" Brenda answered, "what are you talking about?"

"Dinner," he answered, "you want to go to Mo's or have me make my world famous clam chowder?"

"While it is tempting," she said smiling, "it'd be cheaper at Mo's."

Now, for those who aren't familiar, Mo's is a west coast fixture, serving the coast of Oregon for three generations out of small, usually dingy and quaint surroundings. In Newport, at dockside, are novelty shops catering to the needs of tourists, as well as fish processing warehouses, restaurants, and places of special interest.

Among these is situated the original Mo's restaurant, the undersea garden, and the Ripley's Believe It or Not museum. When they arrived, it was if the children had just come from another planet, everything being strange, new, and exciting. They ordered 'family style' rather than by the bowl, each hungrily finishing the first bowl with lots of little oyster crackers floating on the top, followed by a second and in some cases a third, before they were full. They got the tickets for the undersea garden, and found themselves below water level, watching the fish and marine life all around them through the glass walls. Then finally, before heading for the beach house, they made a tour through the strange and unusual at Ripley's.

Bill hugged all the children, kissed Brenda, then loaded his sons into the car and headed for school. Brenda made sure all the children were clean, dressed, and were sitting down eating cereal, then called her supervisor. She gave him a brief rundown of the events of the weekend, beginning with the intervention on Friday.

"Let's hold them out of school another day," he said, "process them into the system today and find temporary homes for them."

She agreed but added, "there's more to this than meets the eye. I fear if we separate them, we will create a whole bunch of new issues and find ourselves paying for years of counseling. If we can keep them together temporarily, I am sure God will provide a way."

He laughed, then said, "Dear Brenda, you are a dreamer. Find a suitable home for all six?" Bert was a good guy, caring and easy to work for, but he was also practical and realistic.

"I have a place, I just need someone to be with them while I look for a permanent solution."

"You have a place for six kids?" he asked.

"Yeah," she laughed. "A little over three thousand square feet on the beach, fully furnished."

"Are we paying you too much or are you selling drugs," he asked jokingly.

"Neither," she answered, "a doctor friend lent it to us for a while."

Bert was smiling, "I'll just bet he did, what's it going to cost us?"

"He volunteered once he saw the children," she said.

"I'll call my wife," Bert said, "see if she'd like a few days down on the beach. I've got some comp time coming and we both like kids."

Brenda was smiling when she and the children filed into the office, nearly filling it. Bert came walking out of his private office with raised eyebrows.

"Kids," Brenda said, swinging her hand in an arc toward them, "this is Bert. Bert these are our kids."

The youngest of the girls hid behind her sister, the rest of them smiled endearingly at Bert, looking like angels in their new clothes.

"Lisa," Bert said to his secretary, "would you take these children down to the 'munch' room and see what you can find while Brenda and I visit?"

Lisa was young and single, a new addition to the office, not yet 'mother' material. She nodded, grabbed some change from a jar on her desk and took Jake's hand. "Come on, let's see what we've got to munch on," she said. They all followed her like baby ducks behind their mother down the long hallway.

Brenda was still holding Timothy when they sat down in his office. "This is Timmy," she offered.

Bert nodded. "I didn't mention a baby to Martha when I called," he said smiling. "We're closer to being grandparents than parents. I wonder how much we have forgotten?"

"Bill and I will help," she offered, "but we can't do 24/7 and find them a home too."

Bert nodded. "Do you really think it is possible? he asked. "I mean, who has the time, room, and stamina to take on six children?"

"Anything's possible," Brenda parroted scripture, "you just have to believe."

"Four days, we'll give you four days," Bert said. "If you don't have something in the works by Friday, they have to go wherever we can find homes."

Brenda hugged him, then began writing down the names of the children and their ages on a sheet of paper. On another, she wrote the address of the beach house and handed him the key.

"They like pizza, pancakes, bacon, hamburgers, hot dogs, and anything put in front of them. They are not picky eaters but know little about life outside of their bedroom. Karen has been mothering them successfully for years, she'll be your best source of information."

Bert started to object as she handed him the baby, but smiled instead as Timothy gave him a grin.

"I'll tell them goodbye, take my own car home and leave you the van, then get to work finding a home for them. Bill and I will stop in after dinner and see how you are doing." With that, and before he could object, she left the office.

Brenda took Karen aside and told her straight out what was going on, asked her to help Bert and Martha out when they needed it, and hugged the children one at a time. She had a tear in her eye when she started her old Chevy Cavalier. 'Dear Lord,' she prayed as she drove, 'only You know the plans You have made for these little ones, for good and not for evil, please help us find a way to keep them together.' She continued to pray as she drove around the small community. Finally she found herself in front of the grade school, so she parked and went inside.

"May I help you?" came the inquiry from a 30-something behind the reception desk.

"Yes, thank you," Brenda said. "I'd like to speak with Mrs. Rice if I could," she said, showing her badge.

"She's in class," the woman said, "I can interrupt her if it is important, or class will be over in a few minutes and she'll have time to visit between classes."

"Thank you," she said again. "I'll just have a seat here until she has a minute." Brenda sat wondering why she had stopped and what she had to say to the woman. Mrs. Rice greeted her warmly right after the bell had indicated the end of class.

"How are Karen and the children?" were her first words.

"They are doing well, thank God," Brenda replied. "We expect to enroll them once again as soon as we find a permanent home."

Mrs. Rice seemed pleased. "And how may I help you," she asked, then added, "I'm sorry I only have fifteen minutes between classes."

Brenda took a deep breath, "I honestly don't know," she admitted. "I don't know why I'm here. I was driving around praying, trying to come up with a plan and here I am."

Mrs. Rice smiled. "Keep your heart and your mind open," she suggested, "maybe someone is trying to tell you something."

Brenda smiled weakly, "I hope so, in my fifteen years the most I've ever been able to place with one family were four."

The bell rang. "Gotta go!" Mrs. Rice said, handling Brenda her card. "Let me know how it is going."

Back in the car, she took a call from Bill. "How's it going?" he asked.

She filled him in on the progress to date. "So, old Bert's taking a vacation at the beach house is he?" he said laughing.

"Yeah, and we're going to stop by and make sure he and Martha are doing alright after we eat dinner," she added.

"The boys have soccer practice tonight," he reminded her.

"I forgot," she answered, "maybe they could catch a ride with the Wilson's."

"I'll give Blake a call at the store and ask," Bill volunteered. "I'll let you know."

When they hung up, she thanked God once again for Bill. She

swung into the hospital parking lot and parked. As she sat, she remembered she needed to clarify the arrangement they had with Doctor Danes. Inside, she was directed to the pediatric ward, and from there to his private office. His secretary took her name and announced her to the doctor who came right to the door and welcomed her into his office.

"Mrs. Nelson," he offered genuinely, "please, have a seat."

To her surprise he joined her in one of the leather chairs facing the desk rather than seating himself behind it. Nurse Baker was right about him, she thought, he's real, not pumped up with himself and his position. A lesser man would have assumed the 'power position' and the safety of his desk to feed his ego.

"How are the children?" Dr. Danes asked, breaking into her evaluation of him.

"They are well physically and enjoying their celebrity status for the time being. They have had so little contact with the outside world that our world, the one we all complain about, seems like a fairy tale to them."

She handed him prints that had been taken at the farm when the children were rescued. They plainly showed the living conditions in which the children existed. He reached into his pocket and extracted his personal check book.

She stopped him. "I'm not here to solicit donations," she said a little too harshly.

He looked at her. "Why then are you here?" he asked gently.

There were tears of frustration in her eyes when she answered. "I don't know. I was praying and felt I should go to the school, then driving around I felt I should stop here. I do want to thank you for your generosity of allowing us to use your house. We should be out by next weekend, if that is alright."

"Just fine," he answered, "you can stay as long as needed."

No one said anything for several seconds, but both continued to sit. Finally Dr. Danes asked, "does this sort of thing happen often?"

"Thankfully, no," she answered, "not here in our area. Maybe in the bigger cities," she continued, "Portland, Seattle, but we usually get two's and three's and most of them from less harsh conditions."

"What is your position?" he asked.

"My position, you mean my title or what I do?" she asked.

"You seem to be in-charge," he offered, "are you the administrator or supervisor?"

I'm a case supervisor," she answered, "one of three case workers who attempt to advocate for children in harm's way. Bert Ellis is our boss, he is in charge of all the satellite offices on the coast, from Seaside south. We are lucky because he lives right here in Newport and calls this home base."

"I'd like to meet him," the doctor said nonchalantly.

Brenda gave him a big grin, "that can be easily arranged," she said, "he and his wife Martha are staying at your beach house and personally caring for the kids while I'm out looking for a home for them."

It was Danes' turn to smile. "Maybe we'll just drop in and surprise them then. May I keep these for a while?" he asked, holding the photos.

"Yes, I can print others," she answered.

She resisted the urge to give him a hug, but shook his hand and then left and walked toward her car.

"Brenda!" she heard someone calling. "Brenda, can I have a minute?" a nurse called from behind her. It was Linda Baker. Brenda stopped and waited for her to catch up.

Her first question mirrored Danes', "how are the children?"

They found a bench and sat together. Brenda went back over the same ground as she just had with the doctor. "May God forgive them," she said of the parents, "how could anyone treat their own children that way?" Brenda just shook her head as she swallowed the lump in her own throat.

"You made all the difference you know," Brenda said quietly. "If you hadn't advocated for them, they'd still be there and sooner or later little Timothy would have died." Linda just nodded, afraid to try and speak, her heart filled with emotion.

Finally she composed herself. "If there is anything I can do for them, please let me know," she said handing Brenda her card with the home phone written on the reverse side. This time Brenda hugged and was hugged back.

In her car again, Brenda felt more at peace in spite of the knowledge she had accomplished nothing toward her goal of finding a home for her charges. She called Bill who was unavailable, and then Bert at the beach house. Martha answered.

Martha, Brenda guessed, was in her late 50's, maybe approaching 60, as was Bert, but looked younger. Brenda had met their two sons when they lived at home, nice kids. Both were in college now. Martha was always genteel, always gracious and genuine in her manner when dealing with people, probably a product of her southern upbringing. There was little left of her southern accent now after all these years living in the northwest, but she still retained her ladylike manner.

"Hello Brenda, so nice of you to call," was the greeting Martha offered. Brenda knew the caller ID had identified her but still it seemed such a nice way to be spoken to. Brenda ignored the urge to brush past the niceties and ask for Bert, instead she returned Martha's greeting in kind.

"It's always good to hear your voice as well," Brenda said sincerely, "how's it going with the children?"

"I love them, every one," she gushed, "but I'm too old to appreciate them as much as I was when I was younger."

"Did Bert mention that Bill and I were going to try and come by?" Brenda asked.

"He did," came her answer, "and it will be good to see you both again."

"Please do give us a call if you run short on anything," Brenda continued, "it will be easier for us than you to shop." They visited for a few more minutes before Bert came on the line. He sounded out of breath.

"Hi Bren," he said.

"Hi Bert, how are you doing?"

"Fine, I think," he answered, "but this must be the only day in history that there's no breeze on the beach. We've been down trying to get kites up without any help from Mother Nature."

"I gave the doctor a heads-up on our situation this morning," Brenda said. "He's okay with our use of the house and wanted to visit with you. He could show up there sometime this week."

"Okay," Bert said, "what have you gotten us into?"

"Nothing, nothing really," she answered. "He said he just wanted to talk with my boss, and you're it. Besides, you'll like him." She could almost see Bert shaking his graying head.

"Bring some ice cream," Bert said, "lots of it, and cones!"

"Roger, boss," she said, "anything else?"

"Not yet, we'll let you know," he answered. "See you tonight."

The pool was neither deep nor wide, Brenda knew that. Those both willing, and able, to foster children were like those willing to donate blood, a small percentage of the total population. Too old, too young, self absorbed, financially unable, physically unable, lacking skills or ability, children of their own, moral or criminal risks, drinkers, drug users, and the list went on eliminating one after another.

She had five fosters and nine kids out in the immediate area, and four others had been adopted and had permanent homes. Salem, Portland and the bigger cities provided more possibilities in the way of adoption, but also had more children needing to find homes. Brenda had always told Bill, 'it's easier and more fun to make 'em than raise 'em and folks found that out while still in high school'.

Bill, Brenda, and their two sons came walking up the steps with three gallons of ice cream and two dozen cones under their arms about 7 p.m. Mike and Beth Danes were already there visiting with the Ellis family and the children. When Brenda entered, she was chastised first by the adults, but warmly welcomed by the children.

Bill and his boys immediately became the center of attraction when they set up an ice cream station and began scooping the quickly softening dessert. Timothy held Karen's hand and walked everywhere with her. He'd even began talking gibberish, which his siblings seemed to understand. They stayed until 9:00 and left together, leaving the impromptu family watching television together.

"Tom?" Mike asked in the manner of two bowling buddies setting up an evening out. Tom being Tom Bannister, the hospital Administrator and Chairman of the Board for the small hospital. Mike, of course, was Doctor Michael Danes, head of his pediatric department.

"Bill? Mike here," was his second call to his neighbor and friend, William Mitchell, the mayor of Newport. Call after call was made, each time in a sincere friend to friend manner.

"Steve, Mike here, when does the school board meet again," he asked of the superintendent of schools.

"Bart? Mike Danes, how's the campaign going? Got a minute to visit?" he asked the incumbent state representative who played golf with him.

In a few minutes he had spoken with nearly everyone with money, clout, or authority within a hundred mile radius. He had spent much time in thought and a like amount in prayer during the past few days. It culminated when Brenda Nelson had dropped in this afternoon and he had seen the pictures. He was a devout man from a rich Christian heritage who had been blessed in many ways, and knew it. He gave God the credit for his good fortune and worked hard to remain humble and faithful.

After coming up against several insurmountable brick walls, God had given him just the whisper of a solution to his problem. It was not clearly or perfectly defined but it was beginning to come together in his head.

"Is this the Baker residence?" Brenda asked.

"Yes," a male voice answered, "who is this?"

"My name is Brenda Nelson," she answered, "I am acquainted with Linda, is she home?"

"Just a minute," Daniel replied. She could hear him calling is wife.

"This is Linda, who is this again?"

"Brenda Nelson from child protective services, do you have a minute?"

"Yes, of course," she said, "is something wrong with the children?

"No, they are fine, thank you for caring. I am calling to see if we could meet and visit."

"Well, I work tomorrow from nine to four."

"I'd rather meet with both of you away from work for a few minutes if you can find the time," Brenda said.

"That is a hard thing for us," Linda said. "Dan does custom farming and I work rotation. You were fortunate to find us home together tonight. Will it take long?"

"No, no more than an half hour," Brenda said.

"Just a minute," Linda said covering the phone. Brenda could hear her talking with her husband in the back ground. "How about right now?" Linda asked. "Dan said TV is just reruns and he'd like to meet you. I've told him all about the children and you and Doctor Danes."

She took down the address and directions, left Bill and the boys a note, $20, ordered them pizza for delivery at 6:00, then left. She prayed on the drive out for God's will and direction. She looked at her watch when she parked, promising herself to keep the visit to the agreed half hour.

The door opened before she knocked, "please come in," Linda said. Daniel was standing behind her smiling.

"This is an unofficial/official visit," she said to her hosts, smiling. "Because of Linda's unique position in bringing the children's situation to our attention, I feel a kinship and responsibility to her. I also have a professional and personal interest in the children." They sat at the kitchen table. Brenda's trained eye took in the surroundings from the time she had parked until she sat down, evaluating and making judgments as she did.

The home appeared to be a modern 20-25 year old structure, between 1,800 and 2,000 square feet, lawn well cared for, home clean and well kept, furnishings modest but fairly new.

"Nice place," she said sincerely. "Do you farm it?"

Dan answered, "yes, we raise a few head of beef, our own hay and a nice sized garden. Once in a while I plant a few acres of row crops to sell when the market is good."

"We have forty," he said, referring to the forty acres surrounding the house. "There's an eighty next to us with an out-of-state owner. Sometimes I lease from him and plant our own crops, sometimes I plant and care for his crops for a fee."

"I see," she said, as though she knew what he was talking about. "How long have you lived here?"

"Twelve years," Linda said proudly, "three more and we'll own it, God willing."

"Nice," Brenda commented, "I wish I could say the same for us, we're only half way through a thirty. Children?" she asked carefully. A sadness came over them, Brenda could see it appear like a dark cloud.

"No," Linda said, "I had a cyst when I was a child, they removed both ovaries just to be safe."

"You are likely wondering why I am here," Brenda said to the couple, then continued before they could answer.

"After having met Linda and seen her heart for children, I am here to see if you may be candidates for our foster parent program." Being intelligent people, the possibility that she had a motive had not escaped them when she called. Both smiled and said, "we had kind of wondered about that."

Brenda nodded and continued, "have you ever considered either fostering or adoption?" They hesitated, so she moved ahead. "I am not here to sell you anything, even if I could, you'd be doing it for the wrong reasons and rather than it bringing you joy it would become a burden." Her comment seemed to ease the tension in the room.

Brenda stood, already over her promised half hour by five minutes. "Thank you for your time, your courtesy in letting me speak freely, and for all you have done for the Brown children already. God bless you."

As she moved toward the front door, Dan stopped her. "How does it work?" he asked. "I mean, if we do find we are interested, how do we find out more?"

She looked toward Linda who was smiling. "You just call me any-time and I'll answer any questions you may have, even let you meet some other foster parents and talk with them privately. They are a tight knit group, always willing to learn from and share with each other what they have learned. None of us are in it for the short term, these children need stability for the long run." She hugged them both and left feeling 'Spirit directed'. It was a good feeling.

Tuesday morning she called, then stopped by the Miller's home. They were empty-nesters, early retirees with no health issues and two grown children living out of state. He, a retired civil servant and she retired from public education as a teacher. They co-owned a salt water taffy shop in town, with a full time manager. That left them both time and a little extra income to enjoy the children who came and went in their lives.

Brenda knew them well, both their strengths and weaknesses. They were well suited to young school age children and had fostered as many as three at one time previously, but lacked the stamina required for infants and teenagers. Brenda knew from experience that preschool and teens were labor intensive and soaked the energy from 24/7 caregivers. She hoped it would not be necessary to place any of the Brown children with them, but desired to investigate the possibility if it became necessary. They were the only fosters in her circle who currently had no children living with them. She was very aware that Friday was only three days away and nothing had volunteered itself as a solution to her problem.

"Mrs. Nelson, please hold for Doctor Danes," came the woman's voice over the phone.

"Brenda, this is Mike Danes," he said just if they had been old friends. "I have asked a few friends to join me for a little get-to-gether this evening and was hoping that you and Bert might join us."

Needless to say, his invitation took her off guard, but his comfortable way of asking intrigued her. "May I ask how the purpose of the gathering would involve Mr. Ellis and I?" She had been careful to refer to Bert in a businesslike manner.

"Why of course. I'm sorry, I have been so busy drumming up support that I completely overlooked including you in my little scheme. I'll explain it to everyone in detail this evening, but for now suffice it to say that I am attempting to garner support for an interim housing facility for children at risk."

Brenda was interested, how would it be funded, who would have oversight...? The questions and problems flooded to the forefront, but she did not ask. "We'll be there," she said.

"Thank you, and bring Bill also if you like," he said before hanging up the phone.

Seconds later she was on the phone with Bert, explaining what little she knew and confirming that he could come. Minutes later Martha was on her phone calling friends and inviting them to join her for an evening at the beach house. She did mention that she wanted to introduce them to some special friends who were staying with her but did not invite them to baby sit.

Mike had faith, faith in God, faith that God's plan included miracles, faith of the ultimate victory of good over evil. It helped him face the unpredictability of medicine and life, without becoming discouraged. He had seen and even played a part in many miracles but had also participated in the inevitability of death as well.

As an elder in his church, he had spent hours by a bedside when the doctor in him said prayer was hopeless. He prayed asking for what he wanted, knowing he would receive what God willed, and had been surprised both ways. Sometimes they were healed on earth, other times in heaven. His faith might have seemed to some as just an optimistic attitude toward life, but he knew it was much more.

When they arrived at the "Beachcomber", they were ushered to the ballroom which had been set up for the occasion in the manner of a high ticket event. A dozen or more round tables, each seating eight, had been appointed with the finest the exclusive club had to offer.

At the entrance, Michael stood in a finely tailored sport coat with open collar, beside a beautiful woman who he introduced as his wife Beth. Well dressed, but not pretentious, she could only be described as elegant. She seemed to share Mike's appreciation and realization of being blessed rather than deserving. Brenda immediately liked her.

It was she who broke free from greeting their guests to invite them to the head table where she and Mike would join them. Bert whispered, "don't you dare tell Martha about this. She'd kill me for leaving her behind to babysit."

Brenda smiled, "same goes with Bill, he took the boys to soccer practice."

Even wearing her best clothing, Brenda felt like a poor relative as those who enjoyed their station arrived in jewels and fur. She watched Mike at the door greeting each as friends, equals, regardless of their position or income. It occurred to her that he might well have shown up in jeans had it not been for Beth. She was reminded of how Jesus had appeared on earth seeming unmindful of the trappings of the world, which He had created. To be comfortable with yourself is the key to not feeling the need to worry about what others may think.

She and Bert had been seated facing into the room, with the portable stage and screen at their backs. As their table filled up, they were fortunate to meet their congressman, a state senator, the mayor and their wives. When Mike and Beth finally joined them, he remained standing and thanked them all for coming and invited them to enjoy dinner together. He then bowed his head and blessed the food, and the gathering of friends, before he took his seat beside his wife. Beth smiled at him, love evident in her eyes. She clearly loved and respected this man, Brenda thought.

As each table visited among themselves Brenda thought, this must be the same perspective the Brown children hold of our lives when comparing them with what they know. Some enjoyed wine or drinks, others coffee, tea, or soft drinks, seemingly unaware of each other. She liked that, the pretense seemed to have been left at the front door.

An appetizer was followed by an elegant salad, then by a lobster bisque, as the wait staff moved with fluidity between the tables, setting down and picking up tableware and china. Brenda and Bert watched in amazement, gaining insight into how those in the world of the rich and famous lived.

Mike spoke across the table. "Bert and Brenda, I hope I haven't put you on the spot here. I felt such an urgency that I cut corners in the attempt to make things happen. If God wills, I hope to help provide a solution to those things that are important to all of us. Many of those here have the power and authority to make things happen in unconventional ways."

Several little specialized saucers, fresh from the oven, interrupted the meal, each little indent in the dish displayed an escargot. Nice touch, Brenda thought, I wish I could have a whole plate to myself.

The little guys disappeared, one after another, into the mouths of Mike's friends. Mike stood, gently tapped the side of his crystal water goblet, bringing conversation across the room to a halt.

"Friends," he said, "before we enjoy our entrée and dessert, I want to take a minute to explain the photos which you are about to see on the screen at the front of the room." The lights seemed to dim by themselves as the screen became illuminated, displaying one after another the photos which had been taken at the Brown's farmhouse.

"Please understand that these are not from some third world country, these are from right here in our community. These are real children with needs that have gone unmet, whose dreams have been stifled by want and pain. Lives in jeopardy, not because there is no system in place to help, but because it was manipulated by those who should have cared for them, and used it for personal gain.

The room remained quiet save the sudden intake of breath from a horrified viewer. Next, the hospital photos of the children in the waiting room, break room, and those of little Timothy in ICU were shown. Then finally, several taken candidly during his visit to his beach house showing the miracle that love and good surroundings had made for the children in a very short time.

"Timothy wouldn't talk and couldn't walk when I first met him," Mike said, pointing to him doing both in the pictures. The lights came up, but the photos continued to be shown as their dinner was served. Bert chose the rack of lamb, while Brenda the bacon wrapped filet.

"I'm feeling guilty," she told him, "I wish Bill were here."

Bert nodded while stuffing his face, "me too, but not enough to tell her what she missed."

The photos had a haunting presence to them, probably just as Mike had hoped. They spoke in ways that opened the heart to hear the message that God was whispering to each.

Following the meal, coffee was poured and a variety of opulent desserts were offered. As the wait staff retired with the last of the empty china, Mike rose again.

"Many of you here know each other, and obviously all of you know me." Laughter rose from all across the room. "What I'd like to do is introduce to you a couple of my new friends who have been holding the line here in our community while waiting for reinforcements. Please welcome Brenda Nelson and Bert Ellis."

Both stood, embarrassed, as the room gave them a round of applause. When they reseated themselves, he asked nurse Linda Baker and her husband Dan to stand also.

"Nurse Baker," Mike said, "was the instrument God used to fill the 'gap in the wall' and bring the needs of these children to our attention." The applause was even louder than before. When it died out, Mike continued.

"For those of you who are not Christian, or are lacking in Biblical knowledge, the 'gap in the wall' refers to a time when ancient cities had walls to protect them from their enemies. When a wall was breached it had a 'gap' which allowed the enemy inside. It was a brave warrior who risked it all by filling the gap to keep the city secure." Some nodded, some learned, but all understood his meaning.

"Besides my desire to enjoy a dinner with friends, I have invited each of you here for a purpose. To some, that may mean opening your hearts; others, your wallets; and still others, using your position and influence to facilitate the impossible. What I envision is a 'city of refuge', a place where children are safe from harm, where they can feel secure and loved, where they are provided for not only physically, but also emotionally and spiritually."

"It's more than a half-way house, or children's home, it has to be. That is why each of you have a unique part to play in the plan. It involves private funding and community participation. Not a 'one-time feel-good' project, but an ongoing commitment to the welfare of our children and community. It must (he stressed the word) involve state, federal, and local agencies, law enforcement, existing child protective services, the medical community, and ongoing participation from both volunteers and paid employees."

The senator at the table whispered, "if he runs for office I'm dead meat," which brought laughter from those who overheard.

"Not to worry, Senator," Mike said. "I'm too busy to retire on the government dole." That brought another good spirited round of laughter and comments. His friend smiled and nodded.

"They are passing around slips of paper to your tables, each of you please take one and write your name on it, then privately list how you might see yourself as partnering in this enterprise. If it holds no interest to you, just say that, and no one will blame you. Remember, your commitment can be making phone calls, helping get permits, cutting red tape, facilitating donations, excavation, construction, surveying, volunteerism at the facility, application for grants, furnishings, building products or land donations. Beth and I have pledged our beach house as a temporary shelter to later be sold, with the funds going to help finance this project." Several clapped their approval.

"Now to the immediate need. These six children will be without a caregiver in a few short days. If no one comes forward they will, by necessity, be split up and placed into foster homes. It is paramount that a minimum of additional trauma be levied upon their already fragile psyches. What they need is continuity, time to settle in and heal, not more unsettling change." He looked at Brenda and Bert, both nodded their agreement.

"Bert's wife, Martha, is with them now, loving and caring for them, but her commitment is temporary." Someone stuck up their hand.

"Yes, Bob?" Mike asked.

"Can we agree to finance temporarily, paid care for the children at their current location? he asked.

Bert was shaking his head no. "The state has guidelines that do not include privately funded care unless within a state facility like a shelter or children's home." Eyes turned to the two congressmen.

They smiled, "we'll look into that," they said together.

An attorney present asked Bert a question, "could the shelter be viewed as a defacto foster parent under current law?" Bert agreed to investigate the possibility, giving the man his card for followup.

More and more interaction between individuals was happening across the room, with ideas being offered, endorsed, or rejected out of hand. Mike was seated and was watching the building of the 'hive' as the worker bees seemed to engage with one another. After about twenty minutes, the conversations had run their course, and attention turned back towards the front table.

"When can we have dinner again?" someone asked Mike with a laugh.

"How about two weeks from today, the 15th," he answered. "I'll make the arrangements but we'll go Dutch next time." That brought more laughter.

"One last thing," Mike said, still standing. "Don't keep this a secret, share with friends, family, business associates, invite them to join us, there's a lot of talent out there just waiting to be asked." As they began to leave the meeting, there remained several clusters of people in deep discussion.

Dan and Linda approached Brenda and were introduced to Bert. Linda opened the conversation, "Dan and I have agreed to a few days a week with the children until a more permanent solution can be found. I assume there is paperwork that needs to be done?"

"Yes," Brenda said, "but a minimal amount since we have already had our evaluation meeting."

"So," Dan said smiling, "that is what you call our little visit yesterday? Linda had been thinking, we'll have to check our schedules and see what days we are available. Can we get back to you?"

"I'll call you Thursday," Brenda said, "we can work out the details." The men shook hands and the women hugged as they walked out together.

"Quite a guy," Linda said, looking back at Mike who had buttonholed the two legislators and was talking with them.

"That he is," Bert and Brenda both agreed. "That he is."

Martha' s guests had gone home, the younger children were in bed, and Karen and Jake were watching television with her when Bert came in. "How'd it go?" he asked, kissing her on the cheek.

"It went fine," she answered. "The women love them, and Karen is so good with the little ones. How did it go with you?" she asked.

"Just another business meeting," he said trying not to laugh, "you know how they are. I'll tell you all about it when we have a few minutes alone."

At ten o' clock they roused the sleeping children and tucked them into beds, turned off the television and went to their own room. Bert guessed that all across the town, couples like they were spending the next several sleepless hours discussing the opportunity that God had provided through Dr. Michael Danes.

Martha listened quietly, interjecting an idea or asking a question now and then as Bert described the evening in greater detail. She said, "you know I am beginning to love the children myself, maybe we could stay involved too, at least a day a week or something."

He smiled, "I'll mark us down as subs and see how many come forward."

When Brenda called the Miller's back, they wanted to meet the children before making a commitment, six sounded like more than they thought they could handle. When the superintendent of schools called the principal, he in turn visited with his teachers, several of which had more than a passing interest in the project.

In particular, Mrs. Rice wanted to visit with Brenda and see if there was a place where she could assist in getting the children re-integrated in the school system. The nurse's break room at the hospital was abuzz with conversation of the staff concerning Dr. Danes and his daring idea. Two nurses and one doctor promised to talk with their better halves about the possibility of being somehow involved.

Mike met with his pastor who called a meeting of the elder board in special session to discuss how they may come alongside in the effort as well. They voted to put the measure before the congregation the following Sunday.

It seemed like God was moving powerfully in the little tourist town until Bert got a call from HEW who had gotten word of the proposal and began a turf war, fearing the loss of federal funding. Previously, the two agencies, federal and state, had complemented each other and maintained a good working relationship. The lines of responsibility were not clearly defined in statute, but the Fed always strong armed the smaller agencies, much the same way the FBI looked down on local law enforcement. Bert called Mike, who in turn called his two friends in congress.

He had anticipated that Satan would somehow attack and had been prepared for it. Dan called Brenda, excitedly explaining that they had just received an offer to let them purchase the 80 acres bordering their land at below market value. She was pleased for them but couldn't understand why she had been chosen to share the good news. "Don't you see?" he said, "some of the land could be used for a site for the City of Refuge."

By Thursday they seemed to have the temporary needs of the six children covered, with several families agreeing to pick up the slack. Brenda met with the Millers again and drove them to the beach house where they met Bert and Martha and the children. During the drive, she outlined Mike's proposal and how it may ultimately work into the foster system for the whole area. They asked to be included in the next meeting.

It was hard for them not to love the children, but Brenda could see a hesitancy also. "Five of the six will be in school beginning next week, only Timothy will need supervision during the day," she offered. "This whole situation is such a non-typical thing that I have to believe that it was brought to us as a means to improve our whole foster program. It is forcing us to utilize more than one volunteer to provide for the needs of the children and," she continued, "I think is forcing more of the public to become aware and involved."

It was Martha who found the missing thread. "Why don't you stay on and enjoy the afternoon and eat with us, get a feel for them and they you. I can tell you I was frightened out of my mind when Bert first asked, now it's going to be hard to share them when others come and take their turns."

The Millers smiled and agreed, letting Brenda to get back to work. She liked the idea of letting each foster couple do likewise, getting familiar with the routine before they had to take the reins. Maybe each couple could be encouraged to come the day before their service, get oriented and mentored before they made the hand off. She called and left a message for Doctor Danes with his service, then called the Baker's house. Dan was somewhere on his tractor, Linda said, but she didn't have to work until later. When Brenda offered to buy lunch, she agreed and set the time and place.

A call from the county sheriff's office was to give her a heads-up on the arraignment scheduled for the following morning at 10:00. The prosecutor had hoped to meet today and go over some details with her prior to their court appearance. Brenda made a note to call him after her luncheon. She was pulling into the parking lot of the Clam Digger restaurant when her cell chirped.

"Hi, Mike here," the doctor said. "I'm returning your call."

Brenda quickly laid out the events that were seeming to be happening all around and in-spite of her; the land deal, the school's involvement, and Martha's idea of the fosters mentoring each other into service.

"The hospital is joining us too, it seems," Mike shared. "Tom has spoken to his Board and they have agreed in principle to encourage staff to volunteer time by giving them a tax incentive, and to provide necessary medical supplies and counselors. They are meeting with their lawyers to see if it effects their non-profit status and their other arrangements for indigent care, to get the best bang for the buck."

"You should find that the Fed have backed off a little to give us room to run, but will be keeping a keen eye on it. Agencies are always so jealous of funding they sometimes forget why they exist in the first place."

Before he hung up, he asked her to check with Bill and see if a little private dinner could be planned soon for the nucleus of the group. He began his list with them, for a Saturday evening, before calling others, he said.

Linda was waiting when she took a seat in the booth. Brenda apologized for keeping her waiting but Linda laughed it off. "No problem," she said, "it gave me time to check out the menu."

They had ordered and were enjoying flavored iced tea when the cell rang again. It was Bill. She took it, told him of the dinner invitation, then promised to call back later. Linda shared that she had been contacted by the prosecution and had also been asked to attend the prelim for the children's parents the following morning.

Each woman ordered a shrimp salad, but had a captain's plate delivered to share family style, giving them each a variety of seafood options to enjoy. Brenda could see that they were becoming close friends and liked it, she did not have many female friends outside of the job. It seemed Linda also lacked close friends outside of the hospital, rather choosing to fill her life with Dan and the chores associated with the farm.

When the conversation moved on to the subject of the opportunity to buy additional land, Linda smiled sadly. "Dan's a good man and a hard worker, but he doesn't always understand the reality of finances. He sometimes forgets that the reason his custom farming business does well is because the little farmers cannot each afford to own equipment. If we change our focus and try to grow, I fear we will lose the income from his business because we are tied up in trying to farm more acres for ourselves." Brenda could agree with the rationale.

They visited for a few more minutes, then Linda said, "we have agreed to take Tuesdays with the children. I have made arrangements at work to change my day off and Dan will work his schedule around it."

Brenda took her hand and smiled, then told her of the foster mentoring plan that Martha had suggested.

"That would be great," Linda said, sounding relieved. "Since neither of us have parented, we were frankly a little apprehensive."

"I'll check with Bert and find out who has Monday and let you know," Brenda offered. "You can get coached up by an old veteran. Bill and I could join you if you like."

Brenda called the prosecutor back before she left the café lot, promising to stop by his office on her way back to her own. She was kind of amazed at how she could be so busy and still have time to get it all done, then she remembered Who was in charge of time. Giving God the 'first fruits' was giving to Him first and expecting Him to make it all come together for His purpose. It seemed she was currently operating in His will.

The prosecutor briefly explained what to expect and asked her to be prepared to give testimony if the judge called for it. He also asked if she had pictures available of the scene. She told him yes, before reminding herself that they were in the computer, but Dr. Danes had the printed copies. "Can I send them to your computer?" she asked him, "or should I print them out again? I had given the prints to Doctor Danes to use in a project he's working on in his effort to encourage community participation.

John, the prosecutor, smiled. "How's that going? Word of it is all over town, I am curious if I can be of help somehow."

"I'll add you to the guest list of the next get together," Brenda promised, making a note.

"Good, that will give me a chance to visit with the good doctor before trial."

Back in her office, Brenda answered a few calls, then opened her computer and sent the photos to John as promised, before printing off another set of them just in case. Bill's answer was yes, he was eager to meet the doctor and get some of that good food Brenda had told him about. She called Dr. Danes and accepted the invitation and received directions to his home.

It was after 3:00 before it appeared the fires were all out. She made calls to three fosters, checked on them and their children before clocking out at 4:00. On the drive home she mused... Thursday, no soccer game, no practice, no plans. Family night! Safeway had a Red Box, she grabbed some discs, then went inside and reverse-engineered her evening.

Dessert, she bought fresh berries and ice cream, then fresh vegetables, cubed veal steaks, seasoned Panko coating, four nice russets to mash and cover with gravy, and Rhoades brown and serve rolls. She preferred the frozen kind but didn't have time to wait for them to defrost and raise before dinner.

The boys were home from school when she arrived, still in their school clothes but already doing their homework. "Family night!" she announced with enthusiasm, trying to get their interest. They ran to the grocery bags and pulled out the DVD's, looking them over carefully, two of the four they had seen before but nodded approvingly at the two which remained. "Change clothes," she called over her shoulder as she retreated to her closet to do the same.

Brenda had just finished peeling the potatoes and had them boiling on the stove beside the broccoli when Bill entered the kitchen and gave her a kiss. "What's cookin'?" he asked, surveying the counter top, which held the veal and the egg and buttermilk dip. The boys ran to greet him before she could answer, "family night!" they yelled together.

Brenda smiled, then dipped the veal into the liquid before dredging it in the crumbs and placing them in a frying pan with hot oil.

"Homework done?" Bill asked his sons.

"Yup," they answered proudly as they began to set the table without being asked. Both Bill and Brenda shared a look, smiled, and raised their eyebrows at the boys' resourcefulness, but said nothing.

"Mom got movies," they declared, handing them to their Dad for his approval. "We already saw two of them." Bill looked at the back rather than the front, judging the movie by it's rating rather than the graphics. Brenda would have got nothing but G or PG he knew, but some of the PG's stepped over the line, in his opinion, in attempt to lure a larger audience.

Brenda turned down the potatoes and vegetable, and turned over the veal which had a nice golden brown on it. She dusted it with a little garlic salt and ground pepper while the other side browned.

"Can I help?" Bill asked.

"You want to mash the potatoes? she asked. She drained them while he added the butter, cream, and salt and began to crush them into submission with an old hand masher they had inherited from his mother. She dished the broccoli into a bowl, plated the veal, then began to add flour and milk to the pan with hot oil and cracklins until she had a roux. Within a few minutes the family had blessed the food and was putting it away like the 'last supper'. A traditional meal, it was also one of the family's favorites with the rolls, butter, and honey. Not a scrap remained as the men in her family surveyed the barren wasteland that had held the Lord's bounty.

"How about dessert?" Brenda asked, knowing the answer. "Do you want it now or later with the movie?"

"Now!" was the consensus of opinion. She dished the ice cream while they cleared away the dishes, then added the berries, topping each bowl with whipped cream. While Oregon may not be the berry capital of the world, it would run a close second. Blackberries grew by the roadside everywhere; red raspberries, blueberries, strawberries, and others were abundant and inexpensive, well suited to the moderate climate.

The central theme of the movie included a small struggling horse ranch that had been inherited by a spoiled rich kid who had no experience in such things, or desire to learn. He, of course, fell in love with a local woman horse trainer who won his heart and saved him from the big city life. Bill was pleased that the director had not included the mandatory bedroom scene to increase the ratings, but chose to follow a less worldly story line.

With the time already past 9:30, the family agreed to finish up the remaining movie and continue the family night the following evening. The couple may have felt a little guilty knowing they would be enjoying a feast at the doctor's house while the boys had order in pizza and watched movies with friends on Saturday.

Friday morning came with a low overcast that threatened rain, common to the coast. The bleakness of the morning had been the cause for many who had returned inland to live, after a short stay. Brenda met Linda, Bert, and Doctor Danes outside the courtroom as she entered the courthouse at nine o' clock sharp. Bert had left Martha alone with the six still sleeping, promising to return as soon as possible.

John O'Reilly stuck his head out of the courtroom and invited them in, showing them to seats behind him. The courtroom was empty except for the court appointed attorney sitting alone across the room, the bailiff, and John and his entourage. A few minutes before the judge entered and the plaintiffs were brought in, a newsman seated himself near the aisle to get a clear view of the proceedings.

Judge Robert Spellman was announced, causing the bailiff to ask everyone to rise as he entered and took his seat.

Both Bert and Brenda had been here before and knew the routine, Linda and Mike Danes presumably had not. The charges were read into the record and both attorneys were given options to speak before the judge asked for the plea to be entered. Sylvia Elam, their attorney, plead not guilty and asked for release pending trial. John objected and asked for bail, citing their lack of ties to the community and the nature of the crime involving their own children.

Judge Spellman called bail unusual in this sort of proceedings and asked the attorneys to approach the bench for clarification. Defense reiterated her claim that bail was both unwarranted and an unnecessary financial burden on them. When John looked over his shoulder toward the gallery, Brenda nodded and held out the photos she had brought. He smiled and nodded as he took them from her and presented them to the judge.

It was obvious to those gathered that the judge was displeased by what he saw. He hesitated, asked the accused parents to rise and pronounced a $50,000 bail on each of the six charges. Their attorney's pleas fell on deaf ears. The judge set a trial date for three weeks from the date and ordered them into custody as the gavel fell, closing the proceedings. The newsie snapped several shots of the two as they were led away in cuffs.

"Thank you all for coming," John said to the assembled group. "I'll try and arrange a time to visit privately with each of you before the trial starts so we are clear if you are called to testify."

Brenda voiced her concerns, "there is no chance the children will be forced to testify, is there?"

"Certainly not by us," John said, "such a thing is often emotionally crippling to children. A sharp defense attorney will often use the threat of calling them, in an attempt to get a plea bargain. I do not know this public defender and won't know if she has a sense of decency or just a loyalty to her clients."

Brenda could not imagine how much emotional damage being forced to testify against their parents would inflict upon the children. Her face turned to stone when she said, "Karen is strong, they may not want the court to hear what she has to say."

"Unlikely they would call either her or Jake for that very reason," John said. "More likely the younger ones who have mixed allegiances. The twins, who just turned six, have never attended school, knew nothing of the outside world, and would be unable to represent the abuse clearly, knowing nothing of real life and humane treatment."

Bert proposed an idea. "What if that newsman were to interview and have access to some of the photos?"

"No, no." came the quick reply. "The court would have grounds to change the venue citing prejudicing the jury pool and the judge would bar us from using them in evidence."

Mike spoke for the first time. "I have already used them to help get the proposed children's refuge off the ground. We had a gathering where they were shown to nearly a hundred influentials with hearts to aid our cause. What do we do about that?"

John shook his head. "The horse is out of the barn but let's don't make it worse by showing them around any further until after the trial. We'll just have to hope that the judge feels that it was insufficient to taint the pool of perspective jurors.

Dr. Danes was, for the first time since she had met him, discouraged and despondent, feeling as if he had jeopardized the case. On the walk out Brenda turned to him and said, "cheer up, you are forgetting

Who is in charge here. This is not about you and me, this is about what God wants for these children, whom He dearly loves.

Mike smiled, then said, "thanks, I needed to be reminded that it's never about me, what I think I can do, or what I want done."

Bert returned to help Martha with the children, a dozen donuts under his arm, after making arrangements to mentor Dan and Linda for their upcoming service on Tuesday.

The rest of Friday was spent just tying up loose ends, following up on reports of suspected abuse, and listening to nosy neighbors point fingers at one another. After she clocked out at work, she made another stop at the market, grabbing two cut up chickens, frozen steak fries, and some shell chocolate to put over the remaining ice cream.

She really didn't feel like cooking. The day and the week had taken it's toll on her, but she knew her family was looking forward to the night together. When she pulled into the driveway, Bill and the boys were waiting in his car. "Hop in," he said, "we've got a surprise for you."

"I've got chicken to cook," she argued.

"Put it in the freezer," he answered with a smile, "I'm taking us out." On the way into the house she said a prayer of gratitude for God's provision.

"John," Judge Spellman said with a harshness uncommon to him, "what kind of an end run do you think you are trying to pull in my court?"

The counselor had no time to respond before he continued. "You used those photos to gain my sympathy and affect my decision on bail, knowing very well they were already on the street and very likely prejudicial."

"Your Honor," the prosecutor began, "I found out only after I had given them to you that the doctor, in his zeal to help the children, had used them to enlist aid for what he saw as a worthy cause."

He was glad that he was not standing in his chambers but rather at home, receiving his rebuke by phone. There was a pause, Judge Spellman spoke less severely as he continued. "John, I respect you as a man and as an attorney, and because of that I'm going to let this one slide. But," he continued, "I am releasing the Browns OR and considering a decision to bar the pictures as evidence at trial."

"Thank you, Your Honor," John said, "I appreciate your accommodation. That said, I fear they will disappear into the woodwork before trial."

"You made your bed," he replied, reassuming his more formidable tone of voice. "What would you have me do in the interest of justice? When the defense gets wind of this, she'll likely ask for a change of venue and this whole matter will come before a less sympathetic court.

John's mind was working feverishly for a solution. "Electronic monitoring," he said weakly, "maybe that would be a fair and just answer to a difficult question."

Even over the phone, he could feel the tension relaxing, when he spoke. "Solomon, remember him?" he asked.

"I do," John answered.

"Do you remember how he settled the dispute between the two women claiming the same child?" he asked further. "Why don't you go down right now to the jail and offer one of them OR and the other the leg bracelet and see who chooses what."

"Okay," he said carefully, trying to see his logic, but missing the point. "And then...?" he asked, trying to draw him into further clarification.

"And then release them as you promised to do," Spellman said, "and see where you have found gain."

He was smart, John thought, too smart for him, too smart to be presiding over county court. He belonged in the state supreme court, in Salem or maybe eventually in the nation's capital. "Yes, Judge," he said, "consider it done, and thank you."

As he drove toward the jailhouse, his mind pondered his choice of words "and see where you have found gain." What did that mean? Did it mean anything? Was he just referring to him dodging official reprimand, or complete dismissal of the charges? That the matter of the pictures as evidence still hung in the balance, or did he see something he had not?

What had appeared as a slam dunk conviction, with justice easily served, now hung tenuously with a real possibility of dismissal or a hung jury verdict. What was he missing, why one OR and the other with the leg iron? What had the story of Solomon's wisdom had to do with it? As he sat in the parking lot of the county jail, he took the Bible that he has hastily grabbed and searched for the proper passages.

He finally found a passage in 1 Kings 10:21. It described two prostitutes, both with infants, one of which had died. Then both had claimed the remaining child as their own. Solomon's judgment was to have the baby cut in half and give each of the mothers half of the dead child. When one then offered to give up her part of the child to save its life, Solomon judged her as the true mother since she had shown unselfish love for it.

Neat story, John thought, how could I apply it for "gain." A thought struck him, Solomon found the answer by threatening to divide the child. What may happen if he were to break the bond they shared by favoring one over the other? Is it possible that they might turn against each other, even to the point of offering testimony?

He called their attorney at home, informing her that he had intention of signing their release, before asking if she wanted to be present. She was surprised and pleased with his decision but saw no reason to interrupt her evening to witness the event. He did not feel it necessary to discuss the terms of the release, that would come up at discovery. If it had come up, he was prepared to explain why he felt the man may be more of a danger to the children or the public at large than their mother, given his violent history.

He met with them separately at first, then had them brought in together, as he made arrangements for the release. John explained to her how they would be held equally guilty under the law, suffering the same penalties when found guilty, even though one may be more responsible than the other. It painted a vague picture in her mind that he was dragging her down with him.

When he spoke to her husband, he tried to do likewise, saying that the jury often placed a greater burden to nurture her offspring upon the mother of the children. He, of course, felt less responsible for their day to day care as the 'man' of the family.

John hoped he had set the stage for dissension between them, having given them plenty of time to ponder the situation before being delivered to the interview room. John had arranged for their conversations to be monitored and recorded in the event their counsel questioned it or it proved useful to him. They did not sit side by side, but somewhat apart across from him as he shuffled through the release papers in front of him.

He began, reinventing the private conversations they had previously. "You are aware that I have met with you both separately, are you not?" They nodded. "That's an affirmative nod," he said for the benefit of the recorder.

"And I told you previously during that conversation that you are both being held equally guilty under the law for any charges, is that also true?" This time they said yes. "And," he continued, "that I am making arrangements to have you both released today pending trial, is that also true?" Yes again.

"Very well, do either of you have any questions before I explain the terms of the release?" Neither responded but did turn and look at each other. "I have spoken to your counsel and she has rejected my offer to appear at this proceeding. Do either of you desire to have her present before we effect your release?" John was addressing them as separate entities now, using their first names, speaking and looking directly at each, forcing each to make their own decisions.

John hesitated, then saw a question in the woman's eye. As he turned his attention to her, he addressed her by name, "do you have a question?"

"Where will I go, where will I stay, how will I feed myself?" Valid questions John was thinking, and she was not looking to her husband for answers.

"I cannot say for certain," John responded. "I can say that your house and contents are not an option at this time. They contain evidence pertinent to the charges. Perhaps a woman's shelter," he offered, knowing it further divided the couple.

"And you," he said looking directly in the man's eyes, "have you any questions?" He could see the man bristle.

"And what about me? She gets three hots and a cot and what do I get?"

"You have the freedom to care for yourself, impose on friends, or look for a men's shelter, as long as you don't leave the county." Since the man was the most incensed already, John focused on him. "Are you familiar with electronic monitoring?" he asked.

"What?" came the answer. "I thought I was being released, free and clear."

"Yes," John said, carefully structuring his reply. "You are being released, but you are neither free or clear until after the trial. You will wear a leg bracelet which will show your location 24/7."

"How about her?" the man asked, nodding to his wife.

"We are not talking about her now, we are talking about your release," John answered. "I can have the deputy install the device, explain it to you, have you sign and you are free to go."

"Do I have to wear one?" the wife asked, nearly in tears.

"No," John said with satisfaction, "that will not be necessary. After our earlier conversation I feel that you do not present a substantial flight risk or a danger to the community at large."

Her husband attempted to jump to his feet but was restrained by handcuffs to the table. "You mean she walks, gets bed and board, and I have to wear this thing and look out for myself!" he screamed. The wife cowered away from him.

"Perhaps," John said, "you'd like a little time alone to discuss this or call your attorney." He knew he was playing the scene for the recorder and the cameras.

"I want my own attorney," she sobbed, tears running down her pig like face, "I don't trust him or his attorney."

John felt sympathy for her in spite of himself. "If you are sure about that, I'll need to advise the court and ask them to assign counsel before we proceed further." She nodded. "Do you want me to call for separate counsel for you?" John asked, forcing her to reply. "Yes, I do!" she said.

"Deputy, please return them to their cells while I contact the court for instruction," John said.

It was after 7:00 when Judge Spellman picked up the phone at his home. "Hello John," he said politely, "and how is your evening going, son?" Before he could answer, the judge continued. "Have you released the Browns as you promised me?"

His tone and attitude caught John off guard. "No, sir," John said, "I did offer but they want separate counsel now so I had them returned to their cells."

"Well done, Sol," the judge said with a laugh. "Which one needs the lawyer?"

"The woman," John answered.

"Let me notify Ms. Elam of her request and contact a public defender. Meanwhile, sign the release for him and leave it with the jailer in the event she wants him on the street tonight. I'll give the defender one myself for Mrs. Brown."

"Thank you, Judge," John said, feeling humbled.

"You are welcome, John," he replied. "And John, we'll leave the pictures in for now, but using them may be grounds for an appeal.

John O'Reilly was 37 years old, and became widower when his wife had been killed by a drunken driver while crossing the road. He ignored God's whisper growing up, in college, and then in law school. Ruth had walked with Jesus from childhood.

After they married, they attended church but he continued to ignore the call to salvation until the emptiness from her loss left him without resource. It was at times like these, when he needed someone to share his heart with, that home seemed so empty. How she would have loved to hear the news of these past days and share in the irony of God's hand at work.

It had been two years now since she been killed, almost as long as they had been married. John grieved that they had just begun to know each other before she had been taken, but was encouraged that they'd have eternity to catch up.

Saturday began with pancakes, bacon, and scrambled eggs at the Nelson household. No rest for the weary, Brenda thought as she called her boys to the table. When Bill joined her, his coffee was still steaming. The boys right behind, they came in like the first snow of winter and filled the room with their activity. Bill blessed the food while Brenda loaded the plates and cautioned the boys to leave some bacon for her.

"Our game is at noon," they said as a reminder of it's significance, "we're playing Westside. They're four and ooh," they added, as an indicator of the seriousness of the encounter. The boy's team had been state champs last year but they had moved up a bracket and now were the small fish in the big pond.

Soccer parents are much like a fraternity, sharing a lifetime bond and closeness, much like what the church youth groups sought to provide. Most of the boys had played together almost since they could run. As Bill loaded the SUV and Brenda the small cooler, the boys checked and rechecked their gear, before heading to the field, more than an hour early. Overcast, a light southeast breeze off the ocean, and a promise of rain when you least expected it, was the daily forecast anytime after September officially brought fall.

As they arrived, newly familiar faces greeted them. Mike and Beth Danes had two sons just finishing up their game in the 12-14 age bracket. The game was tied 2-2 with three minutes left.

Mike volunteered his opinion, "it's hard for me to get excited about any game that doesn't provide for an overtime or sudden death to declare a winner. They boys play their tails off and half of the games end in a tie." Bill agreed with him, while both Brenda and Beth said it was about sportsmanship and teaching teamwork. Women!

"We are still on for tonight then?" Mike asked, looking at the

Nelsons, "about 6:00 or so?"

"Sounds good," Bill replied, "can we bring something?"

"How about buns," Mike said. "I'm doing hamburgers and hotdogs, and the boys are welcome too."

"How many do you expect," Brenda asked, remembering the big formal dinner.

"Maybe a dozen or two," Mike answered. "All friends, very informal. Come as you are." Brenda thanked God, thinking how foolish she'd have looked all dressed up with everyone in jeans and shorts.

Following the game, which they won one-zip, they all enjoyed pizza with the team before going home. "Bren," Bill said, "I think I'm going to like that Mike guy. He seems real, not all pumped up with himself like most doctors or rich guys."

"I agree, and his wife seems down to earth as well, like she knows that they are where they are by grace and not because of something they did."

"I wonder if they are Christians," Bill continued, "we could invite them to church if you like."

"Yes," Brenda said, "I heard he is an elder somewhere but don't know the name of the church." They went back and forth for a while discussing the Dane family and his commitment to both the children and to God as well, as though they could be separated. Their sons were eager to go with them, wanting to hang out with the older Danes' boys and discuss soccer no doubt.

Brenda stopped at the beach house where Bert and Martha had passed the baton to the new fosters, who were getting to know the children. It was a blessing that the children had such low expectations, making them easily cared for. They had hearts which had not yet been spoiled, remaining grateful for whatever they received. It was both sad but refreshing at the same time.

Brenda noted that if mankind could adopt their nature, it would solve a lot of problems and bring them closer to God. She made a mental note to ask Bill about maybe taking them along to church in the morning. She fielded a call on her cell phone on her way home, it was the prosecuting attorney. He filled her in on the events of the previous day with the judge and defendants, then asked her to specifically keep a lid on the pictures and discussions of the case. While he supported their efforts to create a shelter home for at-risk children, he needed to have a jury pool not predisposed or prejudiced before the trial.

Bill picked up two dozen each of hot dog and hamburger buns, and a half lug of Marion berries, and two gallons of Tillamook vanilla bean ice cream on the way home. A hundred or so miles north was the big factory where it and some of the northwest's best cheeses were made. One of the family favorites had always been Brenda's homemade berry pie served hot with good ice cream melting over it.

"What's this?" Brenda asked in mock alarm, "you know we are going out tonight and the berries are too ripe to hold over until Monday."

"Come on, Bren," Bill said in his best pleading voice, "you know the 'rich folks' have never tasted real berry pie and ice cream. 'Sides, we have almost three hours before we have to be there."

She shook her head. She could never resist his little boy pleadings and more than she could her own sons. Out came the flour, shortening, and eggs while the oven preheated. It was a delicate process to combine the hot simple syrup and gelatine with the berries without overcooking and turning them into mush.

She partially cooked the bottom crust of three pies, then removed them from the oven, while waiting for the berry mixture to thicken and cool. At 4:30 she filled the shells and criss-crossed their tops with waiting strips of crust and put them into the oven before hitting the shower and changing clothes. As per her instructions, Bill carefully removed them twenty minutes later, after approving of the golden brown lattice that covered the bubbling purple mixture below.

"They need to sit before being transported," Brenda advised, nodding her approval at her husband. The boys joined them in the kitchen and began lobbying to take only two and keep one for themselves, Bill nodded his approval.

Brenda had a favorite quote that she repeated often, "the best gift you can give is the one you want to keep for yourself." It had been used so much no one knew if she had plagiarized it or originated it herself. Bill and the boys put the ice cream into ice chests and the SUV while Brenda carefully put the pies in thermo cases for carrying.

When they pulled into the large circular driveway, several other cars were already parked. A quarter acre of nicely groomed lawn presented a large but unpretentious home. An old tire on a rope hanging from a tree limb attested to its livability and added a homey touch. Both Bill and Brenda noted that they seemed to be working hard to enjoy their prosperity without allowing it to control their lives or present a false sense of who they were.

As other cars were joining them and began unloading their contributions, they headed up the steps and were pleased to see familiar faces among the guests. Dan and Linda Baker were carrying a cooler filled with fresh corn, still on the cob, the Millers with two covered dishes, and others whose faces seemed familiar but unknown to them by name. Beth was at the door welcoming her guests, directing traffic and making room for food in double ovens, warmers, or refrigerators.

Through double french doors Mike and his sons could be seen poolside, looking comfortable, while talking to other guests. Another half acre behind the home was closely trimmed and set up to enjoy for games like volleyball and croquette.

Danes' sons had a half field soccer field set up with a net and were practicing kicking goals when the Nelson boys joined them. Brenda was surprised to see Bert and his wife arrive and took note that several couples from the banquet joined the party also. At about 6:30 Beth put Mike to work on the grill and accepted offers from several women to help organize the tables, drinks, and the side dishes.

Dan gave his attention to a big, single burner propane stove providing the heat to boil a large pot of water for the corn he had brought from his fields, while several of the men gave Mike help with the buns, hot dogs, and hamburgers cooking on the big grill. There were only about ten couples, but with children, the total number approached thirty by Brenda's rough estimate.

Mike asked the blessing for the food while it was still cooking, then began filling plates from the grill... children first. Then he encouraged his wife and the other women to 'get it while it's hot' as the men hung back, waiting their turns. Bill liked that it all seemed organized, without too much structure or ceremony.

They ate, visited, joked and told stories on each other while becoming friends. No one made mention of the proposed shelter, much to Brenda's surprise and joy. While the women cut the offered desserts the men talked and became familiar with each other. One of them, Ben, was Mike's pastor at the Church of God in Lincoln City and another an anesthesiologist working with him at the hospital.

All three pies, smothered in ice cream, a plate of lemon bars, and nearly all of a chocolate bundt cake disappeared in minutes, with most trying more than one dessert. After the tables were cleared and while the women were scraping, loading and sorting dishes, the children began to organize for the various games.

Mike turned to Dan and simply said, "we are here to enjoy the day, but if you have time, I'd like to visit with you Monday. Please call me." Bill noted that he had precluded the chance of conversation about business matters by the way he handled the request.

Teams that included both children and adults were chosen for volleyball, and likewise for horseshoes. Others chose to sit and visit, taking their turns only when someone wanted a rest. The evening seemed to quickly turn to night. The Nelsons and most other guests thanked their hosts and called it a night a little after 10:00.

"That was nice," Bill said. "Yes, it was," Brenda agreed, "they have a knack of making everyone feel comfortable, don't they?"

"They value the people and not the position," he offered. Brenda hugged his arm, "nicely put," she said.

Brenda had forgotten to ask Bill about taking the children to church with them and didn't want to upset the foster's plans for the day anyway. As they finished French toast and crispy bacon, juice and coffee, the boys left the table to get dressed. "Dan said he and Linda are going to foster on Mondays," Bill commented.

"I had hoped they would," Brenda replied. "I hope the Millers will give it a try also."

"They are," Bill said, "but they are sill antsy. They are going to partner with Dan and Linda Mondays for a while before they go solo."

Brenda smiled. "You seem to have been doing more than throwing horseshoes out there," she said, "anything more to share with me?"

"Mike didn't want to talk business, but we visited with each other even so, and I found out that several of the doctors are meeting soon to form a non-profit corp for funding purposes. I presume it has to do with acquiring land and financing construction."

"How do we figure in?" Brenda asked. "Or were you just eaves dropping?

It was Bill's turn to smile. "I didn't volunteer anything but was thinking maybe we could donate the ground work. We have the equipment, I can find the time somewhere, all it would cost out of pocket would be the fuel. Once they have the land and the plans drawn, we can sit down with them and see what all it entails."

For several years Bill and Brenda had owned a small construction company that specialized in underground excavation. In good times he had as many as a half dozen working for him, in slow ones he was able to handle it all himself. They owned the equipment outright, allowing his out of pocket expenses to be limited to maintenance and fuel. She nodded. "Like you have so much extra time already," she laughed.

The four of them entered church right on time, it was a small Baptist affiliate, sporting a modern new name, which had riled her at first. She saw no shame in declaring themselves as Baptist. But the powers that be were following the trend to change the name to sound non-denominational in an effort to invite those in, who may hold some prejudice against a particular denomination.

Coastal Bible Church had changed nothing except the marquee out front, no change of philosophy, no new doctrinal shift, nothing. They were often asked what kind of church it was, always the answer was the same, Baptist. Those questioning them always responded, "why don't they just say so?"

However, they loved their church, their pastor, their many Christian friends, and the message that God continued to fold neatly and slip into their hearts each Sunday morning. The boys had grown up there, had strong personal convictions accumulated from years of AWANA and Sunday school lessons, and a multitude of close friends. Both

Brenda and Bill hoped it would always be so.

Pastor Brent had shepherded the church for fifteen plus years. He and Rebecca, his wife, were like family to the Nelsons. Today he spoke about the seeming conflict between Old and New Testaments regarding how one should respond to their enemies. Lovers of the OT always presented their case using King David, a man after God's own heart, a warrior who slew the enemies of God's people, beginning with Goliath.

NT people liked the seemingly kinder and gentler version of God in the form of Jesus, who preached the "turn the other cheek and love your enemies" philosophy. That Jesus, who will ultimately come in power and pronounce judgment, will slaughter all of God's enemies.

He began with those things on which they could agree, the three 'omni's, and then added 'unchanging' to the mix. Heads were still nodding in agreement, so he continued.

"Do you think then that you, your prayers, or anything can change God? Reluctantly most agreed with the 'no' answer. Many, however, were puzzled at the prayer issue.

"Forget prayer for the moment," Pastor Brent said. "It is unique and far above man's complete understanding. How would you answer the question as to how God's plan for all eternity can be complete and true if He may change His mind? Is there any certainty at all if God is not certain?" The pastor had raised more questions than he had provided answers but had his congregation thinking now, willing to listen, and not focused on defending their own ideas.

"First, let's think about where and with whom conflict began. It began in the heart of man, in the garden. Man, and not God, introduced sin in the form of disobedience. Man, and not God, killed his brother and shed the first blood. The fact that God knew this would happen does not change the fact that it did. That God allowed free will to error does not mean that He condones or desires it. A less loving God would have killed His creation and started over. Instead He made provision for us to learn, grow, and change back into the form He had created. He wants us to be sinless and have the ability to walk beside Him once more."

It was quiet, he had their attention and most were in agreement with what he had said. "Is a baby born complete?" he asked. They seemed puzzled by his question. "Can it walk, talk, run, read and write, can it make good decisions? Of course not. But it does possess the ability to learn to do so." Every parent nodded, many made comments, and several laughed.

"Consider man's time on earth now, a few thousand years, and compare it with the eternity God knows and lives in. Just a comparatively short time, would you not agree?" he asked. "Would you expect that your infant would learn all he needed to know in the first or second year of his life? God's plan includes a slow education for all of mankind, and if you think educating us without controlling us is easy, remember that God started all over with the Flood."

Someone said something about their own children which brought laughter. "So," he continued, "it is not God who has changed, it is man who is changing and hopefully becoming more able to understand and adapt to what we have learned. Eventually the lion will lie down with the lamb, just as it did in the garden, and we will have no need to have weapons for protection, or have a desire to respond to violence, because Jesus will be our protector and there will be no violence."

The pastor had done the best he could. He had studied, planned, written and rewritten his sermon several times. In the end, he knew that it was not his words that would matter, but those whispered into the hearts of God's people.

He was pleased that he had not needed to take a pro or anti gun position or try and explain if man should use worldly means to attempt homeland security or open the borders and trust in God for complete protection. He knew in his heart that the only true security lay in Jesus, but had a belief that man had a part to play also by using the intellect that God had given him. Brent would have been the first to admit that the shepherd struggles with the same problems as the sheep.

"Dad," Bill's oldest son said on their ride home from church, "what do you think about guns and weapons?"

"What do you mean son?" Bill asked.

"I mean, I listened in church today and still am not sure what I should believe," he replied. "If I go to school tomorrow and some bully punches me, should I really let him hit me again?" The car was quiet as Brenda and both boys waited for his answer. Bill thought for a long time before he replied.

"If you are in a race and your competition trips you causing you to fall, do you just lay there or do you get up and run? And if you do run, do you still run to win or just to catch up and trip him back?" He didn't wait for an answer, he continued, letting the question hang in the air.

"What I heard from Pastor Brent, and what my heart tells me, is that we all are running a race with the goal to be like Jesus. At the finish line we are all winners and all receive the same trophy. During that race many things happen which cause us to stumble and fall, some are our own weaknesses, and some may be caused by others who want to harm us by keeping us from finishing."

They waited for him to continue but he did not. Finally the boy asked, "so you are saying that I should get up and keep running, trying to win, but trip him on the way by?" The car filled with laughter, everyone talking at once.

"No," Bill said, "I did not say that. I said that you should focus on the race and let God guide your heart for how to respond. If you try to be prepared for something that may never happen, the only decision you can make is one using your own intellect and likely it will not be what God desires. Run the race, asking always for God's help in how to respond as you go along."

When Monday came, the Bakers took responsibility for the six children. When the Millers joined them, they were invaluable in helping get the children dressed, fed, and delivered for their first day back at school. Brenda was there also, signing papers and helping to get the two six-year-olds oriented and into class. She sat in the back providing a safety net while they became acquainted with the calamity that was called first grade.

The other children had attended kindergarten and were familiar with interaction outside the family, but they were not. After class she discussed with the teacher and counselor, the wisdom of possibly starting them in kindergarten this term. The consensus was that without a foundation they would struggle and ultimately fail to become a part of the class. They would likely cling to each other, separate themselves from their peers, and always be on the outside looking in. Arrangements were made to start them the next morning in the preparatory class.

Since Karen had been withdrawn before the end of the year, she was re-enrolled in sixth grade with her friend and teacher Mrs. Rice. Jake and the other children were forced to pick up where they left off as well, having missed the final month of school. It was hoped that with some mentoring they could rejoin their previous class at semester and not repeat the entire year.

Shared responsibility was the term Brenda used with the Bakers and the Millers as she urged them to compliment each others' strengths and weaknesses. Dan and Linda were younger and had stamina but no experience with children, while the Millers brought experience and knowledge but not the vitality of youth. They each made a verbal commitment to continue the arrangement, providing continuity to the child care problem for one day a week. When she called the office, Bert told her that although some of the commitments were a little shaky, they had a couple covering each of the seven days. He and Martha called themselves backup.

As one day became another, each challenge was met and over come as another took it's place. Our little circle of friends participated in life, reached out to each other, and moved forward toward the trial date now only a week away. The children seemed more and more well adjusted to their new lives, looking forward to the 'changing of the guard' and the unique qualities that each couple brought with them.

Nothing further surfaced regarding the proposed City of Refuge project or it's progress. Finally, on Thursday, a week before trial, the prosecutor was contacted by the court. The judge required a meeting including both defense attorneys, regarding their request for a change of venue. John had expected it earlier and was surprised at the attempt. He hoped that Judge Spellman would see it as a last minute effort to delay and complicate the trial.

"Counselors, pleased have a seat," Spellman said pleasantly, motioning to the three chairs that had been brought into his chambers. The original PD was a woman in her late thirties or early forties who specialized in family law, divorces, disputes, bankruptcies and civil cases. The new man, Ted Black, was one that John had faced before, an experienced criminal attorney is his fifties who had drawn the short straw in the judge's rotation.

He was a well known partner in a small local firm who lived well and catered to the higher end white collar and non-violent criminal offenses like embezzlement and fraud. John hoped that he would see this proceeding as beneath him and unworthy of his considerable skills with no chance of financial gain.

The defense was given first opportunity to speak, they used the excuse of a tainted jury pool and the impropriety of the photos as their grounds, just as expected. John countered the only way he could, that the pool of jurors was sufficient and those who had opportunity to see the photos could easily be disqualified during discovery. The judge listened patiently, then responded, "does anyone have anything further to offer before I give my answer?" No one did.

"I have had nearly two weeks to ponder this request before it was ever presented, therefore I am confident that I have given it sufficient consideration. I can say that I am disappointed that counsel chose to wait until the last minute to make such a request, therefore posing a hardship on the court if it were granted. Request denied.

When defense started to offer rebuttal, the judge silenced them with a raised hand. "Dismissed," he said. John noted that the two attorneys did not address each other or walk out together, making it obvious they were not colleagues. Although not uncommon, it was unusual to have two cases heard simultaneously by a single judge and jury, but each with individual representation.

One at a time, John met with and prepared his potential witnesses which included two deputy sheriffs, Brenda and her co-worker, the admitting nurse at ER, Nurse Linda Baker, the attending physician in the ER, Dr. Danes, and Bert Ellis.

Witnesses, observers, two newsies with cameras, and both

defense counsels with their clients were seated in the courtroom when John and his paralegal entered and were also seated. One of his little quirks was to arrive at the last minute to keep the opposition wondering if they'd gotten the wrong date or time.

Approximately thirty prospective jurors were first seated, then asked to stand with the assembly when the judge entered and took his seat. The charges were read, the jury thanked for their service to the community and asked if the proceedings posed personal hardship. Only one hand raised, that of a single mother with a nursing infant, who was dismissed without objection or discussion.

Judge Spellman proceeded to educate the prospective jurors about the weight of their responsibility, the need to judge using only the facts presented in court, and the need to not discuss the case outside of the jury room with anyone, including friends or family. He then made quite an appeal for them to consider how hard justice is to find at the hands of man.

"Ask yourselves this." he said. "Are you predisposed to consider the defendants more likely to be guilty because, after careful investigation, they were charged and arrested. Can you honestly say to yourself that you are unaffected simply by the fact that they were indited?

As Brenda listened, she did some soul searching of her own. She thought, isn't it true that few cases without merit never get to court. That the process eliminates most of the innocent because of lack of substantial proof to file charges and move forward? Isn't it the job of the prosecution to not file unless they feel laws have been broken, and the court likewise to drop charges that seem unsupported? Isn't that how she had believed? She could see the judge attempting to wipe away prejudice from his court, helping them try and find an "innocent until proven guilty" mindset.

Each of the attorneys had the right to 'dismiss without cause' up to three jurors. Sometimes their answers to carefully worded questions from the attorneys might lend insight as to their true feelings, other times body language, age, or other intangibles may indicate their leanings. They could come across as too independent or too easily swayed. While the prosecution was looking for an individual with a love for family and a caring heart, the defense was looking for one who believed the state had no right to interfere in the affairs of the family unit.

John was looking for a married woman with children whom she nurtured and loved. And defense; a man without children who thought of his home as his castle and had little interest in caring for anyone but himself.

When the court dismissed for lunch, three jurors had been empaneled and two dismissed. John took note that Black and Elam had left separately without conversation. He would wait until the jury was fully seated, then approach Elam about a possible reduction of charges for her client's testimony. He viewed both she and the less experienced defender as the more easily to be influenced by an offer.

Independently of each other, John and his entourage chose a small sandwich shop across the street from the courthouse where they sat together discussing the events of the morning. Events moved more quickly in the afternoon, the court having found a certain rhythm to the proceedings. Just when John thought he had found a good candidate, Black had questioned her and found evidence of sexual abuse in her past.

At 4:00 the judge closed the proceedings for the day, with half of the jurors seated and five rejected for cause. Judge Spellman thanked those present as though they had been guests at his birthday party and invited them to return the following day for more of the same. One couldn't help but enjoy the judge's dry sense of humor, while operating his court with an iron hand.

Brenda had just enough time to make a few calls to check on her charges before going home to a trio of hungry men. An extra large 'caveman' with extra cheese and two liters of Coke were waiting as she entered the house by the rear door. The boys poured drinks while Bill cut the pizza and seated Brenda before saying grace. Fifteen minutes later you couldn't have found a scrap to eat if you were starving.

As Brenda got to her feet to get the remaining ice cream and shell chocolate, her sons got quiet and looked at one another. "It's gone," they admitted, "we and Dad had it while we were waiting."

Bill looked particularly sheepish as he tried to dig them out of a hole. "But, I did get the pizza," he argued, "doesn't that count for something?

Brenda laughed, "so you used the dessert to get ready for dinner? Is that about it?" Three heads smiled and nodded. She loved them, which made her wonder, how could someone like the Browns treat their children the way they had?

Neither Bert not Doctor Danes were present, both having cleared it first with the prosecution. John expected to maybe finish jury selection but not call witnesses for at least another day and possibly two. By noon, three more jurors were among the primary group and another had fallen to challenge. It was this court's practice to seat twelve and three alternates, so they were a little over half way in the process.

The alternates would hear evidence and discussion just as would the twelve, but would be without voice in the verdict unless one or more of the primaries were replaced by the court. When Judge Spellman closed his court for the day, they had a full contingent of jurors but lacked backups. They would resume in the morning to choose the alternates, break for lunch, and begin with the prosecution presenting his case after lunch.

At discovery, each attorney was supposed to prepare his opposition by giving them opportunity to know how they were going to proceed. They traded witness lists which gave the other time to investigate their credibility. While it was meant as an effective tool to keep everything above board, it also often divulged strategies which kept the court from a 'Perry Mason' type of surprise ending.

John saw it as two coaches trading game books and expecting the better team to still win. The Judge ultimately had discretion as to how much or how little needed to be made transparent in the interest of justice. While John's plan was to present the photographs, their objections were still under advisement, leaving his case somewhat in limbo.

Bert called Brenda at home and filled her in on the children, the fosters, and situations which demanded her attention, regardless of the trial. She was forced to make one trip and several calls in the evening after she finished at court, to maintain continuity. Her option would have been to hand off some of her cases to another worker who was unfamiliar to the families, the children, or its unique details.

Bill and Brenda spent much of the evening praying together for God's will that night. What often seems so apparent to us in our shortsightedness causes us to believe we know what God is thinking or planning or should be doing. We pray as blind men who think they can see, but need to open our hearts to God and ultimately bow to His wisdom.

Day three, as it was called on the docket, began again with jury selection. There was a gallery of curiosity seekers, interested parties, witnesses, and news hounds present, all with a feeling of anticipation. Defense had ran out of challenges and John used his last one before seating the final alternate. It was only 10:45 when they broke, with the Judge reminding everyone his court came to order promptly at 1:00, with everyone expected to be prepared to begin the proceedings.

The court was called to order, charges against the defendants were read into the record, and the Judge asked for their plea. Their attorneys both plead them as 'not guilty'. It was up to John first to make his case against the Browns. He began by presenting the usual oratory outlining why they should be found guilty and how the prosecution expected to prove their case. Likewise, the defense attorneys told why they believed that the case was without merit and why the jury should find in favor of the defendants.

Surprisingly, John had chosen Mrs. Rice, the school teacher, as his first witness. She was sworn in and seated, then John asked her, "from your personal observation and as a tenured professional educator, what can you tell this court regarding the Brown children?" Defense made no objection.

She spoke in a slow measured tone in a manner that indicated she weighed the meaning and value of each word. "I interacted most closely with the oldest, Karen, who was a student in my 6th grade class. On the positive side, she was bright and easily taught, eager to learn. I never had occasion to reprimand or discipline her. On the other hand, she often appeared withdrawn and stressed, unkempt, with poor personal hygiene and often clothing worn to the point of falling apart."

"Objection." The defense asked "are there other children in school who lacked nice clothes and had poor grooming?"

"Yes, there are," she answered truthfully, "but..." He stopped her explanation with a "thank you."

John reworded his question, "can you make a distinction between how other children in poor families appeared compared with the

Brown children?" No objection was raised.

"Yes," Mrs. Rice replied, "you look beyond the obvious to develop an overall assessment to determine if children are at risk. It is not just their dress but also other factors such as the way they take advantage of the breakfasts and lunches available through the federal and state programs, their lack of supplies, their social development, lack of parental involvement, and their interaction with their peer groups."

"Did you see anything that alarmed you?" John asked.

"Yes," she answered.

"And," John continued, "what did you do about that?"

"I brought it to the attention of the principal, and met with other teachers who had responsibility for them as teachers."

"It that all?" John asked, trying to sound surprised. "If you were so concerned, why didn't you report it to health and welfare or child protective services?"

He appeared to be discrediting his own witness. She did not seem to take offense as she replied, "I, we had come to a consensus to do just that and the family disappeared. Moved from their home leaving no contact information. We were forced to assume they had moved away and would be enrolled elsewhere. As teachers we have no authority or means to proceed further than we did."

"Knowing what you now know, would you have done anything differently?" John asked.

"Yes," came the reply. "I would have fined personally outside of the system and let them investigate. I feel like I let the children down.

Defense appeared to have considered an objection but sat back down.

"Thank you," John said to Mrs. Rice. "How did you finally find out about the situation that we are here to investigate?"

She replied, "I received a call from the hospital from a nurse."

"Do you recall her name?" John asked.

"Yes," Mrs. Rice answered. "Nurse Linda Baker."

"Thank you, no further questions," John said.

"Your witness," Judge Spellman said to the defense.

Ms. Elam stood first. "Mrs. Rice, is it true that you cannot testify personally to the charges being brought here?" She continued. "Did you in fact witness any abuse or hear directly from any of the children of such abuse?"

"No," Mrs. Rice replied, "I did not, I only witnessed their results."

"Objection!" came the quick reply.

"You only witnessed the children's appearance, you have no knowledge of actual abuse, is that not correct?" she asked.

Mrs. Rice took time to carefully word her reply. "I did not witness physical abuse."

Ms. Elam deferred to Mr. Black. "Mrs. Rice," he asked, "to your knowledge, did anyone at the school witness abuse?"

Mrs. Rice was getting the hang of it now. "Sir," she replied, "there are several of them present, I'd rather not testify to what they may or may not have witnessed." John was smiling openly.

When John was allowed redirect he said, "just one last question please, how did Nurse Baker get your name and number?"

Now it was Mrs. Rice's turn to smile, "from Karen Brown," she said. "I was listed as an emergency contact."

"No further questions," John said before sitting.

Next John called Linda Baker to the stand, where she was sworn in and seated. "Nurse Baker," John began, "may we call you Linda?"

"Please do," she said smiling.

John nodded. "Linda, will you describe for the court how you became acquainted with the Brown family?"

"I was working in pediatric ER when the Brown family brought in Timothy, their youngest, for treatment. Because of his condition, the attending physician and I called in the head of pediatrics, Doctor Michael Danes, for consul."

"Would you describe his condition for us please?" John asked.

"He was dehydrated to the point of being life threatening, experiencing high fever and convulsions, and severely undernourished."

"Objection," Mr. Black said standing. "Is the nurse able to say conclusively that the patient was undernourished?"

John had expected the objection and welcomed it. "Nurse Baker, can you give us the parameters as to why you used the term undernourished? Was it a personal or professional judgment?" he asked.

"Yes," she responded, "I think I can. When he was admitted, he was more than 30% underweight for his age and bone structure, there was no apparent baby fat, and at 25 months was not walking or talking yet. He appeared emancipated as shown in the photos taken at the hospital."

"Objection!"

"Sustained," came the Judge's verdict, "on the grounds of facts not introduced into evidence."

"Can you tell the court how Timothy's parents reacted to his condition?" John continued.

Nurse Baker looked puzzled.

"Let me re-word the question," John said. "Did they seem to show the normal amount of concern that you are used to seeing?"

"Objection." Mr. Black said, "calls for an opinion."

John looked at the Judge. "She's a medical professional, your Honor, offering her medical opinion."

"I'll allow it," Judge Spellman said.

"Fearful," was Nurse Baker's answer, "fearful not as much for his recovery but more fearful of the complications of his needing treatment. I guess the easiest way to answer is that no one called or came to check on him for two days."

"Objection," Mr. Black repeated, "the defendants have no phone."

"Overruled," said Judge Spellman without explanation.

"One last thing," John said. "What was his condition when released and do you have knowledge of his present condition?"

Linda replied, "when he was released, he had gained nearly 25% in body weight, primarily from re-hydration. He was alert and taking formula and soft foods."

"And today?" John continued.

Linda smiled broadly. "As of Monday he was walking, trying to talk, and eating solid foods. In three weeks he has gained nearly ten pounds.

"Cross?" the Judge asked, looking toward the defense table.

"Not at this time, your Honor," came their reply. Linda was dismissed.

"Mister prosecutor," Judge Spellman said, "the hour is late, do you have another witness?"

"Yes, your Honor," John replied. "But rather than interrupt their testimony, I'd rather call them in the morning if the Court pleases. The Judge nodded, pounded the gavel and dismissed the court until 9:00 a.m. the following day.

John walked the few steps where Dr. Danes, the attending, and the ER nurse sat. "I'd like to call you first thing in the morning," he said, speaking to the nurse, "and then you also Doctor," he said, referring to the young attending. "Dr. Danes, I'd prefer to call you last, to use your position as head of the department to lend credibility to their testimony. If I can get the court to allow the photos, I'll introduce them at that time, following them up with testimonies from Brenda and the deputies who were on the scene with her."

The system which provided for the needs of the children was, by design, on a kind of auto-pilot, with the fosters coming and going, while providing a stable but temporary environment for them. When Brenda and Bill drove down to check on them, they were mobbed with welcome hugs and kisses.

Brenda had this image of them as spring flowers who had gone from hardly poking through the soil, to moving on into full bloom. She took many candid photos to share with Bert and those who continued to have an interest in them. She wondered also if possibly John may use them to provide before and after photos to the court.

"Ms. Elam? John O'Reilly," he said, "am I calling too late in the evening?"

"No, John," she answered, "what's on your mind?"

"I've a thought that might be worth presenting to your client," he answered. "While I don't think I'll need it, we may be willing to drop some of the charges for her testimony against her husband. In the interest of speeding up the trial and placing the children in permanent care, we can reduce criminal negligence to child endangerment and drop the charges of neglect, fraud, material misrep and the rest."

"Isn't it early in the trial to be offering us a deal?" she asked.

"Not as I see it," he answered. "Once I present my next three credible witnesses, we'll be seeking the full penalty of the law on each of the charges for each child. She could easily do 25 years."

"I'll speak with her and get back to you," Ms. Elam said before hanging up the phone.

John's phone rang while he was pouring his second cup of coffee, the clock read 7:00 a.m.

"Sylvia Elam," she said, identifying herself. "I have spoken with Mrs. Brown and she's willing to discuss your offer, but is making no promises." John could tell she was looking to him to guide her through the unfamiliar process.

"You should call Judge Spellman and request an audience with him," John suggested, "if possible, before court today. I'll be there at 8:00 a.m. whether he will see us in chambers or not. You are under no obligation to share our proposal with your co-counsel, but you should take your instruction from the Judge and not from me."

As he had hoped, Judge Spellman had left instruction for John to join them in chambers as soon as he arrived. When they were seated and offered coffee, the Judge leaned back in his chair and said, "Counselors, Mrs. Brown, let's hear what you have in mind."

John outlined his proposal which he had quickly put to paper the previous night, then stopped talking. Ms. Elam and her client quietly attempted to discuss its ramifications and what it required of her.

"You'll plead guilty to a charge of child endangerment and agree to testify in court for the prosecution. In exchange, the DA is willing to drop all other charges relevant to these proceedings. Child endangerment on six counts has a maximum sentence of 25 years to life and a minimum of five before becoming eligible for parole. You'll do at least five years in state prison."

First she argued, then sniffled, then tried to put the blame on her husband for forcing her. They waited, finally the Judge said, "you can accept the offer, or reject it as you desire, but in ten minutes the Court will convene and the offer is mute." She signed the rough draft which would later be replaced and resigned and entered into the court record.

As Court came to order, the Judge spoke to the courtroom. "A plea bargain has been reached between one of the defendants and the prosecution. Will that defendant rise and make her plea known to the court at this time."

Mrs. Brown and her counsel stood and entered a plea of guilty to the single charge previously agreed to. When John affirmed the agreement and the Judge accepted it, she was led from the courtroom to await sentencing on the charge. Ted Black had turned red with anger and remained so but made no verbal response except to confer with his client.

"Judge," he said standing. "In light of this significant change, I would ask the Court to give us a day to consider our options."

Judge Spellman looked over at John, who nodded his agreement. "Granted, be ready to proceed to trial at 9:00 a.m. Thursday morning. Dismissed."

Five hours later, John's secretary took Ted Black's call and put it through to her waiting boss. "Mr. O'Reilly, Ted Black here. Can we meet to discuss a plea bargain?"

"No sir," John said politely, "there is nothing to discuss. He's guilty. You know it, he knows it and the Court knows it. His wife's testimony makes it unnecessary for us to use the considerable additional evidence which would cause the jury to abandon any thought of clemency. We can meet, however, and I can make it easy for your client to see why he should change his plea and let you get back to your practice. I can meet you downstairs in an interrogation room at 2:00 p.m. if that is convenient," he offered.

Black, wanting to retain his dignity replied, "make it 2:30," then hung up. John felt happy to be putting it behind them as he put the original photos and the new ones he'd just received into his pocket.

Whether the Judge may have let him use them or not, John knew that when Mr. Brown viewed them with his attorney, he could plainly see the futility in continuing.

John had to hand it to Ted Black, who had torn a page from his own book... he arrived arrogantly at 2:45, just minutes before John was to have had Brown returned to his cell. It took them less than ten minutes to discuss and record the arrangement that they would later present to Judge Spellman. Black blustered that the photos would have never seen the light of day. John just smiled and did not respond.

When Court convened at its prescribed time, Judge Spellman asked both counsels to approach, then confirmed that an agreement to change the plea had been arranged. When they had returned to their tables, Judge Spellman asked Mr. Brown to stand before confirming his desire to plead guilty. The Court accepted the amended plea of guilty and set a date for sentencing.

How amazing Brenda found it that God had created the circumstance to resolve the issues without involving her and others testimony, without drawing the children into the web, without a hard fought battle with the potential to divide the community. She walked out with her new friends, Linda Baker and Michael Danes, with a smile on her face.

Mike took note of her demeanor and said, "well, Brenda, now we can get on with the important work of finding a home for the children."

The children were beginning their fourth week in foster care at the beach house and third at school. "Bert, this is Mike," Dr. Danes said as he addressed the director, "are we about ready to move forward to a more permanent solution for care of the children?"

Bert nearly laughed, then answered, "are you looking to adopt?"

Mike laughed also and answered, "I already have... in my heart, just as surely as if they lived in my home. Our friend Steve Moss has agreed to let us use the school to hold our meeting, allowing him to be included in the planning as we move forward," Mike said. Bert knew

Steve as the superintendent of public instruction.

"When?" he asked.

"I plan to run an announcement in the paper Friday and Saturday and have the meeting set for Wednesday of next week," Mike answered. "I hope to get maximum participation and input from the community at large by including them in the initial planning. It could be a valuable forum to present a case for the need for more foster parents. Please let me know if you have ideas or thoughts you want me to include or want to present yourself."

Bert thanked him, feeling cautiously optimistic as he considered how this man had chosen to carry the banner into battle. He thought of how Jesus had championed widows and orphans, those unable to speak for themselves.

When the announcement came out in the paper, it gave just enough information to peak the reader's interest, without giving away the full thrust of the meeting. Curiosity makes strange bedfellows, Mike had thought. Many marked it on their calendars because they feared some new program that would increase taxes, others because it alluded to child care, still more because the community offered little in the way of change and were simply too curious to stay home and watch reruns on TV.

At 6:45 p.m. the parking lot was filling up and a second section of bleachers was pulled out in the gym to accommodate arriving guests. A single rectangular table and a couple dozen folding chairs had been arranged at the head of the auditorium. Mrs. Rice and several of her colleagues had volunteered to give handouts to the arriving crowd.

Brenda noted it was a far cry from the plush appointments of the Beach Comber restaurant she had enjoyed the first time. Hardly anyone had dressed for the occasion and none formally. Even the influentials were seated with open shirts and some in jeans. As before, the room had been prepared with the capability to show videos and a microphone supplied for any who might speak to the assembly.

At 7:05, the last section of seating became a necessity as guests still continued to arrive. Mike wore a lapel microphone which allowed him to move about and appear informal. A stationary one stood ready near where the dignitaries sat.

At 7:15 Mike addressed his audience. "Good evening and thank you all for coming," he said. "In the interest of those who expected the meeting to begin at 7:00, let's get started. My name is Mike Danes, some of you may know me from our children's days in soccer together, and some from the hospital where I am charged with the responsibility for your children's care. He waited for the murmuring to quiet before continuing.

"What has brought us together tonight," he said, "is a need for our community to provide safety and care for children at risk. I do not use the term orphans, because although some are, many are not. Some have parents who have not shown themselves fit to be called such." Again there was a buzz in the room.

"If I may, I'd like to show you what I mean visually, rather than try and explain it verbally." The lights dimmed and the screen was filled with the now familiar photos of the Brown children. "If I may, I'd like to ask Brenda Nelson to explain to you what you are seeing."

Brenda stood at the microphone, identified herself and her position, then set the stage. First came the photos of the children in the hospital waiting room, the pictures of Timothy near death in ER, and his siblings eating like hungry animals in the nurse's lounge.

The scene then moved to the house where she and the deputies had found the children living in squalor, dirty and under nourished.

Finally, the photos she had taken the previous week of them at the beach house. As she narrated the changing scenes, she was forced to stop speaking several times as emotion choked her.

Brenda passed the microphone to Linda who followed her lead, explaining her connection and how she had become involved. The ER doctor took the microphone and explained in more technical terms what he had seen and his involvement in the crisis. Finally, Mike reassumed control and explained his involvement; first as a doctor, then as a concerned parent and citizen.

A hand was raised from the rear who asked the question, "are these the children from the trial last week?"

"They are," Mike answered truthfully, "and we feel the Court has provided justice in the criminal proceedings. While that was necessary and it is very important to find justice, it is only the tip of the iceberg. What we have, as you can see from the more recent photos, are six beautiful children who are eternally bound to one another. Because of their circumstance, which made it necessary to be interdependent, to separate them would cause, in my medical opinion, irreparable harm. Now that begs the question of how one might find willing and suitable foster parents or adoption parents for these six."

There was some discussion as people considered the magnitude of the problem he had posed.

"We have with us today both Bert Ellis, the head of child protective services, and a member of the Health and Welfare department with whom you may visit after this meeting. Both will tell you almost to a certainty there are none such in our little community or likely in the state. I along with several state and community leaders have proposed a possible solution which we hope will involve many of you." More chatter as the crowd saw themselves being prepared to be taxed or solicited for funding.

Mike let them talk for a minute before continuing. "Please be at ease, I have not called you here to levy more taxes on yourselves," he said, "quite the opposite. If you'll let me explain," he added, turning on the projector once more, "I'll do my best to lay out our proposal."

The first photo showed Mike's beach house, which brought envious comments from several. "I expect to sell this property and deposit the money from the sale directly into a newly formed charitable corporation. It will provide the seed money to get the project off the ground and begin construction of the "City of Refuge" center for at-risk children. Initial funding will be from several prominent donors who prefer to remain anonymous at this time, ongoing financing will be from state, federal, and local grants."

The next slide showed an artist's conception of a completed structure. "The building will initially provide interim to permanent housing for up to 24 children. It will provide employment for several full-time and some part-time employees, but will also include opportunities for volunteers as well. Currently, the six children are being cared for seven days a week by seven loving foster parents, working in rotation. You can see from these additional photos that it seems to be working well."

A dozen pictures of smiling faces of both children and adults in various circumstances adorned the screen. "Could any of you believe that none of these children had ever eaten pizza outside of the school cafeteria?" Mike asked the assembly. "The hospital administrator and its board have generously volunteered to cover the cost of medicine and supplies and our foundation has several doctors who have pledged their time to provide medical services to the children."

Next came a picture of Dan and Linda in the foreground, with an expanse of farmland in the rear. Mike introduced them by name to the crowd. "Dan, as some present may know, is an accomplished custom farmer, and Linda is one of our best and brightest nurses. Adjacent to their own home is this parcel of land which has recently been offered for sale."

Mike fielded a few questions from the group before returning to his explanation. "We are considering breaking the parcel into two, with the first to be for the building, parking, recreational area, and on-premises housing for staff and maintenance. With grounds for expansion, it would be about ten acres. The remaining 70 acres could be share-cropped to provide fresh food, and the possibility of animal feed for beef animals or horses. At a later date, animal husbandry could easily work into the children's education.

A comment came from a man near the front, "it seems kind of grandiose for a children's home."

"I hope it is," Mike said honestly. "I hope it provides an environment that helps the children forget that they were ever unloved. I hope that they will grow up and become all that God has planned for them to be, without the extra baggage that they were given by their birth parents. I can picture little Timmy becoming a policeman, doctor, fireman, or a military leader, not an indigent living on the street."

The room became quiet again as Mike concluded his talk. "We have among us many with God-given talent and resources. I am asking you to consider what of that you might be willing to offer to make our community a better place. On the handouts you've been given, you'll see some of the ways, both large and small, that you might choose to contribute. Thank you for your time and prayers." When the influentials stood and began the applause, the crowd joined them.

Ironically, the crowd did not leave right away. They clustered in small groups and mingled with each other discussing what they had just heard. Many visited with the teachers, others sought out the Mayor and other notables whom they recognized. Brenda and Bill stood to the side watching as Mike and Beth moved among the crowd, smiling and nodding their heads. Bill finally said, "it could actually work. With God's help, together, we might pull this thing off."

The Board of the fledgling corporation included doctors Danes and Benson, an anesthesiologist; Bud Wilson, an attorney; Tom Severn, a local bank president; and Bob Bailey, a local architect who attended Mike's church. Mike had drawn Christian professionals together who had the God-given gifts needed to not only set up the corporation but to also fund, build, and manage the project. In addition, it had an advisory board of six which included his pastor, the Mayor, Bert Ellis, Brenda, Dan Baker, and his friend the state Senator.

Four had volunteered their time after hearing Mike's proposal to help in clerical capacities. They were the first to help. They collated the lists of volunteers, made and took calls, and passed needed information on to Mike and the board. The land was secured with a sizable deposit and financing was arranged, pending the sale of the beach house.

The mayor helped in the areas of facilitating zoning approval and was able to cut much of the red tape associated with permits. A well was drilled and approved, followed by the advertised ground breaking ceremony, which included most of the town's residents, who came for the free BBQ. Bill Nelson fired up his track-hoe and amid cheers and jeers, scooped the first bucketful of soil, while the Lieutenant Governor used the occasion as a photo-op for his state-paid trip to the coast.

Meanwhile, Judge Spellman pronounced sentence on both the Browns, 25 years with 5 fixed before becoming eligible for parole for Mrs. Brown and 25 to life for Mr. Brown, with 15 of it fixed without possibility of review. A newsie made a front page story of the complete ordeal, piecing it together, beginning with the children's leaving school to the present time. With Brenda's guidance, it was a tale of tragedy with a silver lining in the form of the community involvement it spawned and the facility that it was helping to create.

With the election year approaching, the suggestion of favorable press by a friend in the state legislature caught the Governor's ear. He championed the City of Refuge as if it were his own idea and presented a Bill to purchase the beach house for one million dollars for a state-owned getaway location for notables and the political elite. Mike found it humorous how some could justify anything and spin it to look like a generous gift for a good cause. They accepted the offer anyway, with the condition that it could continue to be used until the new facility was completed.

With cash in the bank, the construction moved ahead rapidly. Much of it involved community volunteers and the rest provided needed employment in the small community. The blessing multiplied itself over and over in ways, too numerous to mention, both financially and spiritually. Mike's pastor used the circumstance on which to base more than one sermon regarding how God uses the evil in the world to create good.

Foundation poured, floors laid, walls framed, and rafters in place, the laborers began to sheath the roof in anticipation of the oncoming seasonal rains. The coast can easily have more than twenty inches of rain a year, which literally brings construction to a halt. The crew worked feverishly to get the walls wrapped and roof shingled so they could move inside.

As the end of October loomed just ahead, a storm front moving down from the gulf of Alaska hit the Oregon and Washington coast with full fury, dropping several inches of wind driven rain in two days. While the roof was in place and the framing wrapped with sheathing, the siding was not complete and several windows remained uninstalled.

Mike, Dan, and Bill, among others, armed with staple guns, viz-queen, and duct tape, worked well into the night, coming home cold and wet to the skin. After two days, the rain moved inland leaving the coast cold and damp. Massive propane heaters provided warmth to the crews and helped dry the structure, making it suitable to complete the siding and enclose the building.

The next potluck for the crews and volunteers was held inside with just the insulated walls surrounding them. Sheet rock went up quickly with professionals guiding the willing hands of many volunteers, then slowed again as the tape and texture process required time to dry and season.

When the rains returned it was early November and painters were inside having only the high humidity with which to contend. Locals knew they could count on their fingers the number of days without moisture between now and spring and thanked God that the remaining work was being done inside.

I would like to paint for you the image of a structure suitable for housing as many as two dozen children and their care givers, providing for their needs 24/7, including food, shelter, sanitary, and recreational needs. What do you see in your mind's eye? A well designed, modern structure, unpretentious but well built; surrounded by farmland and natural coastal shrubbery and trees, I hope. The majority of the building was single story, the exception being the entrance which had a vaulted ceiling. It appeared spacious while not eating up a lot of square footage. On the second level was a game room, places for group study with WiFi connection for computers, a television viewing room and a library.

Dan and Linda had discussed, and had been considering, the Foundation's offer to employ them as on-site managers. They seemed ideal partly because of their proximity next door, but also because of their commitment to the project and its children. Dan had readied the soil on the extra land for spring planting before the first rains turned them to mud. Only a small perimeter around the building itself had been planted in grass to keep the dirt and mud down. The additional nine acres had been left untouched until need for it presented itself, with the exception of a half acre which would serve as the garden.

Over two months had passed since the day the children had been snatched away from their marginal existence, and they had adapted well. Although interaction with their peer group at school found them lacking, it was not so with the steady stream of adult foster parents they had come to know and love.

Seven couples had come to regard these children as their own, most of them sad to see their day end and eager when it was their turn again. The multiple personalities and management styles were a blessing to the children, who lacked life experience. Brenda wondered and worried how it would change when they moved to the new location. She thanked God for the miracle He had performed, for the guidance and direction they had all received, and for whatever the future still held.

When the board met, the consensus was that they should proceed with all haste to complete the building and occupy it before Christmas. It seemed only natural that the children would celebrate their first Christmas ever in their new home. That meant that although the structure was complete, it needed to be furnished. Mike's volunteers called upon their own experiences to make lists of necessary items ranging from toilet tissue to silverware, from beds and bed coverings, to tooth brushes and paste.

One of the vacant rooms was designated as the dispensary and was outfitted, with the hospital's help, with necessary medical equipment and supplies. The kitchen, by code, had to be restaurant quality and by necessity, furnished with a variety of large volume pots and pans. It fell under the commercial designation as a shelter home, much like an assisted living home for the aged.

An interesting side note was that Brenda began getting flack from some of her fosters, wondering if they may loose their jobs when the shelter opened. Many depended not only on the little income it brought but also had the desire to continue in service. She met with Bert and Mike and posed the question as to how the transition might work.

With their focus on the six Brown children, both had overlooked how the changing complexion may look to their current providers. Mike made the suggestion, to which Bert readily agreed, to meet with all those concerned to give them a voice in decision making and try and stay as transparent as possible with them. When Brenda suggested that the foster children should be involved as well, it was decided that they'd use the occasion of the Open House to meet with them.

Mike suggested that the current fosters might enjoy the status of an early opening just for them, a day before the general public. They could also utilize that meeting for their discussion. Word went out the next day to each of the fosters, both Brenda's and her co-workers', that they were invited to a "special exclusive Open House" on December 15th.

With only ten days left to prepare, final inspections were done, occupancy was granted, and supplies, equipment, and food stuffs began to arrive daily. Linda was hired to oversee their receipt and to coordinate their placement and storage, as she took vacation from her nursing duties. Both volunteers and day laborers were called to duty working under Linda's watchful eye.

What seemed to remain as a major stumbling block was someone to coordinate the kitchen. They needed the expertise of an experienced professional cook. As is the nature of that business, the good ones are always in demand and draw good salaries, the poor ones are transient and often not trustworthy and dependable. No single housewife, no matter how accomplished in her own kitchen, would have been a good fit to walk into that atmosphere and be expected to survive long term.

The sheer volume of food necessary to feed three meals a day to two to three dozen individuals would require someone with skills to plan, order, prepare and cook in large quantity. It seemed like another impossible hurdle as they brainstormed together, with time running short. It was Linda who came up with a couple of ideas. She volunteered to check with the hospital cafeteria staff for recommendations and to call Mrs. Rice and ask her to do likewise at the school.

Mrs. Rice found gold her first try. The lead cook of many years had retired early two years before so that she and her husband could travel. When he had died prematurely it had left her alone, without meaningful relationships, and possibly a little short in the finance department.

Linda called Mae Wilson and found her a charming, vital 62-year-old woman needing human contact, that evidenced by the fact it was hard to get her off the phone. When Mae arrived at the new shelter she and Linda formed an immediate bond. She and Mike negotiated a starting salary with an agreement to review it in six months, and she was hired on Linda's recommendation over the phone.

Mae went right to work, surveying the kitchen, taking notes, making suggestions, and adding to the shopping list already begun for the Open House. When Mae asked about the possibility of living on-site, Linda knew God had provided just the right person.

"As many as several hundred," Mike said, when Mae asked how

many were expected at the formal Open House, "we're not quite sure."

"And for the pre-opening?" she asked. Brenda filled in the number for him, a couple dozen adults and as many children. Mae smiled, "piece of cake," she said, about the first one. "I'll need two helpers and some-one to run the dishwasher, no experience necessary. The big one I'll make some calls to my old staff and see who needs a little extra spend-ing money. How much can we offer them per hour?"

Mike nearly laughed, having no clue of what the job was worth. "You offer them whatever you think is fair, I'll back you up and make sure they're paid," he said. He liked the way she looked him right in the eye when she spoke.

"Done," she said. "Anything else I need to know? Do you want a hand in planning the menu or do you want me to handle it?"

Mike handed her his business credit card, gave her a smile and said, "you handle it."

Mrs. Rice had brought three other teachers with her when she showed up early on the afternoon of the 15th to help Mae serve at the Open House. For the first few minutes, it was old home week as they visited and caught up with each other. Then Mae showed them around as proudly as if she owned the place. Finally in the kitchen, she explained the menu, gave each an apron and an idea of what was expected of them.

There were many kinds, shapes, and colors of Christmas cookies already baked and decorated, finger foods, cheese trays, fancy pastries, fresh fruits, and two flavors of punch. In addition, there was a mountain of freshly baked and thinly sliced roast beef and turkey with a variety of breads and condiments. Whether coming for a snack or trying to replace dinner, no guest should leave hungry.

Linda perused the spread, nodding her approval, and grazing as she went around making sure everything was in place. Only twelve of the twenty four bedrooms were furnished and ready for occupancy, the second twelve stood clean but empty awaiting the need to be used. Linda had hired William Thomas as a combination janitor and maintenance man part-time, with the anticipation of needing him full-time as they filled. Today he had volunteered to work in the kitchen and run the dishwasher.

Mike and Beth, Bert and Martha, Bill and Brenda, the majority of the Foundation's board, and other supporters began arriving before the 5:00 p.m. start time and were shown around. When the fosters and their children arrived, each were greeted and introduced, then taken personally on the tour by one or more of the early arrivals. When the Millers arrived with the six Brown children, Brenda and Bill made them their priority showing them to what would soon become their own beds and bedrooms.

Given the size of the town, almost no one didn't know everyone else in some capacity or another. But none the less they mingled, were introduced over and over until there became a general sense of family, especially among the children. As soon as they became comfortable, the questions began, many of which presented new challenges previously not considered. One child asked, "if I stayed here, how would I get to school?" Another seemed to be concerned about their relationship with their current foster parents.

Bert stood first, then asked Brenda to speak to some of the issues. She gathered the children around her, sitting them in front of the roomful of adults. "First," she said looking each child in the eye, "our goal for each of you has never changed. It is for you to have loving and caring permanent mothers and fathers and for you to be happy and well taken care of. Your foster parents are a shelter from the storms that have come into your lives, but they are not and have never been the permanent solution. All those you have met here are involved because they love you and others like yourselves."

One little girl raised her hand and broke everyone's heart, "will I ever see my momma and daddy again?" Brenda knew her parents had abandoned her and her brother before disappearing.

"I hope so," she answered as truthfully as she could, "but until they come back, we want you to be safe and happy."

An older boy asked, "do I have to come here or can I stay where I am?"

"No and yes," she said answering both questions. "Neither your foster parents or you children will be required to do anything they do not want to. Those who want to be a part of The City of Refuge will be welcome to do so, both fosters and children, those who do not will not be forced."

"Most of you have met Karen Brown and her brothers and sisters here tonight," she said motioning toward them. "For the past several months they have had the good fortune to share seven foster parents." Most of the parents knew of the arrangement, but most of the children were not aware.

One boy asked just the right question, "how does that work?"

Brenda said, "let me answer your question two ways, first it provided for the children a place with food and shelter, but what made it really work were the volunteers who came each day to love and care for them." She leaned close to Karen and spoke to her.

Karen stood. "I'm Karen," she said, "I'm a sixth grader, these are my brothers and sisters." She continued, "the last three to four months have been the best of our entire lives. Until Mrs. Nelson helped us, no one but our teachers at school ever said they loved us." She was looking directly at the boy who had asked the question.

"Mike and Beth," she said looking over at the doctor, "loaned us his neat house on the beach because there were too many of us to go to a single foster family. Every day we had a new Mom and Dad." She smiled as she looked around the room at her care givers. "Each of them are a lot different but all of them love us. It was cool," she said, "we have fourteen Moms and Dads." The children especially seemed to embrace the idea.

Jake stood without invitation and said, "I'm Jake. The neat part is that none of them are ever in bad moods, at least not when they are with us." There were tears in some eyes as conversations sprang up here and there.

Finally one of the fosters spoke up, "will it work the same way here as it did at the beach house?" he asked. "Will my wife and I come here and stay the night, then go home the next day?"

Mike stood and fielded the question. "We are all just getting our feet on the ground here, learning as we go, but to begin with, the answer is 'yes'. We'll have a full-time coordinator who will work with Bert, Brenda, and the foster parents with scheduling issues, welcoming of new guests, and taking care of school issues and medical needs. We already have on staff Mrs. Mae Wilson, who prepared all this wonderful food and Mr. Thomas who maintains the building and grounds. Linda Baker is our current coordinator, and our volunteers tonight are Mrs. Rice and her fellow teachers from the school. The room erupted in applause.

Before Mike sat he added, "we expect to celebrate Christmas here with our first guests being Karen and her brothers and sisters. As other children and parents wish to join us, we will make any necessary accommodation to welcome them also. Any requests for change from your current status should go through Bert, Brenda and Linda."

The evening news and weather had already begun as Brenda returned home to Bill and her boys. "What's he saying about the weather for tomorrow?" she asked as she seated herself and kicked off her shoes.

"Rain with light winds 10 to 15 miles per hour in the morning, with rain decreasing during the day," Bill answered, parroting the weathercaster's words. "How did the Open House go?"

"It went surprisingly well, food was great as you'll find out tomorrow with the rest of the town," she answered. "Sorry about taking so long. The boys already in bed?"

"Yup," he answered, "but I'll bet they're not asleep." Brenda went up the stairs where she ruffled their sleepy topknots and tucked them in for the night.

Linda called Mike Danes at his office. Working together outside the hospital had cut away the formality of the hospital as she said, "Mike, this is Linda. I'm worried that we will not have room for all of our guests tonight."

"I was thinking the same thing," he said. "We had, what, 50 last night, and were about full up."

"Mae is cooking for two hundred," she said. "She suggested that we get a pavilion tent from one of the rental agencies and set it up for a hundred with folding tables and chairs and set up a donation jar for those who might seem inclined to help out financially."

"Good idea," he said, "but I'm not sure about the jar."

"I like the idea of giving people a way to help out," Linda said, maybe I can think of something a little more subtle."

"Good, go with it."

That is what she liked about Mike, he could listen, analyze, and make a decision without calling for a poll or a committee to consider all options. That is also what made him a good doctor.

Four men with four pickup trucks showed up just as the fog began to replace the light morning rain and began unloading. It took just over an hour to erect the tent and another to attach the side panels and begin unloading chairs and tables. By 2:00 p.m. a dozen tables with accompanying chairs filled the interior, and a pair of radiant propane umbrella stoves stood at opposite ends.

With a little urging, Mae convinced Steve that a surplus six-station steam cabinet that had sat in storage for ten years should be cleaned up and delivered to them. The schools had all converted to gas, leaving the electric one useless as a backup anyway. Mr. Thomas, with the help of an electrical contractor friend, ran a temporary 220 line to provide power to it.

Both convection ovens were filled with slow cooking meat; four hams, three turkeys, and two nice barons of beef, which filled the building with their succulent aromas. Mae's former co-workers were busily chopping, slicing, whipping, and mixing. Fruit, vegetables, salads, and sheet cakes were appearing as if by magic. On the stove, gravies and sauces simmered as the afternoon worked it's way toward evening.

Linda returned from the craft mart with a tastefully woven basket with a lid. It resembled a miniature steamer trunk with a slot in the lid which made it suitable to accept donations. She labeled it as such and placed it on a rectangular table in the entry, under a gilded mirror.

There was a four-head soft drink dispenser just off the kitchen near the dry pantry where pitchers of soft drink would be filled and then served. Mae had opted to buy rolls rather than bake for the occasion and held them in the warmer where they stayed hot and moist.

Mike, Beth, Bill, Brenda and their sons showed up early, followed by more of the board with their families, and then both vocal and financial supporters. At 5:00 p.m. the general public began to arrive, first being greeted, then given tours. Thomas lit off the heaters and closed up the tent, allowing to heat as the cold, humid night began its chill. At 5:30 Mike asked his pastor to bless the assembly, the structure, and the bounty the Lord had provided, then asked him lead the food line. Most filled their plates and retired to the pavilion tent where they could eat and visit.

As new guests came, some of the first arrivals said their thanks and left, keeping the population somewhere between 50 and 75 at any given time, in addition to the serving crew. By 7:00 the few stragglers left were filling to-go boxes for family at home. Mae sported the smile of a grandmother having served the last of a Thanksgiving dinner, pride of accomplishment apparent on her aged face.

As cleanup began, Linda went to the basket where she found numerous personal checks and five $100 bills which she had seen Mike try to slip in unseen before the guests arrived. When she took the basket to him he smiled and said "will you ask Mae and her crew to join me for a moment?" Mae, Thomas, and the three from the kitchen crew assembled in the foyer where Mike stood smiling.

"Mae," he said, "the dinner was wonderful. You all worked hard today. What did you tell your friends that we would pay them?"

She looked embarrassed, then answered, "all I said was that it'd be better than what the school pays." It was Mike's turn to look embarrassed as he took the five $100 bills and handed one to each of them.

"Mae, please let me know if this is not enough and I'll see to it they get whatever you think is right." Thomas started to object that he had not worked as long and hard as the others and that he was on salary.

Mike smiled and said, "there's a Bible passage that speaks to that, he said. "Something to the effect that the boss can pay more as he chooses as long as he pays at least the minimum promised."

They all laughed when Linda said, "you really mangled the scripture."

Brenda called each of the fosters who had been caring for the children at the beach house, trying to make sure they were willing to continue at the new location. A couple of them hesitated but then confirmed their commitment to continue. With so little personal things to move, it was not a big effort to relocate the children, they chose a Saturday so she and Bill could help out.

The Millers happened to be the duty couple and agreed to meet at the Refuge for the changing of the guard, and have breakfast together. Brenda took the company van, loaded it with kids, invited the Barnes, the couple going off duty to join them, and headed toward the rendezvous. Bill in his pickup laden with school books, clothes, and uneaten food stuffs followed behind.

Mae had sausage, pancakes, eggs, and fruit to eat with two choices of juice to drink. It was ready for them when they arrived and a little wrapped gift for each child sat by each plate, with the child's name on it. Linda handed Bill a digital camera and asked him to record the event as each child opened their small gift. "A Christmas present," Jake said.

"No," Mae corrected, "just a welcome home gift, Christmas will come next week." Each package contained a hand knitted stocking cap and matching mittens. Mae's kindness set the stage for what was later to become an ongoing tradition.

Linda led the children down the hallway, allowing them to chose their rooms as a wall color or curtain caught their eye. Two to a room worked out well, with Karen preferring to be with Timothy and the two younger girls, Betty and Bonnie, needing each others' companionship.

Jake and Ben filled out the trio. Changeable name plates went up on the doors and their meager personal things were hung in the closets or dressers. The Barnes, Millers, and Brenda and Bill followed along as Linda explained the rules and lay out of the building. One of the rooms lying between the kitchen and infirmary had been furnished for the foster couple on duty.

Across the hall was Linda's office, beside it was to be Mae's quarters if she chose to stay on premises. When the Barnes left, Brenda and Bill did also, leaving the Millers and the six children to adapt to their new home. Linda, Mae, and Thomas remained with them to make the transition less difficult.

On the 17th Brenda received a call from the Smiths, another of her foster parents. Their two, a boy and his sister, wanted to try out the shelter, with the parents eager also to work into Linda's rotation schedule. Blake and Penny had been abandoned by their parents and had been with the Smiths for nearly two years. He was seven, she had just turned six. Brenda called Linda who asked Mae to set the table for an additional four that evening.

When they arrived, they were introduced first to the children, then to the staff. They were allowed to chose a room together only because of their ages. Linda had chosen age ten as the appropriate time to consider gender separation as prudent. The duty couple, who were also on their first tour, welcomed the fostering experience the Smiths brought with them and urged them to stay the night, much to the joy of Blake and Penny.

Looking in from the outside, Brenda could see the fosters and their children all coming together as a family. It pleased her to see their burdens lighten and their commitments growing stronger. On the 19th another couple and their foster son came on board and were seamlessly acclimated into the group, bringing the total to nine children and nine foster parents.

Mike and the board had authorized a budget to purchase Christmas decorations for the City of Refuge, it's guests and staff. Working with Bert and the agency, they packaged it to include both those already in residence and those still in individual foster care. Brenda, Martha, Beth, and Linda, armed with a list of names, sizes, and a vague idea of color preferences, recruited their men to drive the big van and follow them to the outlet mall in Lincoln City for the initial round of shopping.

They began with two toys each, then moved on to the more necessary items like clothing and personal items. Each received a new coat, two pairs of shoes, socks, underwear, shirts, and both play and school clothes. In the end, they expended a little over $300 per child for the sixteen in foster care or about $5,000 total.

Mae volunteered her services for a Christmas dinner to include all the fosters and their children, volunteers, and staff. The Board approved and sent her shopping. She planned her menu with about seventy-five guests in mind, much the same as the Open House but with a sit down dinner rather than finger foods. Turkey, dressing, mashed potatoes, gravy, yam casserole, green beans in mushroom gravy, homemade parkerhouse rolls, baked ham, candied carrots, a cake and four pies. She recruited several friends and Thomas to help in the kitchen and Linda, Beth, and Martha to help the men serve.

The lunch room was too small by itself so the entry hall was converted into a dining room and decorated with a tree and holiday decorations. On the afternoon of the 23rd the presents that had been taken home and wrapped were returned and placed under the tree in a corner next to the stairway.

The place was abuzz with whispered voices and stifled squeals as the children checked out the wrapped presents, searching to find their names. On the 24th, the fosters, volunteers, guests, and other children began to arrive, filling the hall to overflowing. Bert, Mike, Bill, and Dan assumed the greeting and welcoming roles while their wives confirmed the tables were properly appointed and ready.

When all were seated, Pastor Brent was asked to bless the food and their time together. He also offered a short version of the significance of Christmas for the children before they began to eat. Interestingly, exclusive of the staff, every single seat was filled, forcing the wait and kitchen staff to use the lunchroom, where they ate in shifts. Mae had cooked off and on for two days but the meal lasted less than a half hour. It took longer to cut and serve the dessert than to eat it, with the children eager to get to their presents.

The tables were cleared, wiped, and prepared for the onslaught of Christmas packages that were delivered to the children by volunteers. Squeals and laughter filled the room as delighted children with big eyes and low expectations were pleasantly surprised time and time again. Mountains of wrappings were carted away as the fosters began leading the children in Christmas carols.

Two sets of foster parents stayed the night to make sure that each child felt safe and loved in their new home. Some of those listening to the children pray had tears running down both cheeks as they heard the children thanking Jesus for loving them and providing for them.

~ ~

Ten years later, many of the original children had now graduated high school, some from college as well. A few were adopted and have loving, caring adoptive parents and families to support them. Several have married and have families of their own now. Bonnie and Betty are now juniors in high school, Timothy just started middle school. None of them still reside at the City of Refuge, but are there often.

As their siblings grew and left, they were adopted by Dan and Linda and live right across the field with their parents. However, they have strong ties to the Refuge and the other children. Linda works full time as administrator and only occasionally has to fill in at the hospital when they need her.

Jake is in college and Ben in the military, stationed currently in Germany, both remain single and committed to Jesus and family. Karen is married, living in Salem, Oregon, where she is finishing up her nursing degree. They have no children yet. Bert and his wife are grandparents and have retired and moved to be near their children and grandchildren.

Brenda now has responsibility for the program and works daily with fosters, both in and outside of the original City of Refuge in Newport. A second Refuge was opened a year ago in Gresham, a small town outside of Portland. Mae still lives and works at the center but has passed the baton for primary responsibility to a younger woman with culinary skills.

Mike is still Mike, although his hair is now flecked with gray, more active than ever in his church and the community he loves. He and Beth are grandparents, both sons happily married with two children each. Regrettably, Mrs. Rice died several years ago of natural causes, as have both of the Millers. Thankfully, however, they are today walking with Jesus and will soon reunite with friends and family. Mrs. Brown came up for parole and was refused at the five year mark, Mr. Brown remains in state prison for the foreseeable future.

There are currently in residence at the City of Refuge eighteen children of different ages, backgrounds, ethnicity, social class, all with stories to tell, but with a common bond. They know they are safe, cared for, and they feel loved, all because God's plan was worked out through a man who took time to listen and obey.

The Clay Pot

There was once a servant who was given a magnificent clay pot made by his master. Although the pot was not beautiful to the eye, it was a work of love. At first, the servant was pleased and placed high value in his pot, but as time went on it became ordinary and was used to haul refuse and dung. The pot became worn and chipped and sat alone in the corner, waiting to be discarded.

During a visit to the servant's home, the master saw the pot in the corner and inquired of it to the servant. The servant was ashamed and asked the master to forgive him for the poor treatment it had received and asked if it could be repaired. The gracious master took the pot with him to his home and built a great fire in his furnace.

As the refining fire of the furnace licked inside the pot, all the years of debris and dirt were burned away, leaving it spotless and clean. However, he made no attempt to clean the outside, rather allowing the blaze to bake the surface into a beautiful glaze, hard and new, but still showing the chips and scratches of the years of abuse.

The master, returning to the servant, then said "I have made this vessel new again; it is yours, care for it and it will serve you forever."

Conflict

The ominous sound of the gates closing behind them confirmed that reentry was not to be an option. Having been evicted from the only home they had ever known, they were at once homeless and helpless in their strange new surroundings. A road less traveled, in the modern vernacular, stretched endlessly before them, trailing off into the darkening shadows that lay ahead.

Frightened and alone, they traveled onward until finally finding a suitable place to rest in the forest. Fruit and berries provided for their immediate needs and the late summer weather made shelter unnecessary. A pristine brook flowed from the manor which they had just left, meandering between trees and greenery. Small fish teemed just under its surface waiting to be harvested as their food. In a sense, it seemed that they were still being provided for.

As they continued to walk on the second day, putting distance between them and their former home, the terrain became less hospitable and the summer sun more harsh. The trees were less vibrant and the land provided less and less food the farther they progressed. The clear bright stream became choked with moss, causing the fish to lie rotting on its banks, its water putrid and undrinkable.

At the end of the third day, summer was turning to fall, a cold breeze began to cause them discomfort and pain, forcing them to seek shelter among the rocks and scraggly desert brush.

"Surely," she said, "we can return the way we came. We can find our way back and make amends for our mistakes. Is what we have done so serious that we should be left to die in the desert?" He just hung his head, unhearing, feeling lost and alone. Overhead the sky darkened, storm clouds threatened rain, as thunder and lightening assaulted their senses. Great bolts of energy filled the sky with jagged lines, momentarily illuminating the foreign terrain, to be followed seconds later by the crash of great conflict from the heavens.

They cowered, wept, and huddled together, seeking solace and protection from the storm. They were cold, cold to the bone, with little clothing to preserve their body heat. "Are we going to die?" she asked him. "Will we be like the fish beside the stream? Oh God, save us," she wailed into the tumult.

A bolt of fire struck a tree, it exploded into flames, the light blinding them. Fear filled their hearts, as the rain stung their flesh and the earth beneath them shook. Then at once it was over. The wind stopped, the rain ceased, and the heat from the burning tree warmed their nearly naked bodies. The fire that had caused terror became their friend and he gathered nearby branches and sticks together. In the darkness they sought comfort from one another, lying together by the fire as man and wife.

Just enough. They struggled to find just enough, to sustain them each day, gathering and eating what little the earth had to offer. Eventually, he learned how to plant and harvest meager crops, how to snare and kill small animals; and she, how to cook and prepare what he brought her. He built a shelter, and then domesticated wild animals for both food and companionship. In time she bore them a son, and later another, but life continued to be harsh and unyielding as their sons grew older.

The first son was bitter because of his suffering and became jealous of his younger brother, who seemed better adapted to their pitiful existence. A stranger visited him often, gaining influence over him, while he labored alone in the fields. Often the stranger pointed out how his brother was favored, causing bitterness and anger to grow between them. His mind dwelt upon the injustice that he perceived and not on how well their abilities were suited to their tasks.

The older son often ate the best of his crops by himself and brought to the family only what was left over, while the younger boy would always bring the best of his animals to butcher and share with them all. Because of this, he found favor with his father, while the other did not, even though he loved them both.

On a particularly hot day, while he was laboring under the relentless sun in the fields, and having forgotten to bring water with him, the older son was visited by his brother. That brother offered to share his own water, but when the older one took it all, an argument ensued.

When it was over, the younger brother lay dead at his feet, another victim of the poor choices his own parents had made years earlier. He and his friend ran away to join others like themselves, to live a life of self indulgence.

Country Kid

It's funny how a feller learns. Lookin' back on it, most of life's lessons didn't seem like learnin' at all. You just kinda soaked it all up as you lived it. Some folks don't seem to pay attention though and don't seem to learn nuthin'.

Helpin' was one thing which Pa taught us first thing. He said you needed to open your eyes and to see other folks as they really were. Don't make fun o' nobody. Wasn't as much a lesson as just being taught how to see things different. Came as second nature to just notice when folks needed a hand once you got the seein' down.

Another thing which was right important was bein' honest. Pa always said "a man's only as good as his word". When we was young we didn't know what that meant exactly, but we knew it was true 'cause the other older fellas said the same thing and nodded their heads. Those fellas always said Pa was a "straight shooter", and that meant about the same kind of thing, I suppose.

We kids kinda sat back aways and listened to the older folks talk and got the hang of how things were supposed to work. Some of us older ones then would tell the youngins what we heard and give 'em instruction so'd they'd know stuff too.

We was farmers, not ranchers. There is a difference you know. Sometimes city folks think they are the same. Farmers can grow stuff besides cows and horses, but ranchers can't. We'd grow stuff and eat it or sell it to other folks who didn't grow it. Sometimes we'd trade for 'store bought' stuff like sugar and flour 'cause it was too much trouble to raise it ourselves.

Ma would sew for other folks who didn't know how, Pa would help other fellas with their chores when they needed it. That's another thing, chores. Lotsa folks don't understand chores. Chores is stuff that's gotta git done, no excuses. If you don't git the chores done when you're 'posed to, then there's the dickens to pay 'cause usually it gits harder the longer you wait.

Chores mostly aren't real hard, just regular, but need to git done, like feedin' the animals. Animals depends upon us for everything, food and even water most of the time. In the winter they have it hard enough just livin'. In the summer tho, they can git most of their food from the pasture and water from the crick.

Carryin' wood for the fire is a kid's chore and even the little ones can do it some. Haulin' wood and splittin' it is for the men and bigger kids. One of the things country kids learn right away is that if you need it you can probably make it. God gave us mostly everythin' a body needs right out in the open.

I never saw a store bought toy till I was eight. No need. Pa showed me how to make a 'flipper from a tree fork, a whistle from a willow, and a sling from the tongue of an old boot. The sling was jus' like the one that David killed the giant with. I could sling a rock real good with it after a while.

'Nother thing you learn on the farm is about livin' and dyin'. When I was little, I got to help save a calf who was born in the snow and was freezin', I kept her right by the wood stove and fed her from a bottle till she was bigger. I got to learn about being born and was a little 'fraid at first cause of all the blood and stuff. Some folks seem real worried 'bout dyin', not me. I's seen quite a bit of it.

Grandma just went to sleep one afternoon in the rocker and woke up with the Lord, they said so in church. Don't seem too scary to me. But, when they's young it can be real sad, or when it lasts a long time and you gotta see 'em suffer. I don't understand why God let's that happen sometimes.

Ma got real sick and couldn't get her breath good, till she finally couldn't git outta bed 'tall. Even tho folks said a lot of nice things and brung by lotsa food and flowers and such, we was still awful sad for a long time with her gone.

One night I got up to git a glass of milk and Pa was just sittin' by the fireplace lookin' at the fire. He wasn't sayin' nuthin' but I could tell he was missin' Ma. I jus' sat down by him and put my hand on his knee and looked at the fire for a long time too. Pretty soon things seemed better so I jus' went on to bed without sayin' a word. Pa and Grandpa both don't say much, but you kin tell they miss Ma a whole lot.

Pa said I should git my schoolin' done 'cause that would please Ma, so I did. I studied hard and got the diploma. Some of the kids my age went on away to more schoolin' but I figure I'll jus' stay and help Pa and the littler ones for a while. I like farmin' anyway and am gittin' right good Pa says.

We go to the church 'most every Sunday and we are learnin' about the things that people did in the old times. A lot of it hasn't changed much and don't seem to me most folks have learned much either. We are still doin' the same things as they did back then.

Sometimes I wonder why we don't get smarter about God and stuff. Ma was the first one who told me about Jesus and helped me understand about dyin' and livin' all over again. I know she is in Heaven with Him right now. Sometimes I want to go see her. I tell the younger ones all that I remember about what Ma said and that they better listen careful in church. Pa don't talk about God much but I know he knows about Him 'cause I saw him prayin' before.

I hope this helps you understand why us farm kids is different than the city kids.

The Creator and the Creation

I will attempt to tell you what I think I know. I think I was lying down attempting to sleep when an idea for a story crept into my head and filled it. I said I think because the nature of the story makes me less than certain.

My story is about a writer sitting down somewhere to write a story about a writer sitting down somewhere beginning a story. As I sit before my old Dell XP and begin to tell my reader about the writer of that story, I have to wonder if she is sitting down before her own Dell telling the story of me telling the story.

I myself am a writer, or possibly a character in a story being written by a writer, who has written many stories. Several of my novels are published and in print on shelves waiting to be read. As I sit here trying to make sense of all of this, a thought just leaped into my head, am I describing myself or is she describing herself?

Indeed, as I stand back from the question, trying to think it through, could there be a third or fourth somewhere writing about other writers writing about themselves? Is this the way madness begins? Doubting yourself, wondering if what you feel is real or made up by someone?

He walks into the room with a swagger, very aware that those already there are filling their eyes with his beauty and grace. Is he mine or hers? "He's mine," I write hurriedly, trying to get ahead of her fingers moving deftly over her keyboard. "Make up your own character," I tell her in my mind. "I just did," she answers back.

He's not exceptionally tall, but looks so in his black leather attire and slim build, and more so because the others are all seated and looking up at him. I can feel the writer feasting on him as I write, lust and desire apparent as her fingers continue to move. "Why a she," I ask myself? "Why did you choose a female writer character for your story?"

"Choose me?" she shoots back. "Indeed, why did I choose a male character for mine?"

I see the dialogue getting out of hand and force myself to concentrate once again on the man who has entered the room. What kind of room is it I wonder? The answer comes to me... a great luxurious living room in a vast mansion, a room full of the rich and famous, possibly the home of a movie star or Hollywood mogul. The guests tire of staring at him and return to their conversations, filling the air with the hum of worthless words and insincere laughter.

I find that I am getting into the character now and putting thoughts of my clone out of my mind. Did she just whisper those words to me? In my usual manner, the story appears without planning or fore thought, no plot or end in sight. She's sneaking back in, causing me to wonder if possibly she already has a plot in mind.

White-gloved service personnel move quietly and discreetly through the crowd, retrieving an empty glass and serving its replacement, as canapés and paté find their way into waiting mouths. In the background, fashionable contemporary music is playing on the balcony and filters down from above like the misting of a spring rain.

She hesitated, took her hands from the keyboard and emptied the remainder of her glass of iced tea, my favorite beverage. I wonder why I just choose to make her choice of drink that which I also enjoy. Sameness, familiarity, common bonds, and yes we share them, but of course writers often write about that which they know.

Black hair, perfectly groomed and coiffed in the style of the day, with not a single errant lock out of place, and he knows it as he displays himself to the adoring masses. He is not 'in style' – he sets the style and knows that tomorrow several will go shopping to try and imitate his 'look', but unsuccessfully. A song of old enters my mind, "he walks into the party like he's walking onto a yacht," ......and so he does. Who is this man, this man of pride and arrogance, this nearly perfect one who stops conversations with a look and melts hearts of the young and beautiful?

I wait to see if my competing author is writing also, apparently she is not, so I continue while she sits back in her chair watching and reading along.

I look for telltale signs of age, ancestry, or lineage in his countenance but find little help there in discerning who the new guest is or where he is from. Others flock to him, but stay at a respectable distance, not daring to touch him. Like children around a rock star, they fawn and smile eagerly, hoping to catch his fleeting glance.

The music changes and picks up a sort of sensuous Latin beat reminiscent of a Samba or Tango and increases slightly in volume. He seems to grow in stature (she adds before I can) as those around him diminish in size. I wondered if he just stood up straighter and they cowered or was it all just an illusion. He's moved to the center of the room now, with a ring of young women encircling him, gently swaying to the beat of the music.

"STOP!" She wrote plainly on the page before me. "Where are you going with all of this," she asked?"

"Butt out," I answer in kind, feeling slightly foolish as I do so, seeming to be quibbling with a product of my own invention.

"NOW CHILDREN"... found its way onto both of our screens, indicating another had joined the fray, "PLAY NICE." It was enough, more than enough, when the one I am writing about began to write about me, but now a third?

"Who are you?" I asked, not really hoping for an answer. Several moments passed with no reply.

The music stopped and the host taped the side of his leaded crystal glass with a heavy silver spoon. Conversations ceased as attention is turned toward him. A senior wait staff announced dinner was being served in the dining room, but nowhere among them was the dark stranger, as they filed toward the expansive hall.

May I digress for a moment? Do you remember a time while in school, having friends write something in your yearbook? Well, of course you do, it was a rite of passage at most public schools. And, of what did they write? Foolishness mostly, or promises of never fading friendships, undying love, or snide remarks alluding to feats of man (or womanhood) unsurpassed in human history. Intermixing both truth and fable, their words were preserved in ink for all time.

"Your point?" one of my nemeses asked harshly.

"My point is that much of what we say is just for the moment and our own entertainment," I answered sharply, "and most of it holds little lasting value."

"Most of yours holds no value at all," she nearly screamed one byte at a time onto my computer screen.

It took several minutes for the crowd to seat themselves, then turned expectantly toward the head of the table. The host was standing, on his right was the tall stranger still dressed in his black attire, but looking once again like a teen just having finished a growth spurt.

I assumed the host to be in the neighborhood of six feet, dressed lavishly, with thinning white hair and a robust build which made his guest of honor at least a foot taller by comparison. From where I stood, I could now see his full countenance, with what seemed red eyes flashing out from beneath his dark brows, and a smile of irony frozen on his lips.

"Ladies and gentlemen," the host began, "our guest, Mr. Devlin Black!" One by one, the party came to their feet and began slowly clapping, but as the guest's eyes met theirs the tempo of their allegiance increased perceptibly. The host seated himself among his now seated peers, giving his place to the honored guest who remained upright, enjoying the applause.

"It's so good to have you here," he began, "Dining at MY table. No doubt many of you never expected to be here, and yet when you were invited you came anyway, unheeding of the warnings of others."

Before each guest, the wait staff had now placed a covered serving dish. Issuing up from each was a thin wisp of smoke or steam which filled the heavy air with an odorous stench like that of rotting meat. They seemed not to notice, mesmerized by the guest's presence.

"Those who expected to sit at another table, but ignored the warnings, will have a long time to consider your choices," he said loudly as he sat and took the top off his plate. Unnoticed by myself and the others gathered in the room, flies had began to gather, landing indiscriminately upon the food, drinks, and the guests, blackening them.

Each plate seemed alive, teeming with moving, writhing worms beside the entrée of rotting rats, looking as if having been scalded in boiling water with fur still on their foul carcasses. "Please eat your fill," Devlin invited, "there's always more where that came from."

"WELL TOLD," came the words from the third author, "A WORTHY

ATTEMPT, BUT FALLING SHORT IN THE END OF TRULY DESCRIBING THE MEAL. BUT THEN, YOU'LL SHARPEN YOUR SKILLS SOMETIME IN THE FUTURE," he added, "WE HAVE A MILLION YEARS TO TELL IT."

The Dog

I just heard an interesting illustration that fits together nicely with Scripture that requires us to "keep our eyes on the prize" and "our focus on Jesus." Although it is no doubt not new to many, I find it worth sharing.

It goes something like this... a man owned two puppies of the same age. For whatever reason, he favored one over the other, and chose to give it more attention and food. That dog, of course, prospered and grew strong, while the other struggled just to survive. Eventually, the larger, stronger dog killed the weaker one and demanded all of his master's attention. It is similar to the story of a man who enjoyed his alcohol. "First the man took a drink, then the drink took a drink, then the drink took the man."

Clive was just twelve when puberty took him like Sherman took Atlanta. One day he was content to play with toy trucks and marbles, and a short time later he couldn't keep his eyes off the young ladies in his sixth grade class. Almost overnight, he began to notice things about them which had not been of interest before. That those things were a result of hormonal changes going on is his body was of little interest or concern to him. He did not care about the 'why' as much as he did the result.

He did not have an older brother with whom to compare notes or ask questions and was too embarrassed to discuss them with his father. He became secretive and private as his body began to exhibit signs of maturity, while his immature mind lagged behind. As a young Christian, he was aware that certain of his thoughts and feelings were unhealthy, causing him confusion and regret.

But still, the one dog grew stronger, demanded more of his attention and time. It caused him to push back and distance himself from those in his church who cared about him and would have given good counsel. As he did so, the world began to fill the void. It seemed that everywhere he turned pictures, movies, even television commercials fed the larger dog. He became consumed with the visual representations and stories, sexual in nature.

When Clive turned thirteen and entered middle school, his older and more worldly classmates were more than willing to offer advice and materials to feed the hungry animal inside of him. "The lust of the eyes," he remembered reading in the Bible, became a controlling force, urging him ever forward. Although he still recognized his double life and the sin of his actions, he seemed both unwilling and unable to control it.

The computer added an available and unhealthy dimension to the battle that waged within him, making nearly every kind of perversion just a key stroke away. The excitement that fueled the flame also made him feel unclean and ashamed, unworthy to ask for help from God to quit what his heart knew as wrong.

One day, when he returned home from school, he noticed a book had been placed on his desk beside his Bible. Neither his mother nor father were home to ask. In his curiosity he opened the book titled "Every Man's Battle" and began to read. Inside of the front cover were the handwritten names of several of his father's friends and below them was his own father's name.

Clive read, cried, and prayed, then read some more, seeing himself in the stories inside.

God lifted the burden of sin from his young shoulders, restored him to grace, and armed him with the armor of God. He added his name to the growing list on the page of the book, then set it aside to give to his son sometime in the future.

First Moments In Eternity

All about them, they felt the presence of God. They were blanketed in the soft bunting of His eternal blanket of warmth and peace. Their throats constricted with emotion caused by the great presence of He who is Love. They felt weak and small and unworthy to even exist. Not a word was spoken and yet all knew exactly what was in the heart of one another.

Their minds were devoid of thought, they seemed to be in a kind of 'drift', without focus or purpose, and yet there was a kind of clarity, a direction or purpose as yet unknown and undeclared. There seemed to be no sound and yet they did hear, no landscape or marker around them and yet they could see.

It seemed to come from afar and yet not distant, it was all around them and yet they had no sensation of touch. It was as if they were a part of it all and yet were watching as a spectator might. Oddly, it seemed familiar and not foreign, they welcomed it and took pleasure in it without making a choice or decision to do so.

Deep inside each was viewing, living, and reliving every moment of their lives. There was no measure of time, only the present existed, blended with what each knew instinctively as their past. Occasionally there was a brief feeling of regret as something of the past brought with it a memory, but it was not pain for there was no pain, only the overriding presence of Joy.

It seemed just natural that you could be both a spectator and actor in the same play, somehow. A thought crept in for just a moment, a singular question, was each seeing the same thing in the same way and what did it all mean. It was not a question to answer however, just a passing thought, not needing an answer. It seemed odd to be seeing it from the perspective of others and yet living it as it had been lived by each. That gave each a dimension and feel for how they had interacted with others and the feelings of others without condemnation, just an additional view, almost like another dimension.

This, they all thought simultaneously, is how God thinks. His camera shows every detail from a thousand angles in a single instant and His eye absorbs it all and understands it all.

Did they have bodies? Another random thought in and out quickly, not important and needing no answer at this time. Then another, did they need bodies? But again, it was but a fleeting speck, not needing to be addressed. Without a measure, time did not exist, for there was nothing to compare it against.

As the time ended for each, and the play drew to a close, there was recognition that it was all true, that it had been real, that it was not a rerun of an old movie but a reliving of their lives from God's perspective, from start to finish. Somehow, its purpose became clear to each, to put it behind them and to look eternally forward without clinging to anything of their mortal life.

Good Times

He lay on the cool damp earth between the rows of raspberries, the summer sun filtering down through the leafy stalks heavily laden with red ripe berries. At that moment, he could not imagine a life better than the one he enjoyed, as he picked and ate his fill of them. In his young mind, he was all alone in the world, no one knew his secret hiding place or shared the joy of being alone and unburdened by its cares or worries. Seven, he was seven years old, due to turn eight the next month, August. His father was at work and his mother inside the house caring for his three-year-old sister... he had the run of the old family farm.

Calling the scant acreage a farm was a stretch by farming standards. The family had only one cow, a few chickens, and a few rabbits in a pen beside the old barn. The family dog didn't count since it was a pet rather than an asset. But the large garden spot provided what the city kids of the time did not have, a connection with nature and a food source waiting for the picking.

His father was already teaching him how to care for the crops, showing him why the weeds needed to be pulled, and the water turned down the rows and allowed to soak into the ground. Even at his young age, he understood the responsibility of caring for his rabbits and the necessity to water and feed the livestock.

When people talk about their 'roots', it is often with pride. How they describe circumstances and conditions that, at the time, were not always pleasant or easy. A time of adventure, discovery, learning and growing, those years when stories were read at bedtime and the bathtub was filled with water only once a week. A time when nature provided enough mysteries to keep a young man's mind occupied and dreaming.

King Arthur and his court, Robin Hood and his merry men, stories from the Bible about heroes like the young shepherd boy David and Goliath, Daniel and the lion's den, and of mythical dragons and gods like Thor and Ulysses, who battled them. Imagination that made a stick into a spear, an old leather tongue of a worn out boot the pouch that held the rock of a sling shot, the old Red Ryder BB gun the weapon of choice when imitating his heroes of the small black and white television. When the heroes wore white hats and the villains wore black, where men tipped their hats in respect to women and good always triumphed over evil.

It was a time where few minded sharing a phone line with their neighbors and felt the pain of friends who encountered hard times. It was a time when you could just drop in on friends and family and feel welcome. A time when sometimes the soup would need to be thinned to accommodate guests, or family cautioned to curb their appetites and let the guests be served first. Honor, pride, responsibility, a man's word, make it right, keep a promise, respect, please and thank you, mister and misses, grandmother and grandfather, and Sunday best were ingrained and part of who we were.

Women were treated with respect just because they were women, no one spit on anyone else, it was rude to interrupt a conversation, to step on someone's shoes, to gossip or to eavesdrop. Our nation's flag was sacred, and duty and honor held value, you did what was right even when it hurt. You never used a first name unless invited to do so or tried to make yourself bigger by demeaning another and making them feel smaller.

When you made a mistake you felt no shame in admitting it and asking for forgiveness. You knew the Ten Commandments by heart and believed that Charlton Heston was really Moses.

Summers were three months long but seemed longer. Going barefoot was expected and cutoffs were the Levis that had outlived their final patch to become summer wear. It was a time when the wealthy owned tents and camp gear, when the public cooked over open fires and sat around it together, telling scary stories, before crawling under heavy blankets and quilts to count the stars until sleep came.

Mumbly peg, marbles, hopscotch, horseshoes, bean bags, sling shots made from tree branches, willow whistles, skipping rocks, arrow heads, jacks, catching frogs, garter snakes, robin's eggs, Howdy Doody, Mister Spud, The Lone Ranger, Ozzie and Harriet, drive-in movies, the Twilight Zone, Wagon Train, Gunsmoke, Raw Hide, My Three Sons, George and Gracie, Alfred Hitchcock, Combat, or the Lucille Ball show.

The test pattern, remember it? "To the moon, Alice!" The Palmer method, 2A2B paper, flash cards, multiplication tables, gum erasers, PaperMate pens with piggy back refills, black boards, PEZ, 3-D movies, Tarzan, kryptonite, recaps, dunce caps, boy scout knives, bumper jacks, service stations, matinees, serial movies, Batman, and hand puppets.

As he reflected, remembered, and relived the past, a sad sweet smile played on his lips. He could almost taste the fresh raspberries once again and feel the summer sun on his face. It felt good to dwell for a time, excluding the more recent past with its cares, worries, and responsibilities, focusing on the sweet memories of childhood. Those days of tooth fairies, butch wax, baseball cards, and made up heroes always larger than life.

When his father was the strongest and smartest man he knew, his mother the best cook who knew all the remedies for every illness. He remembered clotheslines, starched white shirts, and bolo ties.

Seventy years now, a shuffle in his step, glasses on his eyes, and hearing aids in both ears – he was still faithful to his promise to live for Jesus. His parents gone, his sister too, his wife walking with her Lord in grace, and most of his friends also, he continued to endure.

"Father", he said quietly, "how much longer must I wait, what yet is there for me to do, before you take me home?"

"Patience, My son," came the reply, "there are those who have much need of your counsel, many who need what you have been taught. Let your light shine that others may find their way."

"Who are these of whom You speak?" the old man asked.

"I shall bring them to you," the Lord answered, "in twos and threes. Your words will be like the spring rain that nourishes the new crops. The harvest shall be great."

"What shall I teach them, Father?" he asked

The Lord smiled and answered, "all that you have learned, My son."

The Harvest

The soil was plowed, turning under the remainder of the plant debris from the previous season to become humus for the new crop. Then left during the winter months to degrade, it was plowed a second time in the spring, harrowed to break up the clods, then planted and corrugated for irrigation. Over the generations, his ancestors had learned that the best guarantee, if there could be any for a good crop, was the preparation of the soil. Even then, without God's blessing, the crop was sure to fail.

No part of man's labor, planning, or diligence was as important as recognizing that God's Will is always done. Without the rain at the right times, the proper amount of sun to warm the soil and not bake it, and the right soil chemistry, the farmer's best efforts were in vain. Tom knew well both the joys and disappointments that went along with the noble title of "farmer." He was the fourth generation in America of a line of "tillers of the soil" that dated back millennia in Europe.

Modern society in America is so removed from the process that even many adults find it hard to make the connection between what they buy in the market and what they drive by in the fields. To Tom, food was not food unless you could trace its origin to its source. It saddened and maybe angered him a little when school children didn't know that milk came from the cows at the dairy, that hamburger came from their cousins on the ranch, that their French fries came from the potatoes in his fields.

Tom, Marie, and his two daughters lived on the same section of land that his great-great grandfather had farmed after he had claimed it for his own during the great land rush. Tom, like most others, had replaced many of the hand laborers with machinery, but still required skilled men to run and maintain it. Tom found it interesting that the further mankind got away from the soil, the easier it seemed that they forgot Who was the source of all things. There seemed to him, at least, to be a synergy that made him and God almost partners with His creation.

Six days, no more, no less, was the work week. Overtime, if the job required it, but no labor was done on his land on the Sabbath by either he or those in his employ. The twenty mile drive to church each Sunday was a time for the family to visit and catch up on what was going on in each of their lives, and also to reflect upon their blessings. Kris, Kristine Marie as it read on her birth certificate, was eleven, two years older than Krystal Marie, her sister.

The sermon for this particular Sunday was one of their favorites and one that the community seemed to understand better than most, Matthew 13:3-9. It also seemed to be one of the pastor's favorites in that he brought it back to his flock every year or so. Even Kris and Krystal understood Jesus' parable about the sower of the seeds. As small children, they had spent many hours riding on tractors with their father, who always explained in painstaking detail the planting process and the necessity for good soil. Of course the parable was not about planting potatoes, corn, or beans, but about seeds of faith which would grow and prosper and bring a great harvest of saved souls to Jesus.

After sharing lunch with friends after church, on the ride home,

Marie began to question the family about their understanding of the sermon.

"Who is the Landowner?" she asked.

"God," Krystal answered before Kristine could scoop her.

"And who is the Harvester?" she asked next.

Kris was ready, "Jesus of course," she said all-knowingly.

"Okay," Marie said, "what is the crop?"

Tom waited while his daughters pondered the question, then answered for them, "believers, the saved souls of those who choose Jesus."

Marie took out her Bible and was reading from other parts of Matthew in which Jesus explained further and gave other parables to explain the harvest.

Kristine listened, then asked, "When is the harvest? Is it when we accept Jesus or when we die and go to heaven?"

Tom looked at his wife who was already looking to him for explanation.

"Both, I believe," Tom began, "different crops mature and are harvested at different times, but the final harvest is at the end of times."

He quoted the parable about the tares in Matthew 13:37-39, that described Jesus as the sower and the angels as the harvesters at the end of days.

That evening, when the girls were in bed, Marie turned to her husband and asked, "how about us, aren't we sowers? Isn't that the reason for our witness?"

She could almost hear Tom scratching his head, trying to think it through before answering.

"Jesus said that only those called by the Father can come to Him, so that makes me think that though all are called, only some are given ears to hear and eyes to see. Those who are deaf and blind will not choose

Jesus. I think we are to give witness, plant seeds if you will, but some will grow while others will not, depending on the ground that was prepared for it by the Holy Spirit."

Manuel Ortega was Tom's foreman and right hand man. Manny had lived on the farm with his family for twelve years. All seven of his children had been born and grown up calling the farm their home. Maria, his wife, was a second generation American born in Colorado, while Manny was a naturalized citizen.

Unlike many farms and ranches where migrant workers came in season, most of Tom's employees remained year around, living on the farm rent free, even when there was no work for them to do. During the winters when there was no work, and they received no salary, some would travel south to visit family or find temporary work locally to supplement their incomes. As you can imagine, Tom had little turnover or difficulty hiring replacements when he did.

Kris and Krystal had both learned Spanish from Manny and his family, who learned English in return. They were like extended family to each other. When Maria had miscarried in the sixth month, it had been Tom and Marie who had been there for them, both emotionally and spiritually. When Tom suffered a ruptured appendix and was laid up recovering, it was Manny and Maria who had cared for the girls and looked after the farm.

Unlike a dairy farm or a ranch, Tom's products were row crops and each variety had a need for specialized machinery to plant, cultivate, or harvest them. With the retail outlets and the wholesalers often making more per pound than the farmer who took the risks and made the investment, Tom operated on a thin profit margin, which required sound management. He often wished he were like Joseph to whom God gave the vision of seven years of plenty followed by seven years of crop failure. Unfortunately, the only lesson he could take away was the one to fill the storehouses when you could and trust in God.

When the soil was too wet to work, or it was too cold to plant or harvest, Tom often allowed his workers to maintain the buildings and equipment to keep a paycheck coming in, although many other farms did not. Even though the farm's gross was well over a million a year, its net allowed them to live comfortably, but even then, not without good financial planning.

It was just after 3:00 a.m. when the light that seemed to be dancing through the bedroom window finally jolted Tom awake. It was if it had been part of his dream at first, a surreal dance of demons. Clad in their red and orange dress they ebbed and flowed as the structure became more and more involved. Smoke was pouring from the vents near the gables of the old house, causing him to believe that it had kindled in the wiring of the attic. Tom yelled the house awake, giving instruction first to Marie and then the girls.

"Call the fire department," he said automatically, already knowing the 20 mile trip would make their arrival much too late. "And then call the rest of the men, tell them that Manny's house is on fire."

He threw his old felt hat and blue bandana in the bathtub and turned on the shower while he pulled on his insulated coveralls and then joined them under the cold water stream. He stood for several minutes until sodden and shivering from the cold.

He first beat on the front door, then hearing no sound or receiving no response, put his shoulder against it. As the door gave way, the fire seemed to be energized by the influx of fresh oxygen. He called out several times before hearing sounds from the back of the house. When he got to the main bedroom, Manny was lying on the floor where he had fallen after becoming overcome with smoke, with Maria beside him.

Tom grabbed Manny by the belt and Maria by one limp arm and attempted to pull them toward the door. He finally picked Maria up and carried her from the house into the front yard before returning to drag Manny out.

Gathered in the front yard were the other workers and his family holding a garden hose and looking hopeless. After they wet his clothes once more, he reentered the house a third time and headed for the children's rooms. In the first bedroom, three frightened children huddled together under their bed, wide eyes staring. Tom knocked out the window and began handing the children to waiting hands. The smoke was noticeably thicker now and the heat had already dried his clothes, threatening to ignite them.

Next, Tom went to the room adjacent to their parent's bedroom where the youngest children were. The baby lay on it's side in the crib while the two and three-year-old huddled in the closet nearby. As Tom grabbed them and headed out, he heard screams from the back of the house.

José, the twelve-year-old who slept on the back porch, was apparently trapped. Just outside of the front door Tom collapsed into the yard with the three children. Waiting hands grabbed the kids and someone hosed him down just as smoke began rising from his coveralls. The wet bandana and old felt hat were dripping when he attempted to reenter the house. The heat and smoke pushed him back.

As Tom ran around the house, he could still hear the screams of the young man as he cried out for help. Tom and two of his men, using an ax and shovels, began tearing at the wall of the porch as the sound of the living room ceiling falling allowed the fire access to the rest of the structure. Badly burned and barely breathing, José was finally pulled from the wreckage, just minutes before the bedroom door imploded in flames.

Tom hardly remembered being manually disrobed in the yard before blackness shut off the sights and sounds of the holocaust. When he awoke hours later, he and five of the nine Ortega's were in the hospital, José had been flown to the burn center in Salt Lake City, and the three middle children were with Marie and the girls back at the farm.

~ ~

God was gracious, over the next six months the family slowly recovered, emotionally as well as physically. José had a total of four trips to Utah for skin grafts and follow-up visits before he was pronounced healthy and able to resume normal activities. The baby was at first thought to have a possibility of brain damage because of the lack of oxygen, but has since showed no signs of a lasting disability. Both Maria and Manny finished therapy to restore lung function and returned to work. The other children are well except for anxiety associated with the ordeal, that may take years to correct. Tom has some scarring from burns on his hands and arms but is also well and grateful for God's mercy.

During the four months that the two families co-inhabited in Tom and Marie's home, while the other was being rebuilt, they gave daily witness of their faith and love. In the end, with the Lord's leading, the entire Ortega family accepted Jesus and was added to the harvest.

Hero

What is a hero? Our nation, and indeed our world, has forgotten what makes a person a hero. Our youth grow up today looking up to those with feet of clay, morals of an alley cat, and a thirst for personal recognition and monetary gain. The term 'unsung heroes' applies correctly to most true heroes. They do not seek, and in most cases shun, the limelight.

The typical hero does what is right because it is right and because others avoid doing it. The typical hero honors God, country, and integrity. He values his reputation, the value of his word, the commitment of a handshake or promise made. Family, friends, and those in need are his priority. He understands personal responsibility but does not understand the lack of it in others.

Greed is foreign to him, as are deceit and treachery. He is dogged in his commitment to his values to the point of death. He may be a soldier, a police officer, or an office worker whose moral compass keeps him doing right, even when unpopular or dangerous. He is the guy who helps the elderly shovel snow when exhausted, who labors for little reward to raise a family, or who gives his life for a friend. He is the one who will one day stand before the Lord and accept his reward, "well done, good and faithful servant."

Humility

His stained felt hat had seen better days, its original crown barely recognizable, his denim jacket frayed at the cuffs and torn at one elbow, still providing warmth and protection, but reeked of the smell of burning hair and barnyard. It had been a long day already, with the sun still above the low-lying mountains that back-dropped the ranch. There were thirty more head of calves still waiting in the lower corral to brand, inoculate, and castrate, when he signaled the men to take a break.

With three men, all good hands with a rope, it should only take another hour or so for those on the ground to finish up the job. The "header" had the easy job, to get a loop on the animal's head, but the "heeler" had to be a man with a little more finesse to catch both rear legs. Afterward, the horses would stretch the animal out, where the hot iron would hit the right hip with the Circle C, a second man operating the needle, and yet a third either banded or cut the young bulls.

None of the six men helping him had less than a dozen years in the saddle, and most twice that much. While society in general had moved away from the traditions of the past, the farming and ranching community maintained a comradeship that spanned generations. The 'barn raisings' of the 18th and 19th centuries and the attitude that made it all work still existed in the small community of Indian Creek. Each man had a need for occasional help and each man was the answer to another's need, as they moved from ranch to ranch each spring.

Tom drove the old Chevy up to the main house and stuck his head in the door, "Claire, how's dinner coming? We should be done and ready to eat in about an hour."

Claire smiled and answered, anticipating the question, "it'll be on the table when you get here," she said.

She and Tom had grown up together in the valley, had gone to school together, raised three and lost one child, and lived on the ranch he had inherited from his father for nearly thirty years. There was little about the life that surprised her or escaped her notice.

"Tore your elbow again," she declared as he walked away, "leave it tomorrow and I'll get it washed and mended."

Claire knew it would take her less time to mend it than to get him out of it. She was a vital woman, with inner strength born of tradition and strong spiritual conviction. She had lost a son to drowning, one breast to cancer, both parents and a sister, but still she trusted and believed in God and His promises.

Many, when facing those tests, had failed and turned their back on God, blaming Him for their trials, but not Claire. She was of the opinion that the worst we face was but a small part of what we should and would face if God had not kept the evil one in check most of the time. That attitude had stood her well through many times of grief and allowed her to thank God when things seemed bleak.

"Sarah," she yelled, "check the oven, the rolls smell like they are done."

Sarah was nineteen, had graduated and would begin college in the fall, 'God willing'. Claire always tried to add the last two words to acknowledge that she recognized God's sovereignty.

She returned from setting the table and found Sarah removing the last dozen rolls from the stove. She was pleased by how nicely they had raised and browned on top.

When her daughter took one Claire ignored her, knowing it was a family ritual to steal one and eat it with butter and honey before dinner.

"Want half?" Sarah said smiling, holding half out to her mother.

Claire took it, smiled, then said, "Guess I should make sure they are good enough for the boys."

Claire would be fifty-four in August, a year younger than Tom. Her hair, once auburn, was nearly half gray now but her face remained youthful and her skin belied her advancing age. Sarah had tried in vain several times to introduce her to Miss Clairol, but she claimed the right to look her age. Sarah's two brothers Ben and Ed had come home to help with the branding, much to her delight. She expected to be teased and maligned in ways that only siblings could, before they returned to their homes.

Meat and potatoes, the staple diet of America in early days, had not changed a great deal in rural communities. A well seasoned cut of prime beef lay resting, waiting for Tom to carve, a trickle of red in the juice beneath it. A large red bowl was filled with freshly mashed potatoes, with a boat of gravy beside it, and glazed carrots from the garden rounded out the meal, and of course the hot rolls. Claire marveled at how much like little boys Ben and Ed still acted when together, pushing and shoving as they came into the house. Behind them followed four others and Tom who entered last.

Claire stopped them on the porch and scolded them until they took off their dirty jackets and hats, then let them into the house to wash up.

"Smells good," Tom commented first, and then was echoed by the others.

Ben tried to grab a roll but was swatted by his mother and ushered down the hall to one of the two bathrooms. Ed, the oldest, maintained decorum long enough to make his brother look bad, then helped himself to a celery stick on the way by the table.

The assembly was seated together at the long table when Tom asked for God's blessing on the food and began to carve the roast. He began with Claire, Sarah, and then worked his way around the table as plates both empty and full were passed. The room became quiet for a few minutes while the plates were being emptied, then filled again with conversation as the food settled in their stomachs and they refilled their plates again.

"Heard Mark Hagen was killed," Ed said, "turned his tractor left in front of a car as it was passing him."

The others had not heard of the tragedy, and asked for more details. Discussion about his age, how many kids he had, and about their opinion of what the family would do without him dominated the conversation.

"Molly's pregnant," Ed said smiling, waiting for just the right time to announce their good news. "Two months is the best guess, haven't seen the Doc yet."

"About time," Ben said, voicing the standard reply always to at least one bystander. "I thought I's gonna have to take you out and let the bulls show you how things work."

He got a punch for his comment and a laugh from all those present.

"What's the count," someone asked Tom, referring to the number they had branded.

"I make it forty-nine heifers and thirty-four steers," Tom answered, "and three yearlings we missed last go around."

"Eighty-six," Ben said, showing his proclivity for numbers, "not a bad day's work."

Everyone seemed to agree as they pushed back from the table.

"Let me get the plates and I'll bring us some dessert," Claire said.

Sarah stood and began helping to clear the table.

"Hey sis, that red haired kid living down on the old Baker place still hanging around?" Ben asked laughing.

Her face colored in spite of herself, "he doesn't hang around, he comes and goes as he chooses, not that it's any of your business," she said. The brothers tried to get more mileage out of the subject but were hushed by their mother.

A hot peach and apple crisp made it to the table, followed by a gallon of ice cream. Tom began filling bowls while Claire added the ice cream and passed them around. Sarah brought coffee.

"Nice spread," one of the hands said to Claire as he stood to go, "you always set a nice table."

One by one they left, until just family remained.

"Thanks, boys," Tom said looking at his sons, "we appreciate your help."

"We just come for the food," Ed said smiling, giving his mother a hug.

"Speaking of food," Ben added, "got any left over to send with me?"

After both of his sons left, Tom complimented Claire on another fine meal. Then as he stood to go to the barn, he lost his balance and went to one knee. By catching himself with a chair, he did not fall to the floor. He tried to make light of it as he climbed back into the chair, but Claire saw through his bravado and told Sarah to try and catch her brothers. By the time she returned with them, Tom seemed fine and was downplaying the incident.

Ed was a fireman in Somerville, a small town nearby, and well trained as an EMT.

"Squeeze my hands," Ed said to his father, "now stick out your tongue at me."

It took less than a minute to decide that Tom had had a minor stroke and they called 911. As Tom took the offered aspirin and settled into his easy chair, the family stood around with worried looks, speaking in hushed tones, as though Tom wouldn't hear.

"I'm still here," Tom said with a laugh, "and I can hear every word so why don't you include me in your conversation?"

Ed took the lead.

"I think you've had a minor stroke, Dad," he said. Adding, "at the hospital they'll run some tests to confirm or deny my diagnosis.

Over the next two days, tests showed a minor blockage in the blood supply to Tom's brain. Standard procedure was to watch and wait while his body reabsorbed clots; blood thinners reduced the possibility of additional clots, and his body re-routed blood supplies around the affected area.

Ben, being single, found it easy to take time from his job and move home to help Claire and Sarah with the day-to-day operation of the ranch. Ed was able to come every few days to help as well while Tom remained hospitalized.

As he continued to improve, Tom began rehabilitation therapy under the watchful eyes of the rehab staff. The priority was to rebuild strength in his left leg and arm, and in doing so to regain balance.

Outwardly, he seemed to bounce back quickly. After only a week, he walked to the waiting car unaided, his limp almost unnoticeable. But inside, Tom knew that each step was a struggle, that he was less of a man physically than just a week before. As a southpaw, he had always prided himself on his grip and physical strength, now his left arm and hand were noticeably weaker than his right, and clumsier as well. He had to concentrate to force his left side to do what it had always done naturally.

Tom had never considered himself a "prideful" man, but he had always felt "capable," equal to the task at hand, able to get the necessary job done. Now, however, as he gradually returned to the routine at the ranch, it was apparent to him that it was unlikely that he'd ever be 100% again. The first time he'd tried to saddle his horse he had failed, and using innovation to rather the brawn had felt like defeat.

Likewise, when he'd tried to mount, he lacked the leg strength to do so in his usual way. Even though he had chosen to do both alone in the barn, he felt little victory in riding out of the barn to the house knowing that he couldn't dismount and remount without help. It didn't help his male ego to see Claire carefully watching his every move to see if he needed help. It seemed her focus now was on his current weaknesses and not on past accomplishments.

It was hard for him to forget that he had successfully quarterbacked his team to the state championship, that he'd ridden broncos; team roped and had a championship buckle for his trouble. Even as the years had slowed him a step or two, his experience and determination had allowed him to maintain his competitive team roping skills.

When the neighbor's call came soliciting help with their branding he had accepted over Claire's objections. He and both sons arrived before day break, with the expectation of a long day ahead. Morris, his long time friend and team roping partner, met him as they unloaded their trailers.

"Tom," he said in greeting, "thank you for coming, Molly's got breakfast waitin'"

Tom, Ed, and Ben went inside where Molly was pouring coffee for her sons and a couple of local hands. Morris asked God to bless the food and the day that lay ahead, and then the crew set to work on the eggs, ham, hash browns, and fresh buttermilk biscuits covered with gravy that filled the table.

As the food disappeared and napkins were tossed on the plates, Morris said, "Tom, if you're agreeable, I'd like you to help me with the cuttin' and brandin' this morning. Figured I'd give the young-ins a chance to throw a loop or two."

"You're the boss," Tom answered, feeling both relieved and disturbed. Secretly he had wondered of he'd be able to rope and keep the pace needed to get the job done. He hadn't looked forward to trying to mount and un-mount his horse in the view of spectators either. What disturbed him was the thought that Morris, or possibly Morris with Claire's help, had felt him not up to the challenge.

"Got only seventy-four this morning needin' our attention," Morris said as the eight walked toward the corrals, "God willin' we can have an early supper together. Joshua, will you and Ben see if you have learned anything from your Pa and me over the years?"

Tom saw both of the boys smile as they saddled, then mounted their horses, and shook out their loops. He regretted that he had not spent a lot of time trying to pass on his roping skills to his sons. The traditional wood fire in the center of the arena had been replaced with a propane fired one that worked efficiently but didn't hold the charisma of the wood one. Morris had the elastrator, the knives, and inoculating needle on the tailgate of his truck that stuck between the rails of the corral for easy access.

"You want to run the iron to start?" Morris asked, "Or would you rather stick 'em and cut 'em?"

Tom smiled at his friend. "I'll burn 'em for a while and see how it goes," Tom answered.

"You're gettin' modern on us," Tom said, pointing to the burner, "next thing I know you'll start using a squeeze chute and take all the fun out of it."

"Thought about it," Morris answered, "but it's about the only chance I have anymore to cowboy."

Ed turned the first three calves into the corral and closed the gate behind them. Joshua and Ben cut out one and got a loop over its head but missed its feet twice before snagging one. Everyone laughed and gave the boys a verbal spanking before getting to work on the calf. The two boys had found their stride, with Ben handling the heads and Joshua scooping up the rear feet regularly. When they broke for lunch they'd processed forty-three, a shade over half.

"Looks like they wintered well," Tom said as they filled and refilled their bowls with beef stew and fresh hot bread.

"Yeah, only lost two by my count, wolves or a cat, I imagine," Morris answered. "Rest of the herd looks good and will be glad to get back on the summer range."

After lunch, Morris took the iron while Tom the knife, Ben and Josh changed ends on the calves. At three o'clock the calves were back in the field and horses reloaded into their trailers when Molly called out that their early supper was on the table. By 4:00 they were on the road toward home, full of food and the satisfaction of a job well done.

"Did a good job today," Tom said to Ben, "you showed some real promise with a rope."

"He didn't get tangled up in it too bad," his brother added.

Ben was smiling when he punched him in the ribs.

As Tom reviewed the events of the day in his head, he discovered that he hadn't missed riding as much as he had thought he would. He had enjoyed watching his son prove himself. "Thank you, Lord," he thought, "for letting me live to see this day."

Church on Sunday was a blessing and the sermon hit Tom right between the eyes. God has a way of getting our attention, he thought. Like Moses, who had sinned when bringing water from the rock in the desert and was not allowed to cross the Jordan, Tom felt that he was also being taught a lesson for his independence and pride that had kept him from to depending upon God.

A part of his strength had been taken away, giving him opportunity to depend more completely upon others and God's provision. But, he was given the blessing of seeing his children prosper and Joshua take his place heeling up the calves.

Judas

Matthew 27:51-53 *"Then, behold, the veil of the temple was torn in two from top to bottom; and the earth quaked, and the rocks were split, and the graves were opened; and many bodies of the saints who had fallen asleep were raised; and coming out of the graves after His resurrection, they went into the holy city and appeared to many."*

Hebrews 9:27-27, *"And as it is appointed for men to die once, but after this the judgment, so Christ was offered once to bear the sins of many."* NKJ

~ ~

Often a fire appears to be extinguished, only later to reignite unexpectedly, its embers having been fanned by the winds, and once again bursting into flame. And so it was for the man who had borne the scorn of the world for thousands of years. Having known and walked with his Savior, having shared food and shelter, having expected a conqueror to lead them in battle, but found instead a man of peace.

Judas had done what he had been created to do, betray his Master. Judas Iscariot, like his peers, had been chosen by Jesus, each for a purpose and each having the strengths and weaknesses of character inherent in all mankind.

Judas fancied himself a warrior, a militant in today's terms, a rebel with a cause. He knew well the Scriptures that promised the Messiah, but misunderstood what the term 'freedom' really meant. His oppression came from the Roman government, he did not understand the teachings of his Rabbi which spoke of the captivity of sin. While he was amazed by Jesus' strength of character and His ability to do miracles, he was disillusioned and disappointed that Jesus didn't use His power to overcome Israel's oppressors.

What he had expected to do was to force Jesus' hand, not to cause His death. He had become weary waiting for the freedom which Jesus promised. He felt that using the jealousy of the Jewish leaders and their clout with the weak Roman leadership would place Him in a position where He must act, and act forcefully.

Too late, Jesus' words became clear to him. Too late, he understood only too well what his Master had said and meant in His teachings. It was too late when he returned the ransom, and to stop the raging tide of anger and hate that called for Jesus' death. What he did not and could not understand was that had he asked, Jesus would have forgiven him his deceit.

It was the same master that asked that he may "sift Peter like wheat," when he had fallen to the weakness of the flesh in denying Jesus, that held Judas firmly in his hands. But after the act was done, it was he whose scorn sent Judas to a tree outside of the city where he hung himself in disgrace and self loathing. It was he whose fingernail had split the putrefying body, letting the insides fall under his lifeless carcass.

~ ~

From darkness into light, from nothing, to the familiar trappings of the city from which he had just recently departed. Judas stood alone beside the disturbed ground that he had just recently been vomited from, still wrapped in death cloths. It was from the 'potter's field', the very field that was purchased by the unholy bounty that he had accepted for his betrayal of Jesus, that he had been rejected. His body now, once again whole, looked circumspectly around him as he fought to remember where he was and why he was here.

Overhead, the sky was darkened as if it were night, beneath his feet he could feel the roll of the earth as it moved like someone in a disturbed sleep. Somewhere, distant cries of anguish and pain came from unseen lips. He unwrapped the gauze-like cloths which encircled him and freed himself enough to move and walk. He was drawn toward the city which stood in the distance by some unknown force, and began walking toward it. Three days had passed since the crucifixion when those raised began to appear in the city.

Romans 8:11, *"But if the spirit of Him who raised Jesus from the dead dwells in you, He who raised Christ from the dead will also give life to your mortal bodies through His Spirit who dwells in you."* NKJ.

There were those whom he recognized and others like himself, dressed in burial cloths, who wandered about among the disjointed crowds, who were wailing and crying. Everywhere there was talk of the crucifixion of Jesus, with some bemoaning it, others championing its necessity. It became clear to him that after he had hung himself, others had similarly hung his Master on a cross where He had just recently died.

For over a month, word of Jesus' resurrection and witnesses who claimed to have seen and spoken to Him filled the city and surrounding area. During this time Judas lived in limbo, begging for food, sleeping beside the roadway or under a tree, without resource or direction. One night he had a vision in which the Spirit of God spoke to him and enlightened him.

"Judas," He said, "although your weakness and lack of faith condemns you, your Savior, whom you have betrayed, has pardoned you and offers you eternal life in His service. Although you have died at your own hand, you will not see death again, but will rise with the faithful when He returns to claim His final victory."

"What does this all mean?" he asked, awed by the presence of the Spirit.

"You have been raised, as was your Master, in fulfillment of Scripture, and will never die. He who entered into you has been cast out, no longer to have dominion over you. You will serve the Lord only and will never share the joy of another kiss with man born of woman."

~ ~

Always the supporting actor in the play, the bit player without mention in the credits, Judas and thirty five others raised at the crucifixion continue to roam the earth in God's service. Angels they are not, but often doing the works attributed to angels. In physical form, but with the power of Jesus giving them strength, they help balance the forces of good and evil upon the earth. They walk among us.

Letter from Home 11 AD

Hello, my name is John, I am 6 years old. I live near Jerusalem with my family of 2 sisters and 4 brothers. My closest friend is the carpenter's son, Jesus. We have our household duties and our schooling but when that is done, we like to spend time together.

My father, Zebedee, is a fisherman, and he often lets us come with him while he works. Both Jesus and I enjoy the sea and even help with the chores while in the boat. We usually just sit alone and talk which is fun, but many times Jesus speaks of things which I do not understand. He laughs and says they will make sense to me one day when I am older. I think he likes to tease me because he is already 11 years old.

His mother is nice, but very quiet and thinks Jesus, her oldest son, is special. She doesn't explain why, but usually the oldest son has a special place in the family in our tradition. Maybe that is what she means. I like Jesus because he is quiet and does not treat me harshly like some of the other boys. I think next year, when he is 12, Jesus will learn to become a carpenter like his father, Joseph.

Sometimes I get confused when we talk because Jesus speaks about his Father as though he lives somewhere other than here. He tells me often that his Father loves me, which I think is kind of strange, but yet I am happy knowing that I am loved. I hope we will always be the best of friends.

Signed, John

Memories

Presumptuous. One might think it presumptuous that a person without training, with limited education, and without exceptional talent might set down to write a story. And justifiably so, if we do not consider that the author is just a 'ghost writer', working under the hand of the Master story teller, God Almighty. How can anyone with limited first hand experience and average intellect weave the reader so intricately into the fabric of a story as to immerse them and make them feel actively a part of it, they cannot. Then too, the final and most important element of the equation is that the story provides value to the reader, beyond just entertainment. We shall see if I am to be so blessed...

~ ~

Sentimental was the word that best described how he felt. That feeling of melancholy which lingers after one is emotionally drained. The recollection of time spent together, of laughter, and of poignant moments now frozen in time, never to be relived again, except in memory.

They had all left the family, the friends, and well wishers, most of whom they had known together for a good part of their lives. He sat alone, like a butterfly in a field of flowers, his mind refusing to settle on any particular thought, bouncing from one to another. Then a fleeting thought came to him, when he had lost her he had lost his focus, his reason to look forward. He wondered when, if ever, life may hold meaning for him again.

Can you picture him, head hanging, shoulders slumped, eyes veiled and unseeing? Can you feel his numbness and lack of emotion? To live life fully is to feel the joys of the summits and to suffer the anguish of the valleys. The same happiness, born of love, is that which brings the pain and despair of loss. Clayton may have sat for hours, hardly moving, before finally falling into to a fitful sleep.

~ ~

"Clay, come see what I have," she beckoned.

He got up from the lounger on the patio and walked the several steps across the yard to where she was working in her flower bed. The morning sunshine brought out the highlights in her blonde hair that accented the deep blue of her smiling eyes. On her finger, crawling along its length from her wrist, was a fuzzy caterpillar. He matched her smile and wondered at how she had overcome her fear of insects to pick up the furry little creature.

"It's a caterpillar," she said, as might a six-year-old, stating the obvious.

"I see that," Clay answered, "is it something special?"

"Yes, of course," she said, "he's special because God created him for a special purpose."

Clay loved the way his wife viewed God's creation with childlike wonder. After nearly twenty years together, she still was the same inquisitive thirteen-year-old that he had met and fallen in love with when his family had moved to town. He could still picture her sitting in the tire swing in her front yard waving as they passed by in the U-haul truck.

"Oh, I see," he said playing along, "and what is that purpose?"

"To grow and change and someday become a beautiful butterfly," she said with conviction.

"Is that all?" Clay asked, still playing the role.

"No, of course not," Beth answered, "that's just the beginning. Once he has become a butterfly, his real work begins."

"What work is that?" he asked, "what can a butterfly do?"

She stopped and stared at him for a moment, her freckled nose scrunched, apparently trying to gauge the sincerity of his question before continuing. Then, like an eight-year-old explaining to a younger brother one of life's mysteries, she continued.

"First, he'll bring joy and happiness to anyone who sees him. He'll bring awe and wonder to children of all ages who have watched him change, and hope to those who see him become a new creature."

Her eyes sparkled with excitement as she paused to take a breath.

"Then, he'll move from flower to flower, giving and receiving what God has put there for him to spread," she continued.

Clay was entranced by her beauty and charm, and amused by her perfect interpretation of God's cycle of life.

"And then..." he said waiting for the finish.

"And then, he'll lay eggs to start the whole thing all over again, and then he'll die," she finished.

"Sounds sad," Clay observed, "that after doing all of this work, he had to die."

"It's not sad at all, silly," she said smiling, "after he did what God created him to do, he got to rest from the work."

~ ~

As Clay awakened, he looked around the darkened living room and could tell that night had fallen while he had slept. He was confused for a moment, wondering where the sunlight had gone, then he remembered it had been just a wonderful dream. He wondered if it would be worth his time to retire to the empty bedroom where he was sure to lie awake, or if he should just close his eyes where he was and hope to return to where he'd been.

~ ~

"Do you have a shoe box?" Beth asked, walking into the garage where Clay was working at his workbench.

"Maybe," he answered looking up.

She walked carefully toward him, her hands together in front of her, almost as if praying.

"I found it in the flower bed," she said, her hands opening to reveal a new born quail. "I think his mother deserted him."

The pitiful creature was barely feathered out, probably just newly hatched, and hardly self sufficient. It could stand and only walk a few steps before shivering and falling on its side.

"Were there others?" I asked her, "or was he alone?"

"He was all by himself," she said, "I'll bet he got separated from the others and got lost. Can we feed him?"

"We can try," Clay answered, "but it's a long shot that he'll live."

They found a small box, put blanket batting into it, then set it on a heating pad. Clay dug some earth worms while Beth found an eye dropper, then smashed them and added warm water to the mess. They took turns holding its mouth open and giving it drops of the makeshift meal before returning it to the box.

"I wish we knew how to care for it," Beth said sadly. "I'm afraid that when it wandered off and its mother and father didn't find it right away, it was sure to die."

"There are always a few who wander away and are lost," Clay commented, "but some stay with the parents and live and complete the cycle of life."

~ ~

She called from the gray shroud that enclosed him as he slept. "Did you see the news?" Beth asked him from the kitchen.

"No, I was watching the game," he answered, "what's going on?"

"I read in the paper that there was a terrible fire downtown," she said. "Many people were killed."

"That's terrible," Clay agreed, "how did it happen?"

"They haven't determined yet," Beth said, "it was in an old apartment complex, and it happened in the middle of the night. A lot of people didn't pay attention to the warning when the smoke detectors went off. They slept until it was too late."

Clay considered what he had just heard then said, "I'll bet they try and hold the landlord responsible somehow for not forcing them to leave, even though they were given ample warnings."

"One man was overcome by smoke and died after going back three times to save his children," Beth said, "he gave his life for them."

"I'll bet he loved them so much he didn't even consider the risk," Clay answered.

~ ~

The old hall clock chimed 3:00 a.m. and woke Clayton from his dreams. He used the bathroom, had a glass of milk and an Oreo, then covered himself with his wife's comforter and lay on the sofa. Within a few minutes, exhaustion wrapped him in its arms once again and he began to dream.

~ ~

She had just turned sixteen when she asked, "Clay, how long do you think forever really is?"

Clay lay beside her on the grass, looking up at the blue sky, feeling the cool earth against his back. He had just turned seventeen and like most young men found it difficult to think past the end of the week. He tried to think of something profound to share but found nothing.

"A long time," he finally said, wondering at how girls were so adept at asking unanswerable questions.

"Do you believe in God?" she asked next.

"Sure," Clay answered, "doesn't everyone?"

"I don't think so," Beth said, "at least a lot of people don't want to admit it. They like to think that they are in charge, that they can determine their own destiny."

"Like our coach who tells us that we can win if we want it bad enough," Clay agreed. "That we can be or do anything we put our minds to."

"I'm saved," she said matter-of-factly. "I accepted Jesus when I was eleven years old."

"Is that why you asked about forever?" he asked.

"I guess," Beth answered, "I still get confused sometimes when I read the Bible about dying and living forever."

"I was only eight when I was saved," Clay volunteered, "I didn't understand it then, but I think I do now."

"Tell me," Beth said.

"We are all made in God's image," he said, "meaning that we, like He, will live forever." "But," he added, "only the saved will live forever with Jesus in heaven."

"I guess it doesn't matter then," Beth said smiling, "how long forever is, does it? You and I will be there together."

Four years later they made her promise official when they exchanged wedding vows.

~ ~

That no-man's land between asleep and awake, the place where you can continue to dream but seem to have some conscious control and editing power over your dreams, exists, and has been given a name by those who study such things. Clearly, it is not a place where one can just will themselves to go, or can stay when it is time to awaken. But, it is a nice comfortable place to dream dreams that please you with their predictable outcome.

Clay lay on the sofa, aware of his surroundings, yet unwilling to open his eyes and embrace the day alone. He struggled to hold onto the last remaining remnants of sleep as they continued to evaporate like mist in the sunlight.

He was attempting to recreate the fond memories of the birth of their son but was having difficulty doing so. Oh yes, he could remember the occasion in detail, but had lost the silky thread of sleep that would have let him relive the event with Beth.

The ringing of the phone cleared the last vestiges of sleep from him as he answered it.

"Hello Clay," his mother said, "just thought I'd give you a call and see if you are alright."

Her concern apparent but unwanted, Clay forced himself to be civil to his eighty-year-old mother.

"Just fine Mom," he said, trying to sound cheery, "I just woke up, didn't sleep well last night."

In her attempt to comfort him she accomplished just the opposite when she said, "believe me, I know how empty the house can be. But you'll get used to it."

Clay didn't want to get used to it and didn't want to cheer up either. He wanted to feel the pain. His suffering made him feel as though he were being loyal to Beth. He couldn't imagine ever getting used to life without her.

"Thanks for calling Mom," he said a little too briskly, "I appreciate your concern."

He felt badly that he had cut her short, but couldn't bear to hear more of her pep talks.

~ ~

With the sting of the hot water on his back and shampoo forcing his eyes shut, Clay heard Tommy say, "I'm six. I'm in the first grade. I'm going to ride the bus to school."

Beth had smiled and then turned her head slightly away, covertly wiping a would-be tear from her blue eyes. Clay could tell this was an emotional moment for her, a cutting of the apron strings, a time of letting go. They had both walked their son to the bus stop and waited there with him until he was safely on the bus, waving at them out of the window. They walked slowly home together holding hands, but not speaking.

Then Beth said, "Jesus must have felt like this when He was separated from His disciples and entrusted them into the care of the Holy Spirit."

~ ~

Clay had always been amazed at how Beth could see God's hand in both the large and small events of their lives. She, better than he, had always seemed to include God in every aspect of her life, never more than a half-step from His side, always able to see the lesson being taught.

He had stepped out of the shower and was toweling his hair dry, trying not to see the reminders of Beth's presence which were everywhere.

Tom and his wife had been forced to catch a flight home just after the funeral. Clay had hoped they might be able to stay a few days but returning flights were booked as a result of the spring break holiday.

Tom had taken a job out of state where he had met and married Teresa, following his graduation. Although they had attempted to maintain a close relationship, the miles and busy lifestyles had brought about the inevitable separation that the Bible called "leaving and cleaving."

The drone of the television provided background noise and helped keep the house from seeming so empty. Although only a few minutes after eight, the mind numbing programming had lulled Tom into the waiting arms of unconsciousness.

~ ~

"We're pregnant," she bubbled, "will miracles never cease?"

That was how he was greeted as he walked into the house after work one fall evening. He had just turned forty-one and she was looking right at the forty. Tom was a junior in high school, with girlfriends, his first car and first job. Clay had been looking forward to a time when he and Beth could spend more time together, seeing sights and doing things that did not include raising children. Apparently he had done a poor job of disguising his disappointment at her "good news."

"I thought you'd be excited," Beth said still smiling.

"I am," Clay lied, "but I would have been even more excited ten years ago when we were young."

"God moves in...." she started to say when he interrupted her.

"Are you certain?" Clay asked trying not to sound desperate, "is it for sure?"

"Pretty sure," Beth answered, "mother nature and EPT agree."

"Who is EPT?" Clay asked.

"Early Pregnancy Test," she answered, "a drug store over the counter kit."

"I wonder," he said, speaking mostly to himself, "if we elected to include maternity benefits the last time we revised our health coverage."

Beth left the room without speaking, he found her in the bathroom washing her face, eyes red, looking solemn. He just stood woodenly waiting for her to speak, she did not.

"I'm sorry," he began, trying to think how he could explain himself without seeming selfish and disappointed. "You caught me by surprise and all I could think about was how it was not part of my plan."

Beth brightened a little, "His plan is the only one we can trust, our plans are always made without us having all of the needed information."

Clay gave his wife a hug, nuzzled her neck, and then said, "We'll be better parents now that we know how to do it."

~ ~

David was born prematurely less than six months later. After a difficult labor of eighteen hours, Beth had delivered by C-section. Even though they had been told months earlier by their doctor, it was still a shock to actually see their son born with Down's syndrome. Not by choice, but by design, they had joined the exclusive club of families raising a Down's child.

Beth seemed able to focus on David's strengths, while Clay more on his weaknesses. Something, he supposed, that was related to the way God had created man and woman differently. Beth delighted in his sunny disposition, his warm and loving personality, his teddy bear like body, while Clay struggled knowing he,d never excel in sports, in academics, or likely not marry and father a family.

While both Beth and Clay prayed often for their son, their requests were far different. Clay prayed for a miracle that God might make him whole; Beth prayed that God would help her husband to see him as whole. David was fifteen when Beth died of cancer.

~ ~

"Dad, are you alright?" David asked, waking Clay from still another dream.

"Yes son, I am fine," Clay answered, "I must have dozed off watching television, why do you ask?"

"Mom told me that you'd be real lonesome after she was gone," he said, "she told me that God made me just to keep you from being lonesome."

"Your Mom was a smart woman," Clay said considering what he had just heard, "a lot smarter than me."

"You're smart too, dad," David said, "but Mom said that being smart wasn't as important as being kind. She told me to always love everyone and be kind to them."

"You do that good," Clay said, "better than most folks."

"Thanks Dad," David answered before giving his father a hug. "I love you."

"I love you too," Clay said, his eyes filling with tears.

"Am I going to school today?" David asked.

"Nope, no school today, David, its spring break," his father answered, "let's go fishing instead."

Money, Have I None

In the time immediately following Jesus' crucifixion, a seemingly rag tag band of young men gathered behind closed doors, fearful of the future. Frightened and leaderless, enemies of the rich and powerful Jewish leaders, they cowered and hid, unknowing of what the future held for them.

For hundreds of years, Israel had been promised a Messiah, scholars of the period hung on every word, predicting the time and place of a great one who would come and lead them away from the tyranny of their Roman oppressors. The great prophets of the past had foretold his coming. But now, four hundred years had passed with no sign of him, none lived to give voice or renew the hope that the promise would be kept. Israel had lost hope in what seemed to have been a myth and rejected the stranger who came from Nazareth without credentials.

~ ~

Present Day

"Tom I want you to meet a man I was introduced to last night," Jim said. "He just moved to town and is kind of an interesting guy."

"Oh yeah? What's he do?" Tom asked his friend.

"I'm not sure, a tradesman I think, maybe a carpenter," Jim replied.

"How'd you come to meet him?" Tom continued.

"My brother John introduced us. He goes to his home church for

Bible study."

"So when do you expect to see him again?" Tom asked.

"Tonight," Jim answered, "Pete and Andy and a bunch of us are meeting for Bible study."

"Oh, alright," Tom said reluctantly, "it's a bad night for TV anyway, what the heck."

"I'll pick you up about six then," Jim said.

When they arrived, the door was open and many of the men were already inside talking. Tom recognized most of them and met a couple more. There were twelve in all. After they had all been seated, their host opened with a prayer, then set out some light snacks.

"I am pleased to see you all here," their host began, "and I welcome those of you who are joining us tonight for the first time. I'd like to begin this study at the beginning, then work our way slowly to the present."

No one objected or questioned him as he began to read, "*In the beginning God created the heavens and the earth...*" From time to time he'd stop and clarify a verse or explain its true meaning, but he moved along with surprising speed, without missing a word. By the end of the first evening they were already beginning Exodus, with the host painting vivid mental pictures, giving each a sense that they were living a current event.

As they left together Jim asked, "Well, what do you think?"

Tom smiled, "amazing, it's simply amazing how differently it sounds when he reads it. I felt like I was right there."

"So, are you up for tomorrow night?" Jim asked.

"Sure," Tom answered, "same time?"

The group met nearly every evening except Sunday for the next month, each eager to return and continue their adventure in God's

Word. What each man found was the Bible was not a dry, ancient history book, but an interesting and appropriate guidebook for day-to-day life, all through the ages. When they finished the little book of Malachi, only four chapters in length, the men were agape at the power and meaning its last few verses held.

Tom was not the only one who noted the change in their host's speech as he began the New Testament. It soon became apparent that he adopted the personage of Christ, changing the words 'he' to 'I' or 'me' in the text, as they followed along. It was as if he was reliving the past from memory and not from the record before him.

Seldom did anyone interrupt the study to ask questions for seldom were there questions which demanded answers after the host read them. However, when he replaced "*His mother Mary*" with "My Mother Mary" in Matthew 1:18, Pete raised his hand indicating he had a question to ask.

"Yes, Simon," the host said to Pete, "have you a question?"

Pete hid his surprise and answered, "Sir, my text reads "*His mother Mary*" and you substituted "My mother Mary."

The host smiled at all of the assembly, then said, "*Have I not been with you long enough that you know who I am? Do you not recognize that it is of Me whom the account speaks?*"

There wasn't a sound in the room as each listened to their hearts speaking to their minds.

He continued, "*Did I not say that I am with you always, even unto the end of the earth? Why then do you seem surprised that I am here among you?*"

Several minutes passed as each man came to grips with the indisputable Truth which sat among them. Finally John spoke.

"God's Word tells us that you will return in the clouds, riding a white horse." He said, "Help us understand how You can be He."

Jesus smiled, and as He did, He began to glow, filling the room with light, then He spoke, *"and so I shall, just as it is written, at the time the Father chooses. But now I am about My Father's work, here among you, equipping you once again to 'Go therefore and make disciples of all nations, baptizing them in the name of My Father and in My name, and that of the Holy Spirit.'"*

One by one, each fell at His feet, tears pouring from their eyes, immeasurable joy filling their hearts.

"If you look for Me, you will find Me," He said. *"If you knock on the door, I will open it for you. Whatever you ask in My name will be done for you."*

The believing will believe that this happened, the unbelieving will never believe, regardless of the testimony of the twelve who were there and witnessed it first hand. I leave it to you to knock and see who opens the door.

Neither Spot Nor Blemish

Across her arms were many short limbs and brush, destined for her cooking fire back in the village. The desert was nearly devoid of any quantity of more sizable fuel, having been picked over many times by others also eager to prepare their meals. She struggled under the load, not because of its weight, but because of the uneven terrain she was forced to traverse, while not able to see ahead because of the wood. She wished now that she had bundled the wood and tied it securely and carried on her back.

Overhead, the early afternoon sun caused her to sweat under her closely woven robe and brought with it an ever increasing thirst. How far had she gone she wondered, in her search for fuel. Much of the scenery looked either unfamiliar or too familiar, depending on how you approached it. Far in the distance, the curve of the earth would have limited her view of the horizon were it not for the mountains that rose somewhere behind it. Because of this phenomenon, those mountains seemed to arise from nowhere, the desert floor having disappeared just before they began.

Underfoot an unseen rock caught the side of her sandal, causing her to lose her footing and twist her ankle as she fell. She lay among the scattered remnants of sticks and limbs on the rocky ground. For the first time since she had left the village, a sense of worry crept into her conscious thought, bringing with it alarm and fear.

Was she lost? Could she walk? Would someone notice she was gone and come looking for her before the wild animals found her?

She had not meant to travel so far from camp, but got caught-up in the search for wood and had not given careful attention to her surroundings. The familiarity of the distant mountains was the only sign that she may be traveling in the right direction.

But then too, she thought, didn't the mountains that ringed the desert all look pretty much the same? Her ankle was already beginning to swell as she sat massaging it, wondering if she could stand. She untied the sash which encircled her slim waist and wrapped it tightly around the injured area before attempting to regain her feet.

"Where is Leah?" Ajadab asked, "Have you seen my daughter?"

Over and over he made the inquiry as he passed through the camp, moving farther and farther from his own tent. It was early yet, he thought, much time remained before the darkness would fall and the night hunters would have the nerve to show themselves. But still, concern for her safety creased the coppery skin of his brow.

As was the custom, immediate family made camp near to each other, with more distant relatives further away. As his own tent came into view, likewise his wife and family, aunts, uncles, and cousins gave him a sense of peace. Surely, one of them must know where she was or where she had gone. His three sons, all older than she, were pursuing their own interests, unmindful of their younger sister. His wife was doing chores and preparing bread for the evening meal. Only the daughters of his brother's family had taken note when she had left camp in search of fuel for her mother's oven.

He was directed to an area where the tents stopped and the desert began. It looked hopelessly vacant and inhospitable as his eyes searched the wasteland with no reward. He had hoped to find footprints to follow, but thousands of feet, both men and animals, had made impressions in the sand before her. The sun in the cloudless sky was rapidly moving to the west and would soon set beyond the mountains and be replaced by the moon.

Ajadab returned to his tent and gathered his family around him, "we must mount our horses and find her," he implored. "Who will ride with me?"

Several of his brothers and his two oldest sons mounted their animals, placed coals from the fire in their clay pots, loaded water flasks and joined him.

"We will ride until the sun is one hand above the mountains," he instructed the search party, "then we will return to camp. Try and stay within sight of each, that no other will be lost."

The small party rode east from the point where she had last been seen, fanning out until they were nearly a half mile apart. At this point in time, God's children had been wandering in the small desert for ten years. This followed their choice not to heed God's instruction at the border of the Promised Land. Only Joshua and Caleb had trusted in the Lord, all the others returned with reports that showed their doubts in God's ability to protect them. This caused God to send them back to wander for forty years until the entire generation of unbelievers had died.

There was hardly any of this land that did not show the mark of the chosen, whom God charged Moses with shepherding. One footprint looked much the same as another in the sand.

Leah was eleven, not a woman yet, but also not a small child. Living a life of hardship in the desert, she had learned much about survival and the necessity to trust in Elohim, God the creator and sustainer of life. Part of her was frightened, afraid of the unknown that would soon be roaming in the darkness searching for prey, but in her heart she had confidence in God and His protection.

She tried to stand unaided but could not. She looked at the limbs that lay about her and chose one with a fork that allowed it to fit under her arm and tried a second time, this time with a prayer on her lips. As she stood, she could feel her heart beating where the sash strengthened her injured ankle and restricted the flow of blood.

She realized that she could no longer carry the firewood but could walk if she did so carefully, while watching her footing. She left the wood behind, but stacked it in a way that it would provide evidence of her having been there. Not far away, the ground rose and ended at a rocky peak. It would give her a vantage point to aid in her search for camp and make her more aware of any danger that might be pursuing her.

With each step, sharp needles of pain reminded her of her injury. A single gnarled tree stood among the rocks at the summit of the small hill having lost its battle to live in the harsh climate. The sky above darkened as clouds gathered, threatening rain upon the parched land below.

Ajadab and those with him had been searching fruitlessly for several hours when Jehovah's voice thundered from the heavens above and the first of many bolts of lightning fell from the skies onto the distant mountains. He knew that darkness was not far off as the sun rapidly approached the mountain tops, which were cloaked now in dark clouds. The lightning was striking nearer now, frightening both the riders and their horses as they turned them back toward the camp. Like Leah, Ajadab prayed to God that He would protect her and care for her, while hope for finding her diminished and despair filled his heart.

The grayness of dusk had just taken away the visual connection between the men of the search party when a fiery bolt from heaven struck the mountain top just above Ajadab, causing a barren tree to burst into flames. Silhouetted in its light was the recognizable image of his daughter, Leah.

All across the camp, word of God's power and faithfulness passed from person to person, as the story of her rescue was told and told again. On the next day a young bull, without spot or blemish, was offered up to the Lord as a freewill sacrifice in thanksgiving.

Never Alone

Alone now, her husband of 59 years had 'gone on ahead and was walking with the Lord he loved', she often told herself. It had been thirteen months since the cancer had been diagnosed and probably as many years before when it had first began in his prostrate. At first, there had been the optimism that spawned hope, later only the reality of the brevity of life.

When Elaine thought back, as she did often, she tried to weigh the benefits of knowing the angel of death waited nearby, as opposed to a single and final event that left no time to prepare and get affairs in order. To some it seemed merciful that one would just lie down and later to wake up in presence of the Lord. Others longed for final moments, heartfelt discussions, and precious memories to be shared before separation. She knew that God's plan was prepared in advance for each of us and was not subject to change.

She, however, was still unclear just how prayer figured into the equation for events already decided. At seventy-eight, she was content to not question as she had been in earlier days, she was more trusting, more dependent upon the truths found in God's Word. She was becoming comfortable with not knowing "why" everything happened the way it did.

The only why that still came to mind occasionally was why she remained after he had been taken. She looked forward to a joyous reunion and saw little that she was still able to do here on earth. What she questioned was her value to Jesus' kingdom and what purpose she still may serve.

She had been a school teacher, and a good one by many accounts. She had felt that she had been able to make a difference in those days, in the lives of the children she mentored. Even later, after she had retired, she continued to tutor many in her home, where she was able to teach without the restraints being imposed by a secular society. But finally the electronic age had made the skills she possessed unnecessary and antiquated.

Who needed to know how to find a square root or use a slide rule when a cell phone could give you the answer without having to think? It had all happened, it seemed, almost overnight, that the value of knowledge had been devalued. Human contact became the exception rather than the rule. The family unit became fragmented and dysfunctional as commitment and personal responsibility declined. Dependence upon God was replaced by dependence upon things.

She laughed to herself. Once the prayer before a semester test had been to "let me remember what I have been taught", now it was more likely to be, "please don't let my battery die." That brought another saying to mind... "there are no atheists in fox holes." Now she wondered if even that were true, where men had began to put their faith in technology rather than God. On Sunday mornings, she was not alone in her desire to roll back the clock to a simpler time when worship was voices lifted up to the accompaniment of an organ or piano, rather than electric guitars and keyboards with synthesized music.

Disconnect, that is what she called it. Mankind had or soon would disconnect itself from the umbilical that still held it to its Creator. They would be adrift just like those floating in space, separated from the mother ship in some movie scene. God's Word had spoken to it in the Old Testament when it described the branches being cut off from the vine, being left to wither and die. She could see it, understand it, but felt helpless to change or stop its progress. How God must grieve at His own creation, she thought, at the suffering it caused to itself by not learning from previous mistakes.

Elaine felt grateful that she was able to drive when few of her friends still did, that her overall health remained good enough to care for herself and maintain her small home, and for the decision made so many years before to follow Jesus. The aches, pains, and physical limitations were just worrisome little things that came with the territory. She made a great effort not focus on them, but to remind herself of the blessings that remained.

Tea, rather than the coffee she preferred, was becoming her beverage of choice, and fruit and vegetables her mainstay. Remembering the times past when everything was eaten with relish and without complication, she marveled at how her body now was much more finicky than when she was younger. She loved dairy products but couldn't enjoy them often now without paying a price.

Her phone rang, interrupting her day dreams, it was her oldest son Ben. Of the three they had raised, Ben was the one who made the most effort to stay in contact with her. He and his family lived a few miles across town, preventing them from sitting down together as often as she'd liked, but could be depended on to call regularly.

"Whatcha up to?" he said, always beginning the conversation the same way.

"Just finishing up breakfast," she answered, "I got up a little late today."

"Whatcha havin'?" he said, repeating yesterday's dialogue.

"Oatmeal and fruit with a cup of tea," she said patiently, anticipating his next remark.

"Well, I'm just checking on you to make sure you are okay, better get back to work now," he said. "Love you, love you too," they said, before disconnecting.

Although it amused her that the conversation could have been a recording, she did appreciate hearing her son's voice and looked forward to it. Her other two sons called less often, but usually with something to share when they did. More often than not, they filled her in on their victories or disappointments before asking about her. All three sons were married and had children, one had a grandchild already, slightly ahead of schedule. Of course in society today, it seemed few made an effort to get married before a child was born, and some never did.

It was approaching 11:00 when she dialed the phone and waited while her friend made her way to answer it. "Morning," Elaine said, "how are you feeling this morning?"

"This Ellie?" the voice asked.

"Sure is," Elaine answered, "who were you expecting, some guy?"

Her old friend laughed, "one could only hope." she said.

"How about lunch?" Elaine asked, "you haven't eaten yet have you?"

"I don't remember eating," came the honest answer, "but if I did it doesn''t matter anyway," her friend said. "I'm hungry again."

"Good, I'll be by in a few minutes to pick you up," Elaine said. "You be ready."

Bessie was never ready when she arrived, regardless of how much warning she was given, Elaine expected it. After thirty years of friendship, they were just like left and right shoes, worn, scuffed, out of style, but still comfortable next to each other. God had brought them together in the workplace, where they had formed a friendship that weathered many storms, including the loss of both husbands. Bessie, the senior by more than a decade, no longer drove or was able to live alone, depending on her family or friends for the few times she was able to get out. Lunch together was always an adventure, often taking up the larger part of the day for the women.

If there was one thing that age taught you, it was patience. With no schedules to keep, no one to answer to, no reason to leave or come back early, life made few demands that required one to become anxious when it took a few extra minutes to answer the door bell. When Bessie finally opened the door she said, "well there you are, I've been here waiting on you." Both of them laughed like school girls.

"Where shall we eat today," Elaine asked, "your turn to choose." No matter whose turn it may have been, they always ate at the same place. Both of them enjoyed Thai food nearby and the friendly faces who served it.

Bessie was thin and frail looking, recently becoming unsteady on her feet, but still had a sharp wit and easy smile. "Winter's acomin'", she said, for the thousandth time since they'd become friends, "cold out today."

Elaine smiled. She'd heard that nearly every month of every year no matter what the temperature, and no matter when, she had to admit winter was indeed "acomin'". As it turned out, it was November and the crisp air, with the accompanying wind, did have a bite to it as they stepped from the car at the restaurant.

Falling in later years and breaking a bone often carries a fear with it, much worse than dying. Immobility takes away the final bit of independence from the elderly and seems to crush the spirit. Both women held on to each other fiercely, unwilling that gravity should provide the final insult to their brittle bones.

Once inside, they looked at one another with a sense of accomplishment, having bested the enemy another time, as they were safely seated. They ordered in a grand fashion, as though they were starving and had not eaten for days. Neither would eat much, but both would take the remainder home for a second or third meal at a later time.

There is a genteel way that a guest can act that makes both the served and the server feel special and loved. The pair had perfected it to the point that the wait staff looked forward to each visit as much as they. The little restaurant closed at 3:00 but made no mention of it as they continued to clean around their guest's table while they visited. At 3:20 both women rose, put on their coats, and argued over who's to-go box belonged to whom, before clutching each others arms for support, as they walked out.

"Ben called," Elaine said as they drove toward home.

"Ben's a thoughtful boy," Bessie answered, "I always liked him."

"Yes, he is," Elaine agreed, "calls me every day."

"You going to vote?" Bessie asked, "not that it makes much difference," she added.

"I'll probably go vote early and mail it," Elaine answered. "I can't stand in line long with my bad legs."

"That's a good idea, Bessie agreed, "maybe we can get the ballots together." They made small talk until Elaine pulled into the driveway and turned off the engine.

"Let me give you a hand," she said, getting out and walking around the car.

Bessie slapped the offered hand gently, then said, "you are just trying to get my doggie bag, aren't you?" The two hobbled up the step and to the door where Bess fumbled with the door key for several minutes, trying to find which one and which side faced up.

"I'll call you," Elaine said, as the door closed.

On the short drive home she knew she had gotten her answer. The answer to her question as to why God allowed her to remain for a while longer.

Pictures in the Heart

The water, in the setting sun, had taken on a golden glow that danced as a light breeze disturbed the surface. In proper season, such as this, the moon sometimes began its arc just before the sun finished setting. Maybe it was the latitude, together with the season, that made this possible, he did not know. But there they were, two giant orbs staring at each other across the endless sky, with the earth between them.

Somewhere far out into the lake, a fish jumped, causing a splashing sound. Nearer the beach, unseen by human eyes, the animals of the forest had begun to leave their hiding places to partake of water from the lake. Others, the predators, would hold back waiting, while the deer and smaller animals ventured from the safety of the forest. They would watch and wait, while moving closer, hoping for opportunity for an easy meal.

It was both the dance of life and of death; life for those whose senses prevented them from becoming a meal, death for the inexperienced and unwary. Yellow eyes with vertical pupils watched and waited for opportunity from the thicket. A young doe took a tentative step, raising her head as she did to 'taste' the air, standing motionless for several seconds. She repeated the scene three more times before she reached the water's edge and dropped her head and began to drink.

For several seconds, as she faced out toward the lake, she could neither hear nor see the danger which crept up silently behind her. Her sense of smell was nearly lost to the cool water while she drank her fill. Warily, she raised her head again; listening, watching, and breathing in the scents of the forest.

Just as the great cat gathered itself to spring, she leaped sidewise several feet, then turned and ran into the thick brush. He would continue to wait, perhaps the breeze would change and blow across the water toward him rather than from behind, and not announce his presence until too late.

The moon was alone in the sky now, the sun having disappeared, a backdrop of stars were beginning to glow behind it. The sounds of the night, familiar and reassuring, murmured across the lake... first a loon, then a Great Horned owl who occupied a perch on the top of some dead snag.

Timeless, or so it seemed, the reoccurring ballet that chose who may live to dance again and who would dance no more. Nearby a frog croaked a message and was answered again and again as others took up the chorus.

The small scurrying animals that dotted the beach were to be left for others, the fox, the bobcat, and possibly the night owl. The great cat was older now, more patient, and less eager to work hard for small gain. He had found that he was ill suited to spend energy chasing a rabbit if other options were available. He waited patiently and was rewarded for it.

The doe had returned with its young at its side to join others at water's edge. In the darkness he could see his smaller cousin, with his tufted ears, also take notice of the young fawn. He would not hesitate to challenge the bobcat if it came to that, if it tried to steal his meal.

Far distant across the lake, the yellow eyes of a cabin announced itself as the human predators settled in for the night. Earlier he had heard them communicating, and seen them frisking along the water's edge. He had considered for a moment how helpless and unwary they seemed, how easy it would be to take one down, carrying it into the forest. Something in him however, had urged caution.

The fawn had wandered a few paces away from its mother, standing closer now to the fringe of the forest, where he lay. The moon illuminated the white spots on its back, making it easy to see in the darkness. He poised himself once more, gathering his muscles to spring.

Before he could, the smaller cat jumped and missed its prey by inches, sending it and the various other animals scurrying for safety. Much like an angry father, he wanted to scold and punish the impetuous bobcat, but just gave it a warning growl instead. A fight without food would have been a waste of effort.

Inside the cabin, Grandpa, Grandma and their two grandchildren were all playing a board game and eating popcorn. The children loved to come to the cabin and enjoy the excitement and attention they lacked at home. They enjoyed the slower beat, the lack of pressure to perform, and the patience that came from grandparents. Both Ned and his sister Carole delighted in the repeated stories that their grandfather and grandmother told. Often, they corrected some detail from a previous telling that had been left out or forgotten, causing everyone to laugh and argue good naturedly.

For the grandparents, it was like raising their own children again, but with more knowledge and less demands on their time. Patience is the gift that God gives to replace enthusiasm and vitality. Not a bad trade-off, they agreed.

"What will we do tomorrow?" Ned asked, his head already full of possibilities.

Bill looked at his wife Kathy and winked, then answered, "let's just sleep in and rest all day."

"Boooo," was the response from both children. "We can sleep at home," they chimed.

"How about a boat ride and a picnic then?" Bill asked smiling.

"Can we fish?" Carole asked, "I haven't fished since last year."

Bill looked at Kathy pleadingly, "what do you think Kath, we might catch a nice trout for dinner."

She smiled, "trout would be nice, but I'll make sure we have a back up plan in case you get skunked again."

They all laughed and continued to let the roll of the dice move them around the board.

Ned was eleven, Carole would be eight on her next birthday, as she always reminded them. She had already claimed it for herself, with it still months away. Both had been spending time at the cabin since they could walk. The children were still alert when the older folks herded them off to bed and turned out the lights, but were asleep just ten minutes later.

The water was nearly clear, the silt from spring runoff having already settled to the bottom. It was easy to see the fish swimming below the boat, except when they hid among the rocks or where fallen trees or limbs gave them natural shelter. Overhead, Ospreys and bald eagles were frequent sights, hoping that an unwary fish might get close to the surface. The north end, where two streams fed the small lake from the surrounding mountains, sported cattails and swamp grass in its shallower water. It was also a nesting place for herons, loons, and an occasional family of ducks or geese.

Bill and Kathy had owned their property for over thirty years, but only in the last dozen since they retired and built, had they begun to use it more regularly. When their own two sons were young it was a place to come and pitch a tent or bring a camp trailer, to fish and relax for a while before returning quickly back to work in town.

The 14' boat accommodated the four of them easily and the little five horses moved it across the water well. Bill had purposely brought several light-weight poles for the purpose of making the 'catch' all the more exciting. It also taught the children patience and finesse if they hooked into something more sizable. The little ultra lights were short and easy to cast, with only four pound line on them.

Kathy was the first to 'hook up' but quickly asked Carole for her help in landing the fish. Of course Carole counted the fish as her catch when she landed a nice 12" rainbow. Ned was next, but was disappointed when his 'bow was smaller than his sister's. As the morning wore on, several more were hooked, some were kept and some lost when they slipped the hook.

Finally Bill, who had spent his morning as chauffeur and captain, hooked a big one. He could tell its size as it peeled off line without slowing down, that it was several pounds. He played it for several minutes before getting even a glimpse, as it ran along the bottom, bending the light pole nearly double. Of course the excitement and noise in the boat was maximized as everyone shouted advice to Grandpa.

Finally, after several grueling minutes, the fish began to tire and gradually Bill was able to coax it toward the surface. However, from time to time, the big fish would make another valiant attempt to free itself of the hook by diving, running, or jumping. Bill held the tension steady, employing his years of experience, feeling both joy and sadness as the fish steadily lost stamina.

He was tempted to cut the line and let it go, but before he could convince himself, it broke water yet another time. As the fish cleared the water, shaking its head, with the sunlight bringing the colors of its scales into view, large treacherous claws closed around it. Even the magnificent bald eagle seemed at first overly burdened by its weight. But after several hard beats of its wings it gained altitude, breaking the fishing line without effort, as it flew away.

The four sat for a time in awe, silent, amazed by what they had just witnessed. Then all at once they became animated, each rushing to share their version of the event. Pictures would have been good, but Bill knew the pictures permanently etched in their memories would continue to give them pleasure as long as they lived.

He was wise enough to know that Ned and Carole would be retelling this story long after he and Kathy were walking with Jesus in heaven. He silently thanked God for the experience they had been provided as he piloted the small boat across the lake to their picnic spot.

They tied up to some small brush after pulling the boat up onto the sandy beach and began to search out a suitable location for their picnic. Ned pointed out to the children the two sets of deer tracks in the sand at the water's edge.

"It looks like a doe and her fawn," he said, "they came down last night for water. Something scared them off, probably a bear or cat."

The imprints approaching the water were well defined, showing that they had been made while walking, but those returning to the forest evidenced a hasty flight, by the way the soil was disturbed. Ned, more than Carole, showed a keen interest and asked many questions.

"Was it a mountain lion?" he asked, as they sat on a blanket on the beach near the water.

"Maybe," Bill answered, "but more likely a bear or coyote."

The children could picture danger now behind every tree and were looking anxiously around them.

Kathy could see the tension in their young faces. "We've never had any trouble with any animals, large or small," she said, hoping to calm them. "God provides food for every animal and we are not their natural choice."

"But," Carole said, "don't people ever get attacked by lions, bears, or wolves?"

"Almost never," Bill interjected, "once we learn about them and their habits, if we use common sense, it is seldom an issue."

"Have you seen them?" Ned asked his grandfather, "did you ever see bear around here, or a cougar?"

"Only a couple of times over all the years we've been coming here," he answered honestly, "and then they were quick to avoid me. We don't feed the animals, leave garbage out where they can get it, or spend time out alone in the evening. Most of the larger animals hunt at night."

"Never," Kathy was quick to add, "stay around if you see a young animal. Even a doe could see you as a threat to her fawn and hurt you. All animals will protect their young and challenge anything that threatens them."

Both children looked back at the tracks they had seen in the sand.

"Do you think she fought for her fawn?" Ned asked.

"No," Bill said, "it looks like they ran away. But she would have if it had been necessary."

On previous visits, when both children had been younger, they had just taken walks, roasted marshmallows, and skipped rocks. They had never really ventured out into the forest. But Bill could see that now was the right time to teach them both a respect and love for nature. After they finished eating lunch, he began by showing them the proper way to clean fish and to dispose of the parts left behind.

"Best way," he began, "is to put the guts back in the lake, as far from shore as you can. They become food, then, for other fish without, attracting land animals."

"Like bears and lions?" Carole asked.

"Like raccoons, bears, or anything with an appetite," Bill answered. "We don't want to encourage them to depend on us for food or come snooping around where we live."

"Oh," she said a little too solemnly.

"You have a dog at home, don't you?" Kathy asked.

"Patches," Carole said proudly.

"What does he eat?" her grandmother asked.

"Dog food," the children answered together.

"Good," Kathy said, "but if you didn't feed him and he was hungry, what do you think he would do?"

"He got into Mom's pantry once and chewed up a bunch of cereal boxes. He made a real mess," Ned answered.

"Does he usually eat cereal? Kathy asked, "did he eat much of it?"

"No," he ate a little, I guess," he said, "but mostly he just made a mess."

Bill had listened to them and saw where Kathy was leading. "Wild animals are the same. They have the natural food that their Master provides and would rather eat it, but when they can't get it, sometimes they are forced to look for something else," he said. "Our job is to not become the box of cereal."

Both children and Kathy laughed.

The day seemed to go quickly. They walked in the forest together, looked, listened, and asked questions about nearly everything they saw. Farther in they came across a beaver dam in one of the streams, with a clear deep pool all around it. Bill and Kathy explained at length how the beaver fulfilled part of God's plan by placing his home as he had.

All were disappointed to not get a glimpse of the resident beaver.

Birds, both large and small, walked, flew, and made their presence known to the quartet, with Bill identifying each species. A large grouse puffed up and spread his tail in the trail ahead, making an unusual noise, while performing a courting dance. Too late, Bill attempted to point out a doe and her fawn who had been frightened from their resting place. They disappeared before he could speak.

Kathy identified a rotting stump full of ants that had been recently turned to pieces and noted that the insects were a preferred diet of black bears, right along with wild berries. The children collected and then abandoned cones, rocks, sticks and other interesting souvenirs as the walk continued. When they stopped to rest and share a snack, Bill cut them each a 'walking stick' from some willows, then showed them how to make a whistle from the green willow as well.

With the daylight on the wane, the four returned to the lake, only to find that a visitor had overturned their ice chest and stolen their fish. Footprints in the wet sand convicted an unseen raccoon of the crime. Both children were upset to have lost their catch but both also had received first hand the lesson that their grandfather had been trying to teach.

"I should have hung it between two trees," he said, "several feet off the ground. It was my fault for making it too easy for the masked bandit."

And so, they returned to the cabin hungry, tired, and happy, but without a single fish for their dinner. Bill beached and turned over the boat, stowing its motor beneath it. Kathy and Carole went inside to begin dinner and stoke the fireplace with fresh wood.

"Grandpa," Ned said, "does Dad know all of this stuff like you?"

"Most of it," Bill replied hearing the unasked question in his voice.

"Why do you ask?"

"Just wondering," he answered noncommittally.

Bill didn't speak, letting Ned take time to say what was on his mind.

"Doesn't he like it up here?" he finally asked.

"He used to," Bill said, "but he doesn't come up as much as he did."

Ned picked up a rock, inspected it as he'd been taught, then side-armed it across the lake.

"Five, not bad," Bill said congratulating him, "you're getting the hang of it."

Inside the cabin, a chicken had been dredged in flour and was beginning to sizzle in the big black cast iron frying pan. On the propane stove, water was boiling in preparation for the potatoes they had peeled.

"Grands!" Carole said with a smile, watching as her grandmother popped open the store bought container of refrigerated biscuits. "Do we have honey?"

"In the bear," Kathy answered pointing to a shelf in the cupboard.

"I'm getting old and lazy," Kathy said aloud, mostly to herself.

"That's okay, Grams," Carole said comfortingly, "they are not as good as yours but they are still good."

It was nearly dark when the smell of food brought the men up from the lake.

"Smells good, Kath," Bill said sincerely.

Kathy smiled and replied, "Wash up so we can bless this food and eat."

The pitcher pump brought the water to the sink where they washed both their hands and faces, while Carole and Kathy placed the food on the table. They sat, before joining hands and bowing their heads. Bill blessed the food, but before he could say amen, Ned added "bless Mom and Dad."

Both Bill and Kathy noted his strange added message but said nothing. The crisp fried chicken was moist and juicy inside, the homemade gravy over the potatoes and honey buttered biscuits filled them full. Afterward, they played rummy, pitch, and old maid before their eyes got heavy and their beds beckoned them.

"What do you suppose is going on with Ned?" Kathy asked Bill as she readied for bed.

"I'm not sure," he answered his wife, "but he asked some questions about his Dad when we were down by the lake that made me wonder."

"Maybe we should talk with him," she said, concern in her voice.

"Let's give him some room, don't crowd him, see what happens," Bill replied. "Maybe just he and I can go for a hike or something tomorrow and spend a little guy time and see what's troubling him."

"Grandpa," Ned said as they walked along the sandy beach, pitching rocks and driftwood into the azure water, "why do people get divorced?"

Bill hesitated, considered both the question and its implications before answering. "You are asking me a pretty difficult question," he began. "But, I'll do my best to answer it."

They sat down on a fallen log and looked out into the lake.

"Ned," he said, "do you still read the Bible?"

"Not as much," Ned admitted, "we don't go to church much anymore."

"When we get back to the cabin we can look some of this up in the Bible," Bill said, "but for now I'm going to tell it to you as I remember it, okay?"

Ned nodded but said nothing more.

"Somewhere in Genesis is the part where God made man and then woman from his rib. Another place He tells us that the two become one, does that make sense to you?" Bill asked looking at the boy. Ned nodded again.

"Becoming one means more than just getting married," Bill said, "it means that you have agreed to love each other and put them before your own wishes." He stopped to make sure he was being understood. "A man and woman make a promise called a covenant that should never be broken, both to each other and to God," he continued. "But God knows that we are not like Him, that sometimes we do not or can not keep our promises."

"Have you and grandma ever thought about divorce?" Ned asked in a very small voice.

Bill hesitated, hating what he was hearing and beginning to think.

"Thought about it, yes, we probably have," he said, "seriously considered it... no. Will you tell me why you ask?"

"My best friend Tommy told me that his mother and father are getting divorced, that he will have to decide which one to live with," Ned said. "Lots of kids in my class don't live with their real moms and dads."

"Are you worried that your own mom and dad might get divorced?" Bill asked gently.

"Sometimes I think about it," Ned admitted, "it seems like Dad is working all the time and we don't see him much. Mom complains about it a lot."

"I see where that might bother you," Bill said, "do you ever pray about it? Have you told God how you feel?"

Bill could see tears in Ned's eyes and blinked back some of his own. "Shall we pray together now?"

Ned nodded and bowed his head as Bill did the same.

"Lord Jesus, you know our hearts, you know our thoughts and the pain we feel inside. You know the fears that trouble us and You are the answers to all of our questions. Although we trust in You, we still worry and that worry is what we ask You to take away from us today. We ask that you put the same love You have for each of us into the hearts of Ned and Carole's mom and dad. We ask that you will bring them closer together in that love. Amen." Bill prayed.

"God," Ned added, "help Mom and Dad to love each other and stay married."

Bill's cheeks were wet as they resumed their walk without further conversation.

~ ~

"With the kids gone, I thought we could spend some time together," Helen said into the phone.

"I've got a closing in the morning, first thing," Steve replied, "big commission. How about tomorrow night instead? I'll buy you a fancy dinner somewhere."

"Just forget it," she said harshly, "I'm not looking for a fancy dinner, just time with my husband." She hung up the phone without saying goodbye.

Helen was feeling the loneliness of separation, and not just from her ambitious husband, but also from her Savior. Steve had worked the last four or five Saturdays, long hours. He used Sundays then to catch up on his rest and do the yard work and manly chores around the house. His promise that it was just a temporary thing, that things would slow down, that they could share breakfast and church services together, had began to fall on deaf ears.

She had began to let herself feel abused, she began to focus on *her* unfulfilled needs, on what was lacking rather than the blessings she enjoyed. Intellectually, she knew that Steve was working for the good of the family, but emotionally it was he that seemed selfish and driven.

What had become of the man she had married?

Steve, on the other hand, felt that his sacrifices weren't appreciated, that Helen was being selfish, demanding, and unreasonable. She enjoyed the freedom that his success provided, the meals out, the nice cars, home, and clothes didn't she? Where did she think they came from if not his dedication to work? It was Biblical wasn't it, laying away stores in the good times for the lean ones that would surely come later? The more he considered it, the more he resented her attitude and unbending demands upon his time. He began to wonder if he could ever make her happy.

~ ~

"Well?" Kathy asked as Bill entered the cabin and Ned ran to join Carole on the tire swing outside.

Bill looked at her for a moment, and then spoke slowly, "it seems that Steve and Helen may be having problems in their marriage and Ned has picked up on it."

A worried look came over Kathy's face, "I haven't heard a word from either of them," she said, "do you suppose that we should say something when we get home?"

"No," Bill answered. "Unless they ask for our help, our best recourse is to pray. Ned did say that they haven't been going to church."

"The devil only needs a foothold," Kathy declared, "if you don't fill your heart with God, he'll fill it with things of the world and draw you away."

Bill didn't say anything more but remembered a time when they'd been drawn into the world. It had nearly cost them everything.

Kathy had been a school teacher and loved it. Because of her personality, she was good at it and 'invested' herself in her students. Over time, she began to give more and more to the job and less and less to her own children and Bill. Taking calls at home, staying late for conferences, bringing papers home to grade evenings and weekends was 'part of the job' she had declared. The boys had filled their time with sports and school activities, Bill with his male friends, fishing trips, ball games, and eventually found himself drawn to a single woman in their church.

Bill still praised God for His intervention. She had, before anything had happened, been offered a job opportunity in another town and had moved. But, not before the seed had been planted. Bill now found himself looking at other women differently than he had previously, having already committed adultery in his heart, and justifying it by Kathy's lack of companionship.

It had been his friend Joe, one of the church elders, who had noticed the change and risked their friendship to take him aside and broach the subject. Bill had been angry at first and defensive, but Joe persisted in love until God opened Bill's eyes to his sin of lust. Many tears were shed when he had told Kathy and asked for forgiveness and many more when she saw herself through her family's eyes. Their sons had never known how close they had come to divorce.

~ ~

"Son," Bill said to Steve on his cell phone, "things have changed, I'm going to have to ask you and Helen to come pick up the children rather than we bringing them home."

"But," Steve began, "I'm buried at work, I don't know if I can get away."

"Sorry son," Bill said bluntly, "you are just going to find a way."

Kathy had been listening and was smiling when Bill put down the phone.

"I thought you were not going to butt in," she said.

"I'm not," he said returning her smile, "We're going to get them aside and tell them a story we have never told anyone, is that alright with you?"

Kathy hesitated, not wanting to re-live the pain of many years past, reluctant to open old wounds, even to family. Bill waited while she considered the options.

"I guess it is our witness," she said. "Just as we witness our faith, we should also witness our weakness and God's mercy and grace. Bill nodded agreement.

Steve didn't sound all that excited when he called back two hours later but said that he and Helen would be up the next morning. With three days left in spring break, Bill struggled with a way to tell the children they'd be going home a day early. 'The truth will set you free' instantly came to mind when he prayed.

"Hey kids," Bill said, trying to sound excited, "guess what, your Mom and Dad are coming up tomorrow." He didn't see the necessity of explaining why.

"Yay," Ned said with enthusiasm, "maybe they'll go fishing with us." Carole, too, seemed eager to share the mountain retreat with her parents.

~ ~

After greetings and hugs were exchanged, both children descended upon their parents as though they had been away all summer. With them both talking at the same time, telling of their many adventures, Bill and Kathy just stood back and watched, smiling.

"We waited breakfast," Kathy said, "We hoped you'd be up early for sourdough pancakes, bacon and eggs."

The menu was hard to refuse, with the clock reminding them that neither had eaten before leaving home. Neither Steve nor Helen said much, just answering when spoken to and then in short sentences. Bill could tell there was tension between them.

"Carole, will you and Ned do me a favor after breakfast?" Kathy asked, "Make us up a nice picnic lunch."

Steve started to object but Bill waived him off.

"What'll we make?" Carole asked.

"Whatever you want, you fill the basket with whatever sounds good," Kathy replied.

When they finished eating and Helen and Kathy were stacking the dishes, Bill suggested they take a quick walk on the beach together while the kids filled the basket.

Bill and his son were walking in front, with Kathy and Helen following. The sun had cleared the nearby mountains and began its daily chore of warming the land, replacing the chill of the night. Steve seemed to relax as he looked across the mirror-like surface of the lake. Bill supposed that he was reliving times in his childhood. Helen too now seemed less tense and had taken interest in nature's beauty as they walked.

"Do you remember the time when we brought the old truck and camp trailer up and lost a water pump on the way?" Bill asked his son.

"Yes," Steve answered, "you were about as steamed as the radiator as I recall."

"How old were you?" Kathy asked.

"I guess about ten or eleven," he said, "Tom and I were both still in grade school."

Bill stopped and sat down on a fallen log and when the others joined he said, "I'll bet you didn't know that your Mom and I came up here in a last ditch effort to keep our marriage together."

No one said anything for some time, then Bill and Kathy began telling their story, while the others listened. They told the details, shared the feelings that had caused the rift, then as it ended, Kathy said, "that was thirty two years ago."

Tears were in both Steve and Helen's eyes when Bill stood and said, "we'd better be getting back before the kids begin to think a bear got us. Your Mom and I are headed back to town right after lunch, you and the kids are welcome to stay as long as you like."

They waved goodbye to the four right after lunch and headed back to town, neither of them speaking for several miles. It was two days later when the phone rang, it was Ned.

"Grandpa, we just got home, we had a great time," he said, "we showed Mom and Dad all of the things you showed us."

"Mom caught a fish," Carole added, "but Dad threw it back because it was too small."

Steve took the phone from his children, then said, "thanks Mom and Dad for the best advice you never gave."

Quell the Raging Storm

The hand of God was raised over the earth, below Him the earth writhed as if in pain. He watched for a time, then spoke, *"be still and know that I am God."* Nature bowed to her Master, her King, her Creator, as God answered the frightened prayers of His children. His love knows no boundary, His power has no limit, His promise no end.

Bodies and debris were found as far as two miles inland from the shoreline. The island had no natural boundary to contain the ocean's fury. Moving with the speed and stealth of a cheetah, but far more deadly, the 18" high wave had moved nearly a thousand miles across the open ocean from the point of the earthquake, hardly noticeable to anyone who had been at sea.

As it neared the shore it began to gather itself, to pile water upon water, as the shallow beach provided resistance. When it broke free, it was a wall of water fifty feet tall and several miles wide. Many on surf-boards, a half mile out, watched as its fury mounted between them and their homes along the coastline.

The wind circled like a great cat trying to get behind its prey, while its force mounted. Where the earth's heat met the cool air of the great ocean, it began to rise and fall like the panting chest of an animal. As one force was overcome by another, it began to spiral and rotate, gathering strength as it did, like the dance of two unseen performers.

It was nature's orchestra that played the tune for the dancers, helping them to further gain speed and momentum. No other force in nature rivaled it in size or power, no preparation adequate, no prevention possible. The dance would be danced until the partners tired of their game, showing its disdain for man and his all of accomplishments.

A crack first appeared, like those in the mud of a parched riverbed. At first it seemed to open, then close itself, as if unsure how to proceed. But once the decision had been made, the fissure in the earth's surface opened with lightening speed, moving ever forward, unstoppable, immeasurable.

The great crack in the earth's crust vented steam and gas from its core far below, but neither quickly enough nor in sufficient quantity to prevent the pressure from building. It ruptured and exploded with forces akin to those that birthed the universe so many years ago, filling the air with dirt and ash. Molten rock poured out an inexhaustible quantity from the raw sore that was the volcano.

The winter's snow, stacked high on the mountain peaks, lay dormant, drifts like peaks of whipped cream, a joy to see. Like a savings account, banked for later use, they waited for someone to make a withdrawal. The Chinook winds swooped down as might a bird of prey... caressing them, warming them, and turning their crystalline flakes into water.

Like a snake gathering itself to strike, drop added to drop, rivulet to rivulet, until trickle by trickle each depression in the mountain became a stream. Each stream joined with another as it cascaded down the steep mountainside, gathering speed and power as it did. Far below, nestled at the foot of the mountains, a ramshackle nest of homes gave man shelter and security from nature's seasonal rain and snow.

Days, then weeks, and finally months had come and gone and yet not a single drop of rain had been released from the white clouds high overhead. The heat of the summer sun had dried the earth's crust and milled it like flour. Reservoirs and streams had long since given up in their battle to exist. Hot, dry winds scoured the earth's surface, also looking for water to send upward to the thirsty clouds waiting patiently above. First the plants, then the animals which depended upon them, and finally all of mankind who had claimed to be sovereign over the land, suffered and died.

With a roar like a hundred distant lions or a convoy of a thousand trucks, it came shaking, like a massive dog drying itself after a swim. Unknowing, uncaring of its surroundings, it shook off like fleas the puny attempts of man to construct lasting monuments to himself. Buildings, both great and small, became rubble in an instant, their occupants lying dead or running and screaming in terror. Lasting but moments, it remained in their hearts forever, like the echo of the devil's laughter.

Crack! Then again, it came, filling the stagnant air with ozone. Crack! The sound akin to a dry tree breaking its back, followed in just seconds by that of a massive base drum. Jagged shards of light filled with energy unleashed it and raised its broken fingers in the air like the hands of a dead man imploring God for release from his torment. Dry trees and plants added to the fury as they burst into flame, flame ravenous and relentless, wanting, needing to devour.

Unbridled, untamed, the earth vomited, attempting to rid itself of the sickness that mankind had brought to it. Only God has the power and wisdom to bandage its wounds and heal it.

Question

"You expect me to believe that?" he said scoffing. "Why should I believe a word you have to say?"

"Because, because it's true," she answered, "Because I never lie."

"Okay, calm down," he said backing off a little, "assuming it is true, what would you have me do about it?"

She took a minute to collect herself rather than just plunging ahead. Although young, she was wise enough to know that just because something was important to you, it was not necessarily so to others.

"Are you sure?" he asked in a more concerned voice.

"As sure as I can be," Amanda answered, "I was there, I heard him say it."

"Maybe he was kidding," he said, "in poor taste yes, but maybe he wasn't serious."

"Sounded as serious as a heart attack to me," she answered, "he was smirking and looking her over like a piece of meat when he said it."

"Let me get this straight, he came right out and said that if she slept with him, he'd make sure she passed his class?" he asked.

"He said what I told you," she answered. "You are failing my class, I see no chance of you passing unless you choose to come home with me tonight."

"Maybe he was offering to tutor her, give her special help," he suggested. "That's exactly what he'll claim he meant by it if I go to the dean.

He'll say he offered to go above and beyond and she misunderstood."

She looked defeated. "So what can we do? Both you and I know what he meant, and she does too," she said. "How many do you think he has said that to behind closed doors and gotten away with it?"

Amanda could tell that Professor Maxwell believed her, but she could also tell he was unwilling to go up against a tenured professor his first year at the university, and risk his career without proof of wrongdoing.

"Give me time to think," the professor said, "meanwhile, tell her to make sure she's never alone with him and ask around discreetly if any of the others have received similar offers."

~ ~

Amanda was a freshman, only eighteen, and spending her first year away from home. Her grades had provided a partial scholarship, which gave her parents enough financial help to allow her to go away to the university rather than living at home. The local community college had been only a two year school and had questionable value when one attempted to transfer credits to an accredited university.

She lived in a dorm on campus, a five hour drive from the home where she had grown up. Without transportation and extra finances, she found it easy to concentrate on her studies. She spent most of her time on campus, either in the library or playing volleyball. As a walk on, she was readily accepted and allowed to practice with the team regularly.

Her skills were apparent to the coach, he wasn't however, willing to waste one of his few scholarships on her until she had proven herself. She practiced, made friends, and increased her skills, almost as a form of entertainment.

It was on the court where she had first met Becky. Becky was also a freshman, but on an athletic scholarship that demanded both commitment and a good GPA to maintain. As it turned out, it was the two classes they had together and a common interest in volleyball that initially forged their friendship.

Since neither of them had finalized their educational goals, both had taken liberal arts courses, hoping to find just the right place for them as school progressed. Amanda envied those whose course was charted for them, those following in their parent's footsteps or those who had been blessed to know what they wanted to pursue in life.

While Amanda came from a larger town, Becky was rural America all the way, coming from a small farming community in eastern Oregon. While she was not a 'hick', she was a little naïve and less assertive than Amanda. This, Amanda believed, was the main reason why Professor Williams had chosen her to be his victim. Knowing that English was a core class and that she needed it to maintain her scholarship, he must have felt he held the upper hand.

They sat together in the library studying, speaking softly so as to not incur the ire of the matronly librarian.

"I've been thinking," Becky said, "maybe he was just trying to help me out. Maybe we read him wrong. Maybe I should take him up on his offer. I can always walk if he comes on to me."

"No way, José," Amanda said with emphasis. "You know better than that and so do I. If you go, whatever happens would be just your word against his, and he would win. He'd claim it was you who solicited him for better grades and deny the whole thing."

"But, what can I do?" she asked, "If he flunks me, I loose my scholarship."

"I spoke to Prof Max about it," Amanda said, "he's giving it some thought, and said to stay way clear of him."

"Will Max help? Did he believe you?" Becky asked.

"He did, I'm sure of it," she answered, "but he's afraid to take Williams on without more proof."

~ ~

"You squeaked by, I gave you a break," Professor Williams said as he laid the English test in front of Becky, with a D- across the top. "Better give some thought to that tutoring we spoke about. I don't want you to lose that scholarship," he added with a smirk.

Subjective, much of the creative writing they were currently doing in English, gave considerable latitude to allow the professor unlimited discretionary power. Unlike math or other subjects that were more black and white, both young women knew they could never prove a case against him.

Six weeks into the semester, Becky had a 2.2 in English, well below the 3.0 she needed to maintain. Amanda, on the other hand, had a 3.4, with their work showing very little material difference.

"Mr. Maxwell, you've got to help," Amanda said, Becky standing by her side. "Someone has to do something."

Max liked both of the girls, and both were doing equally well in his history class. "I've given it some thought," he said, "even talked to one of my old professors at my alma mater, without using names of course. He suggested that you ask for a transfer into another class."

Becky was near tears, he could tell when she spoke, "I asked, all the English classes are full. My only chance would be at semester and by then it'll be too late."

"Let's pray about it," Professor Maxwell said, surprising both young women. "Sometimes we try and take on more than we are equipped to handle and need God's strength and direction."

Amanda watched as Becky smiled for the first time in weeks, then bowed her head. None of the three prayed aloud, but all three of them prayed from the heart and asked God for guidance.

~ ~

Amanda could tell that Becky was off her game at their first scrimmage, when they played against each other. The coach also was critical of her performance and spoke to her afterward about focus and commitment. Amanda, on the other hand, was able to exploit their weaknesses and shined like a new bulb. She felt guilty about it afterward.

When they went into history class together, Professor Maxwell motioned Becky to his desk and handed her a slip of paper, a name and number written across the top.

"What is it?" Amanda asked her friend.

"He said it is a private detective, that I should call him, he has already talked with him."

"I went to college with Professor Maxwell," the young man said after introducing himself, "we roomed together. He asked me as a favor to look discreetly into a matter of concern to you."

"We don't have a lot of money," Amanda said for both of them. Becky was nodding her agreement.

"Consider this a favor for a friend of a friend," Dean Black said smiling. "I owe Prof Max a lot, he helped me find salvation when I was headed in the wrong direction."

"Do you have any ideas?" Becky asked.

"Let me snoop around quietly, ask a few questions, look into a few things that might be of value," he answered. "He probably thinks he's bulletproof, so he has probably not covered his tracks very well."

Neither woman had any idea of what things Dean may be referring but trusted him because they had little choice.

"Time is critical," Amanda said before leaving the meeting, "semester comes up in three weeks and it appears that he'll fail her if we don't do something."

Becky said nothing but her brown eyes were rimmed with tears.

"I'm on it," Dean said smiling, "Pray for God's direction."

~ ~

"A trend, but hardly concrete evidence," Max said to Dean as they sat at Starbucks sipping coffee. Several papers lay on the table between them.

Dean looked disappointed by his friend's comment.

"Look at the difference between men and women," he said pointing. "In my experience women are usually better in English then us men. However, his women students either seem to excel, transfer out before semester, or flunk out at semester. With the male students, the stats are more as one might expect all across the spectrum, with few transfers."

"What is that saying to you?" Max asked his friend.

"Possibly that those who reject his tutelage are forced to either transfer or risk failure, and look at how it stacks up when you factor in the ones on scholarship," Dean added.

"Wow!" Max replied, "Those on scholarship either seem to rise to the top or drop off the chart completely, nothing in between."

"Exactly," Dean said, "that's the way I read it."

"So what's your plan?" Max asked.

"I need to get access to information about those who failed or transferred," Dean answered, "and pray that some are willing to be forthcoming with me."

"Let me make a call or two," Max said, "I don't want you hacking the system unless you have to."

A few days later they met again.

"A dozen, I have a dozen names," Dean told his friend, "but so far only three of them have agreed to talk with me."

"How about students who no longer attend the university?" the professor asked, "drop-outs or transfers? If they were forced out, they may feel some incentive to get even."

"I thought of that," Dean agreed, "but I wonder if a woman's scorn is really a legitimate tool and how credible they may seem to a board of inquiry."

Maxwell nodded agreement, "I see your point. Even so, if you find others, their testimony would add more weight to the charges."

"Let me interview the three and see if we have anything," Dean said, smiling. "I'll get back to you."

~ ~

Becky was clearly struggling in volleyball, her personal situation had directly affected both it and her other studies. She told Amanda in confidence that she was considering dropping out and going home. Amanda encouraged her to discuss it with their pastor first and to hang tough while Max and Dean pursued it from their end.

To make matters worse, after two miscues back to back in their first game, her coach pulled her and put Amanda in her place. Amanda felt guilty when she played well, causing Becky to look worse than she really was.

"What made you decide to transfer?" Dean asked the young woman.

She looked down at her feet nervously, "it just wasn't a good fit. My professor and I didn't really communicate well."

Dean could tell that she had more to say but was reluctant to do so to a stranger.

"I've heard the same from several young women," he said, stretching the truth, "but never from any of your male colleges. The professor must relate better somehow to men."

"What did the others say?" she asked, tears beginning to form in her eyes.

Dean looked at her, sensed her pain and answered carefully, "they said he offered them accommodation to help themselves raise their grades."

"Accommodation, is that what they called it?" she almost screamed. "Accommodation, that's a nice word that makes it sound almost like he was doing us a favor just for sleeping with him."

Dean let her vent for a few seconds, then asked, "Is that what he said?"

"Not at first, at first he just seemed interested in helping me raise my grades to keep my scholarship," she said. "It was not until I went to his house that it became apparent what the price of his help would be."

"Did you tell anyone else?" Dean asked.

"I was too embarrassed. I felt so stupid and degraded. I knew it was his word against mine and no one would believe me. I was lucky that I could transfer, others could not." she said.

"How did you do in your new class?" Dean asked.

"3.4, no problem, I was able to keep my scholarship," she answered proudly. "And my dignity."

"Do you know of others who were not as lucky?" he asked.

"Several, I suspected," she answered, "but we never openly discussed it."

Dean nodded, wanting to ask for names but hesitating.

"I always wondered about Gina," she said seeming to reminisce, a sadness coming into her voice. "She couldn't get a transfer, so she stayed in his class, kept her scholarship but committed suicide right after semester. She got into booze and drugs."

"How well did you know her?" Dean asked.

"We were on the same team. She had the talent to go to the Olympics," she answered, "but things changed for her when she began to be tutored. She lost her fire, her concentration."

Dean had been taking notes but now stopped. "Would you be willing to speak to the police about this?" he asked. "Other young women will be victims too if we don't stop it."

"I know two who lost their scholarships and dropped out," she volunteered, "maybe they'd come forward."

"Please talk to them for me while I sit down with the police department and find out where all of this is going," Dean said. "But I caution you to keep it all quiet so word does not get out."

~ ~

By most standards, it was a small town. The taxpaying residents were outnumbered by the students four to one, leaving the police department long on supervision and short on funding.

"Detective Morgan," the tall, aging man said with a smile, sticking out his hand, "how may I help you?"

Dean introduced himself, showing his investigators credentials, then got right to the meat of the problem. Morgan took a few notes and asked several questions before leaning back in his chair. He was in his early 60's, flecks of gray were replacing his once black hair and his waistline was several belt notches over optimum, but there remained a certain vitality about him that made him seem competent.

"I'm a grandfather," he volunteered, "my oldest granddaughter will graduate this year and hopefully attend a university next year herself. I can't imagine what it would be like for her if she were in this situation."

Dean knew that God had provided just the right man to look into the allegations.

"Do you have a financial interest in this investigation?" Morgan asked point blank.

"I do not," Dean said with emphasis, "I was asked by a friend to try and help out, but I can see now that this needs to be more than an internal investigation by the school, not to be swept under the carpet."

"You're quite an astute young man," Morgan said jovially, "ever thought about going into real law enforcement? You have the makings of a good detective."

Dean laughed. "That a job offer?" he said.

"Let's try and work through this thing together," Morgan said, "and then we can discuss a career change for you."

~ ~

Four young women were in the apartment when Dean and the detective arrived. Morgan had made it clear that he wanted Dean to introduce him, then gradually withdraw from the conversation and let the detective do his job. Dean introduced Detective Morgan and Melissa introduced her three friends.

Two had been forced to drop out of school and were working in town trying to get money to return to college without scholarships, the other, like Melissa was still in school and on scholarship. She, however, had acquiesced to William's demands and continued in an objectionable relationship with him in exchange for a 3.9 GPA.

"Who will begin?" Morgan asked, "Who will tell their story?"

Melissa began, with Morgan carefully recording her dialogue. Several times the others interrupted to agree with what she was saying. Next Alice, who had lost her scholarship, told a similar tale, adding that repeated tries to transfer before she became academically ineligible had been refused. Dean noted that Cathy, the current victim, was crying softly as she heard and evaluated what they had said.

Bess followed Alice and repeated nearly word for word the shameful facts as she remembered them. Cathy was in tears, realizing that the others had taken the higher road, even at the expense of their education and dreams.

It was Cathy who Morgan focused on. "Together we can stop him, stop him from hurting anyone else, and maybe put him in jail. But," he added "it won't be pleasant for any of you or any of his other victims who are called to testify."

He waited for it to sink in before he continued. "You've got to stand together, lean on each other, and take strength from God."

He paused again, then asked, "How many of you knew Gina?"

Morgan had played his one and only trump card, hoping that they'd realize that their decisions may mean life or death to another young woman like themselves.

~ ~

"Max," Dean said from his cell, "I have someone I want you to meet. Starbucks at 6:00?" He'd caught his friend off guard but Max agreed.

Professor Maxwell was sitting alone at a table when Dean and Detective Morgan arrived. They ordered coffee and began to visit, with Morgan taking the lead.

"For the most part," he said looking at Max, "you'll be kept out of it. The prosecutor agreed that the court's focus would be directed away from you and toward Williams and his accusers."

Max looked relieved. "It's not so much that I don't want to help," he said, "but what I have to offer is mostly hearsay, as the court would term it."

"You did the right thing, got the ball rolling," Morgan said. "Your friend here did a nice job getting it together," he added, nodding at Dean. "Now it's up to us to make sure Williams gets what he's got coming."

~ ~

The judge honored the prosecutor's request for a change of venue due to the nature of the charges, and the probability that both sides of the case might be adversely effected because of the college's influence. Just previous to discovery, five additional witnesses came to the prosecution of their own volition, ready to testify. Looking at a lineup of nine known witnesses and the possibility of other unknown ones, the defense attorney began looking to cut a deal.

The deal fell through when it was determined that one of the nine had not yet turned 18 when the professor had solicited and then been with her. The new charges now included statutory rape. The trial lasted nearly three weeks but the jury was out less than an hour before coming back with a guilty verdict. Williams was sentenced to 20 years fixed without possibility of parole and then charged for wrongful death by Gina's parents, who sued for punitive damages in civil court.

Upon hearing of this, the university was quick to try and make reparation to the victims, offering full scholarships and individual monetary settlements, in an attempt to dissuade further law suits.

Praise God, Maxwell thought to himself, that the nightmare had finally came to a close without him being directly involved, and that the young women could go about the business of getting an education. Dean was interviewed, tested, and hired as a rookie with the police department, and had both a mentor and friend in detective Morgan.

Amanda graduated with honors and pursued a career in criminal law, Becky and her peers went to the NCAA finals and took second place. Melissa, Cathy, Bess, and Alice returned to school and completed their education before disappearing back into the fabric of society.

Retribution

Half enough, that was the amount of change that remained in his pocket as he walked toward home, his head hanging in defeat. He had expected a different outcome, that he'd be going home and greeted as a hero when he walked into the apartment. Less than an hour before, he had walked this same street, going in the opposite direction. In his pocket had been the last few dollars of his mother's meager salary and a list of groceries he was expected to return with. Those few things were to have provided for them until next Monday when she was paid again.

Nate had felt the desire to impress his mother and sisters by showing himself as wise and resourceful. He had wanted to provide for them in a more grandiose way than his mother could afford. He could picture, as he walked confidently away from home, returning not with a just quart of milk, a pot roast and a few vegetables, but also with fresh bread, ice cream, and pastries.

They had lived, since his father was killed, a life fraught with difficulty, seldom feeling secure and confident in their future. They had lost their home, unable to make the mortgage payments, and had sold their old car to provide food and rent until his mother had been hired at the Five & Dime down the block from where they now lived.

They had never been wealthy, even when his father had been a foreman at the mill, but they had lived comfortably and securely. He and his two sisters each had their own rooms, closets with more clothes than necessary, and a mother that could go to the market and buy, within reason, whatever struck her fancy for the evening meal.

Nate's father was forty-two when he was killed by a mishandled bunk of lumber being loaded onto a flatbed trailer. Without other witnesses, the responsibility of the mistake was not born by the machinery operator who lived to tell his story, but by his father who, it was claimed, had purposely placed himself in danger. Because it was termed suicide by the investigators, no family benefits for either death or worker's compensation were paid.

They had little time to grieve, their house of cards fell apart quite quickly, and without warning. Their meager savings was barely sufficient to pay for the funeral, leaving nothing for them to live on. On the 60th day of delinquency, they were escorted from the house, which was later sold at auction. On the street, with little money and no local family, everything they owned was in or on top of their Oldsmobile station wagon. None of the three children had ever lived anywhere else, making the eviction very personal and traumatic to them.

It took Beth two weeks to find a part-time job that paid only minimum wage, then two more before she got her first meager check. Their church and a few friends had helped at first, but it seemed as the days dragged on that help evaporated and finally disappeared, leaving them living in shelters with others, also homeless.

Nate was fourteen, he should have been thinking about dating, getting a driver's license, and playing sports, but instead he found himself being tutored by others like himself, but who were more worldly and experienced. They taught him how to survive on the street, take what he wanted, and become hardened and critical.

When the car needed repairs, they lacked funds to fix it so Beth sold it to the mechanic for enough to rent an apartment near where she worked, and buy food. Nate began stealing and selling small things, then gambling with the money, while his mother was working. When he lost he didn't see it as a loss, but when he won he saw it as gain since it was not his money at risk. His sisters had each other, his mother had her job, Nate had no one except his pals on the street, and none of them had any joy or happiness in their lives.

Three card monte, also called street hustle, was the game of choice in their new neighborhood. It required little skill from the participants, just a desire to earn easy money without labor. The dealers were practiced in their art and even if they hadn't cheated, could easily outsmart and outwit the local neighborhood kids.

The hustle was to let the new guy win, building his confidence, expecting that he would always return for more easy money. When they did return, they always brought and bet more than before, with plans to hit it big.

Nate had left the apartment with $20, the last few dollars of Beth's check, he was supposed to buy a few items, then return. It was the first time he had risked 'family' money, always before he had risked money that had come to him illegally.

"Nate," was the only acknowledgment of his arrival when he joined the group gathered around the 'dealer', working off a TV tray in the alley behind the market. When the dealer mentioned him by name, he felt important and a part of the group, accepted. He watched several rounds as money changed hands, eager for his turn. The younger ones played for 'change', the older kids used 'green'. Nate fingered the $20 bill in his pocket nervously, knowing that he should leave and go to the store. Yet he stayed, mesmerized by the cards, and encouraged by his ability to read them.

Then he found himself the center of attention, the 'man on the bubble'. The dealer had broken the twenty down, two fives and ten ones. Nate had always just bet quarters and an occasional $1, but felt embarrassed to go small now among his peers. He bet a $1 and doubled it, feeling good, he bet two and lost. Nate looked at it as having lost only a dollar so he bet two again. Again he lost.

He began to sweat, feeling anxious, and found it hard to keep his eye on the cards with a five riding on them. When he lost the bet, he panicked and bet the final two, he lost and was now down ten. It had taken five minutes to lose half of his family's food budget for the week.

Since his father had died, he had both lied and stolen, now he had stolen from his own family. He felt dirty, lost, and without hope. He could see no chance of ever returning to the life of joy and happiness he had known. For a moment, he wondered if he would be better off dead. Then, as if in answer to his thoughts, a Voice filled his head, "I love you, I have always loved you. You cannot earn My love, you do not deserve My love, but I give it to you freely and unconditionally."

Tears filled in his eyes and ran down his cheeks, he began to sob. "Return to me," the Voice said, "and I will return to you. I will never leave you nor forsake you."

Nate continued to cry as he remembered those words from long ago, when he and his family had accepted Jesus' salvation. "Forgive me Lord," he said out loud, uncaring of who might hear, "forgive me and take me back."

Soul Harvest

He gazed in childlike wonder at the tall stately figures before him. They seemed to have a kind of regal bearing about them as they continued in their tasks, walking to and fro. They worked efficiently, hardly making a sound, as though being attuned to one another. Pleasant looking, but not overly attractive, they were individually different, yet shared the same general appearance, as often do members of a family.

Almost nothing was said but an occasional nod seemed enough to communicate what needed to be done. He felt kind of guilty for not helping, and yet he knew he would just get in the way and slow their progress if he tried. They were not oblivious to his presence, but neither had they chosen to visit or make small talk with him.

Their steps were purposeful and they seemed to have a certain economy to their movements. From his vantage point, he could see for miles, and strangely, as he concentrated, the things at a distance became as distinct and recognizable as those closer had been. He thought, it was like a movie camera zoom lens, how things would draw nearer as he focused on them. Each worker would nearly disappear into the distance for a moment and then return with their package to add to the now sizable and growing number already there.

He really had no sensation of time and idly mused at how long he had been here and how long their task would take. Not that it mattered to him, he had no pressing issues and there seemed some urgency to what they were doing. He knew instinctively he would not leave until they were done, until the soul harvest was complete. He shared the joy which each felt as they were collected, as each new believer was brought near to present to Jesus.

Timeless

A linear dimension, having a beginning and an end, a normal progression indicated by a definable movement. Without some sort of measuring stick, gauge, or quantifier, time cannot exist.

Can you imagine a world or a life where time has no relevance? I think not. What if humans were all born age thirty two and never aged? What if there were no markers to indicate the end or beginning of things. What if they just appeared or disappeared without ceremony.

What if all knowledge came with the package at birth, with no more to accumulate or lessons to learn. It would be like buying a car or computer with whatever options came with the model.

He wasn't, and then he was. That is how it worked. One moment there was an empty space next to her, and then next he stood beside her talking softly and looking at her with concern in his hazel eyes.

"Are you well?" he asked.

"Yes, of course," she replied, "why do you ask?"

"I thought that I discerned a sense of confusion in your face," he answered.

"Certainly not confusion," she said with conviction, "possibly surprise."

"I see," he said trying to conjure up a definition of surprise without success. "What was the source of your surprise?"

"I am a hold-over," she admitted, feeling a little inferior. "And, although I have been reworked to exist and function in our world, I still retain memory."

"Memory?" he answered quizzically, "I am not familiar with that term."

"I am sorry;" she apologized, "that is a term from an earlier time, from before."

"Earlier time, before?" he said, looking at her oddly, "are you sure you are feeling well?"

"Yes, quite well," she said automatically. "I think I may have opened a can of worms full of questions I cannot answer."

"Worms, canned worms?" he said shaking his head, "why would anyone can worms and why would you want to open them?"

"Never mind," she answered, tiring of the conversation. "Let's move on."

"Move on?" he repeated, "Where should we move to?"

"Stop it!" she exclaimed, "You are driving me crazy. Please just stop talking for a while so we can try and communicate effectively."

He had taken on the look of a pet dog, eyeing her curiously. She half expected him to tilt his head to one side with questioning dog-like eyes.

"That is better," she said after several minutes had passed. "What is your name?"

He remained silent. She waited. Still he did not answer. Thinking back, trying to rationalize his lack of response, a phrase came to mind, "for a while." A while, an indeterminate length of time, in a place where time did not exist, she thought. He had no concept of when he should resume conversation.

"Please talk," she said, enabling him to resume.

"You speak strangely," he observed, "is that a result of you being what you call a hold-over?"

"Yes," she admitted, "I think it must be.

"Jack," he said.

She wanted to laugh, make a joke, have a little fun, but restrained herself from saying, "you don't know Jack."

A part of her longed to return to the time of memories, to the time when life made more sense, a time familiar to her and yet no longer her home. What she desired most was kinship. To find another like herself with whom she could converse, share memories of the non-existent past and dreams of an already known future.

"Automaton, are you familiar with that term?" she asked her protégé.

Indeed," he answered. "A being lacking self will, a puppet, a creation without the ability to make autonomous decisions."

"Would you define yourself as an automaton?" she asked curiously.

"I would not," he answered immediately. "I make decisions and carry out the considered application of them, and stand ready to defend the results." He sounded quite indignant at her question.

"And yet you already know the results when the decision is made, and knew that you would make the decision, and know its results," she observed. "There is no margin of error, no question of outcome, no small deviation possible from what is already known by you, is there?"

He seemed to be evaluating her statement, unseeing of the question in it.

"Do you ever get bored?" she asked, knowing he would have little concept of what she really meant.

He looked at her blankly.

"You appeared," she said, "you just appeared beside me from no where."

Again there was no response.

"Listen carefully to my speech," she instructed, "I said you appeared, did I not?"

"Yes," he answered.

"Do you agree and understand that statement?" she continued.

"Yes," he responded, "I think I do."

"Alright, now consider the word 'appeared' as I said it. It indicates tense, past tense, which is a measure of time," she continued. "You claim that you have no memory, that you do not understand the concept of time, and yet somehow you do."

Jack continued to grapple with what she had said, continued to try and understand the point she was attempting to make.

"'Now' is a word that indicates the present moment," she began as would a primary school teacher. "We are talking 'now'."

Jack smiled and nodded, indicating that he was not asleep and that he was listening carefully.

"'Before' is an unfamiliar word to you, which indicates something that has previously happened, as when I asked about when you appeared," she continued.

Jack looked understandably confused.

"Memory is what I have that you claim not to retain, memory is a record of things that are not now or in the future," she said. "You said that you stand to defend the results of your considered decisions. Results are those things that happen after the decision is made."

Jack seemed eager to embrace the concept she was describing, even though he did not understand it. "I appeared," he said. "I appear now."

"Yes, yes," she agreed excitedly, "your memory is of appearing, that is in the past. It has already happened, you cannot change it."

"How do you know these things are true?" he asked.

"Because as a hold-over I have memory, I can remember things from before, a time when things were not as they are now," she answered him.

"Is this a good thing?" he asked her. "Should I want to have memory or is the 'now' enough?"

"I'm not sure," she answered, "but something inside of me misses the way things were before."

"Explain the 'before' to me," he said.

"Let's sit down," she suggested, "it will take me awhile."

"What is 'awhile'?" he asked, returning to his earlier mode.

"Please just listen," she said. "Don't interrupt, just try to understand."

"When you appeared you had knowledge already given to you. It seemed full and complete, without any need to add to it. When you disappear, that knowledge will go with you. It was not always so," she said. "When I appeared, I was not as you see me now, I was without knowledge."

"Where did you gain knowledge then?" he asked.

"I was given it by God, a small portion each day as I lived," she answered. "A day is a measure of time."

He was shaking his head. "No, just the 'now'," he was saying. "Time is now. God is now."

He gave her an idea. "God is forever," she said.

"Yes, God is forever," he agreed, smiling like he had won a victory.

She felt that she was making headway; he had a concept of forever.

"Forever is more than just the 'now'," she began, pointing down at the floor, trying to indicate a point of reference. She took a small object from her pocket and placed it on the floor between them and repeated 'the now' while pointing at it. Then she moved to the far side of the room away from him and laid another like it down, saying, "the before" and pointing at it. Finally, she moved back past 'the now' to the distant side and laid a third on the floor, then said, "the after."

He looked at her, confusion apparent on his face.

She pointed to all three markers, encircled her hands as though to include them within the circle and said, "forever."

He smiled and nodded. "You know the forever?" he asked her.

"No," she answered truthfully, "only God knows the forever. I know the before, and the now, but no one but God knows the after."

"Will you teach me?" he asked her. "I want to know the 'before'."

"Let me read you God's own words that describe the 'before'," she said, "and some that tell of the 'after'. Pretend we are standing at the 'before'' and walking toward the 'now' as I read to you.

"In the beginning God created the heavens and the earth..."

Unusual Circumstance

I opened my eyes, finding myself standing on a sidewalk in the darkness with my wife, both of us facing a well lighted house.

I heard her ask, "Where are we?"

I answered, "I'm not sure."

We stood quietly together for a few moments without speaking, finally she asked, "is that us inside?"

Her question, or maybe statement, jolted me as I realized we were looking at ourselves inside our own home. "I... I think it is," I answered in a shaky voice."

"How can that be?" she asked softly.

"I'm not sure," I answered her truthfully, continuing to watch the couple as they moved about the room.

Slowly, gently, a small part of memory returned to my consciousness, answering some and confusing others of the many, many questions that filled my mind. It was Friday night, or had been when I last remembered, our night to watch Bluebloods together at 9:00 p.m. MST.

As we had aged together, we found our tastes more and more similar, or at least we were willing to sacrifice so we could enjoy time together. I did note however, that she found things to do elsewhere when WWE was on, and I when the infamous Wheel of Fortune made its nightly appearance. But tonight had been different, hadn't it? I recalled how we had been invited to a friend's home for dinner and had stayed late to visit. Late, of course, meant staying past 10:00 p.m.

I could still taste the roast beef, brown gravy and mashed potatoes. But of course, it was the company that had brought us, and made us linger on. Over the years as partying, dancing, and child rearing had faded into the background, so had much of our social life. She joked often that we had none, and I was more and more content with that.

I was awakened from my thoughts by my wife who made yet another observation, "I think the local news just came on," she said, "I can see the reflection in the picture behind us, I mean them."

Sure enough, she was right. The talking heads were visiting with each other and looking at the camera with faked smiles and laughter. Next the weather dreamer appeared for one of his short visits, telling only part of the story and making us wait to hear the rest. They knew very well that if he told it all up front we'd have all cut it short and gone to bed early.

With all the scientific advancements and radar this or that, he was still wrong as often as right, and was forced to change his predictions several times a week. I had always taken offense at the "chance of rain or snow" thing, with them assigning a percentage as though they could read God's mind. Often it had already been raining by the time he announced his 20% or 30% chance of rain on any given day.

Inside, we seemed to be talking with each other, discussing his "weather guess" and how it might affect our plans for the morrow. I found it interesting that one could nearly guess the program's content well enough to not need sound at all. The picture of a car crash, house fire, or other event with captions made the news team nearly superfluous. Neither of us spoke, gathering the information presented and wondering about humanity's need to always know the "breaking news."

As if a door had opened in my mind, the reflected images of the car and burning house rushed into my consciousness. I recalled driving homeward from our night out, losing control on an icy corner and the car slamming into the house on the corner, our house, and bursting into flames.

She took my hand and turned her attention from the house for a moment, looking directly into my eyes. "They'll go to bed soon, where will we go?" she asked questioningly.

God's plan, I thought quickly, was that man should lead his household. Why? No one seemed to know for sure. The feminists fought it, but in the end it was up to us to answer just this sort of question, without any clue of the correct answer. Right on cue inside the house, she stood, then he followed behind, turning off the lights as they left the room. We stood there on the sidewalk for a few moments staring into the darkened house, seeing nothing but our own reflection in the darkened windows.

"There are times," He said smiling, "when we are not quite prepared to leave and yet not ready to arrive."

We must have been looking downward, because hearing His voice, we both looked up and into His eyes. He resembled something out of a stage play or movie, seemingly backlit by unseen lights. 'Aura' best describes the faint but effective glow that pulled Him from the darkness and showcased Him before us.

He seemed large, maybe bordering on huge, but not just in height, which appeared to be several inches more than my 6'2", but in his overall character. Possibly like meeting your favorite movie star in person and not being disappointed by what you saw.

When neither my wife nor I responded, He continued to speak. "It is true that I have prepared a place for you, as I promised, but it is also true that all things happen in the Father's time," He said quite pleasantly, with a touch of humor in His voice.

I finally found my tongue, but was trying to organize my response before speaking, when He answered my thoughts. "Yes, of course. You, like I, were dead, but now you live."

I heard, or possibly sensed my wife gasp beside me as His words became clear to us.

"Fear not," He said plainly, "for no one can snatch you out of My hand, those the Father has given to Me belong to Me."

My mind was racing, a million questions to be asked and yet none seemed important enough to voice.

"Yes," He affirmed, "I am He whom you have served; I am the One who loved you before the beginning of time, before you were in your mother's womb."

Tears of emotion were streaming down our cheeks, we dropped first to our knees, then fell forward prostate on the ground before our Savior, Jesus the Christ. All at once the ground disappeared, light filled very portion of the horizon, nothing of our former encounter remained, no house, street, sidewalk or earthly structure. The outlines of translucent shapes and forms surrounded our Lord, singing praises of worship and joy. Huge crystalline structures began to appear, looking much like skyscrapers made of glass block, shining like the sun.

"In my Father's house," He began, "are many mansions..." I finished saying with Him in my mind, without moving my lips.

– DANisms –

- Advice from many is simply criticism in disguise.
- To become strong you must suffer the testing of your strength.
- Cling not to those things which have brought you here, but to those that will move you forward.
- Sadness, like joy, lives in the heart waiting to be nourished.
- Strength is a sign of weakness and weakness a sign of strength.
- To have what you do not have, you must do what you haven't done.
- A callus is a sign that you have lived and worked. To be callus is a sign that you have never worked at living.
- Sadness is a time of rest while you are awaiting a time of joy.
- The language of love is always understood by the loving.
- Hate is a stone in your boot and a briar in your saddle.
- Being a simpleton is neither simple or easy.
- Take comfort in that you have lived through the worst that has ever happened to you.

AVAILABLE NOW

The Cady Miller Series

SHIELD OF FAITH

"One more thing, Red, then if you want I'll shoot you, okay? Thing is, if you should beat me, I go to Heaven to be with the Lord, but if I beat you, where do you suppose you'll go for all eternity? Have you thought about how long forever in Hell might be?"

Red cursed again. "You don't worry about me miner, you worry about your little family here after I shoot you!"

SHIELD OF HONOR

Amid the explosions and aerial displays that marked our nation's Independence Day, he heard a yell followed by a louder and sharper report that was closely followed by a second and third. Cady, in his blue uniform with Kevlar vest and duty belt, was lifted off his feet by the impact and fell fifteen feet from the pier into the East River.

SHIELD OF JUSTICE

Unknown to others, Cady Miller was a dangerous man, having the physical and technical abilities to inflict mortal injury. His lean stature and rapidly advancing age belied his physical prowess. His pale blue eyes now retained their 20/20 vision by the use of contacts lenses, but more importantly he used that vision to see things others often missed. Skills honed through years of training and discipline allowed him to maintain an edge others frequently lost as the years caught up with them.

These and other offerings available at the Author's website:

www.danneyclark.com / www.danscribepublications.com

– ALSO AVAILABLE –

Chronicles of the WIDESPOT CAFÉ

After college, nine years went by quickly, I moved from job to job, town to town, never having a close relationship or a feeling of belonging. I worked in every industry, every position, in every field garnering small success but feeling alone and empty inside.

To my credit, I lived on my earnings, not touching my investments, but spending all that I made. I drove taxi, waited tables, painted houses, sold shoes, installed computers, cooked, drove truck, did construction, or whatever came along.

Young, healthy, and able to learn quickly, I was easily employable. I have never owned a house, a car, or been married. Like King Solomon, I searched for the meaning of life, and like him, I didn't find it. I had many friends, none close, no ties, few responsibilities, felt no kinship to anyone except possibly the friend and partner I knew in college. But he had now moved on and marched to a different beat.

Then one day I stopped by the Widespot Café intending to just have a meal... that day, it all changed for me. I met Mae and Jib.

These and other offerings available at the Author's website:

www.danneyclark.com / www.danscribepublications.com

Made in the USA
San Bernardino, CA
11 July 2014